Molly '
I Remember When

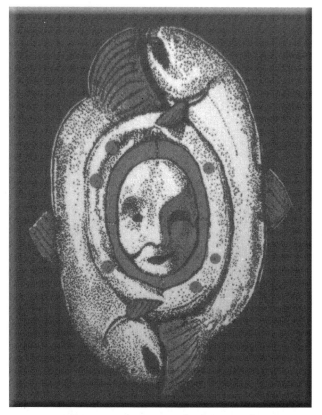

Growing up in Alaska on the
Kwiguk Pass of the Lower Yukon River
Molly Hootch Hymes

PO Box 221974 Anchorage, Alaska 99522-1974
books@publicationconsultants.com
www.publicationconsultants.com

ISBN 978-1-59433-267-8
eBook ISBN 978-1-59433-268-5

Library of Congress Catalog Card Number: 2011944738

Copyright 2010 Molly Hootch Hymes
—Second Edition 2011—

Photos by Molly A. Hymes
Maps created by Michael Locke
All Scripture quotations are taken from the Life
Application® Study Bible©

Manufactured in the United States of America.

Dedication

To my sons Alvin Eugene Hymes and Daniel Alvin Hymes

Acknowledgments

This book would not have been possible without the encouragement of my husband, Alvin Hymes. I have never written any major literary piece before, especially a book. It took the combined efforts of both of us to make it possible. It was he who inspired me to write about that portion of my life which, I realized, was of a time now only kept in my memory. It needed to be remembered as a legacy I could pass down to my two sons Alvin E. and Daniel A. Hymes. My sons were also encouraging me to write this book so they could remember their mom during her younger years, growing up along the Kwiguk Pass of the lower Yukon River.

I also want to thank the following individuals for their assistance in making this work a reality. Their guidance and encouragement was priceless.

Emily Mathew for her help with the overall writing of this book. Debbie Graves for her help with the technical presentation of the material. Audrey and Patrick Guilfoile for their assistance with the organization of the stories. Michael Locke for his help with the maps that were created. Glenn Schmidt for his assistance with the cover layout. Ula Hoffer for her ever-present enthusiasm which kept me inspired during the writing of this book.

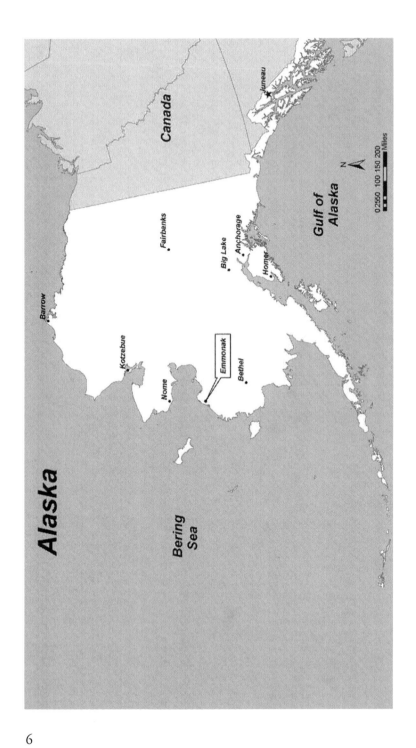

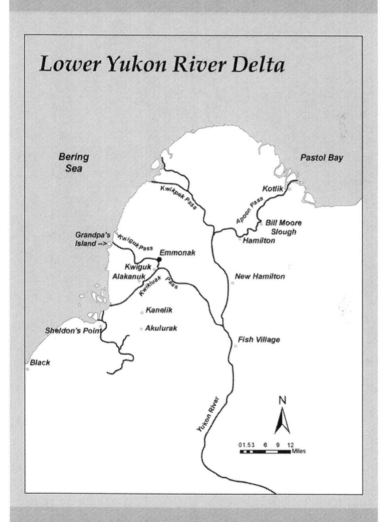

Lower Yukon River Delta

Bering
Sea

Pastol Bay

Kwikpak Pass

Kotlik

Apoon Pass

Bill Moore
Slough

Grandpa's
Island -->

Kwiguk Pass

Hamilton

Emmonak

Kwiguk

Alakanuk

New Hamilton

Kwikluak Pass

Kanelik

Sheldon's Point

Akulurak

Fish Village

Black

Yukon River

N

0 1.5 3   6   9   12
Miles

Map displaying points of interest mentioned in the book.

Contents

Introduction

The purpose of writing this book is to recount the experiences of my life as a little girl growing up on the Kwiguk Pass of the lower Yukon River. This collection of stories includes my memories of those events occurring during my younger years growing up in the Yupik Eskimo village of Emmonak. These were my years as a grade-school girl in the 1960s. That time of my life was occupied with spending time with my family and the experiences I had with them. We lived the Eskimo life as it was during a time solely devoted to a subsistence existence.

These stories are also about remembering the life my Pa lived. He was my hero and the idol of my life. I looked up to him as I was growing up as a little girl. I wanted to write this book as a remembrance of his life. This work is more about my Pa's life than it is about me. Both of our lives were deeply connected as one. I wanted people to know who my Pa was as an individual who devoted his life to a subsistence culture. It needed to be written down as a legacy to him.

My Pa passed away July 18, 1997. He could not speak any English, only the Yupik language. With his passing I realized that a generation of memories was lost. How my father's generation lived and worked out a subsistence lifestyle is gone forever. Little of that time was written down. I did not want that to happen to my generation that transitioned from an entirely subsistence existence to a modern society now lived by my contemporaries in Emmonak.

I want to pass along my memories to the next generation of the life which I lived while growing up on the lower Yukon River as a little girl. I want my sons to know how their mother grew up. I want them to be able to experience my life as a little girl during a time which did not have the modern conveniences which we take for granted today. I want them to be able to experience, with me, fish camp, berry picking, running the trap line and witness all the activities God so blessed me with during my youth.

I need to share with my siblings the wonderful times we spent together as a family. It seems so long ago and during a time which remains only as a memory to me. We experienced many family moments together as we lived a subsistence lifestyle during our youth. Those family moments we spent together represent a time now long past, existing only in my memory. Today modern conveniences make our life so different.

I also desire to share a portion of my life associated with the years before and after the Molly Hootch Case. It was a time which not only affected my life but also the lives of all high school age children throughout rural Alaska. I want to tell that story from my perspective as I lived it and saw it happen. I feel honored to have had that legacy to leave behind for future generations.

One of the most difficult decisions I had to make was how to organize my memories of the past. As a little girl dates and years had no meaning to me. I just didn't need to remember what year a certain event occurred or what moment in time I experienced it. I knew they either happened during my grade school or high school years. That made writing about my life in a chronological order too difficult if not impossible. I decided to organize my memories according to the seasons as I experienced them. It was according to the seasons which our lives were most affected. My memory of the events of my life held more value to me through the passing of the seasons rather than the passing of the years.

I begin each story with a Yupik word and its English translation. I also include my personal thoughts about each story as a brief introduction. I end each story with a forget-me-not flower and a proverb from the Bible. The forget-me-not was my favorite flower to pick on the tundra as a little girl. Every time I see one it brings back the memories of my younger days on the delta. It is also the state flower of Alaska. I selected a proverb from the Bible to provide a thought provoking message for your own personal reflection.

The following pages represent the stories and experiences of my life while growing up a young Yupik Eskimo girl on the Kwiguk Pass of the lower Yukon River. I hope you find them informative, enlightening and entertaining. These are the memories which I have of those times that I can say, "I remember when."

Molly Agnes Hootch Hymes

Imangaq

It existed as a slough off the north bank of one of the middle mouths of the lower Yukon River. The slough meandered north and west through the flat, treeless tundra connecting the Bering Sea to the Kwiguk Pass of the Yukon River.

It was best known for its population of blackfish. It was home to one of the largest breeding grounds of blackfish in the lower Yukon River delta. The Eskimos called this fish imangaq. They grow to about seven inches in length. They are elongated with a dark olive-brown coloration. Their belly is white and the fins have reddish-brown speckles. They eat the larvae of such insects as midges and mosquitoes. They especially like to live in tundra sloughs and lakes with vegetation for cover.

Their hardiness is legendary. They survive the cold winters by moving to deep water when the surface becomes solid ice. They have large gills protected by gill covers helping them to survive the harsh winters of the lower Yukon River delta by burying themselves into the bottom mud.

Alaska Blackfish
Dallia pectoralis

During the old days no one inhabited the land adjacent to the slough. People lived further upriver. It wasn't until the village of

Kwiguk began to erode into the Yukon River that people began to migrate to this portion of the delta. Eventually all of the people of Kwiguk, and some people from the upriver territory, moved to settle the land surrounding the slough.

The people called the village established around the slough Imangaq. The settlement was later given the English name of Emmonak, which meant Imangaq in Yupik Eskimo.

It became the village of my birth. The land surrounding this blackfish slough would provide the backdrop for the many memories I have of growing up while a little girl along the Kwiguk Pass of the lower Yukon River.

My Family Tree

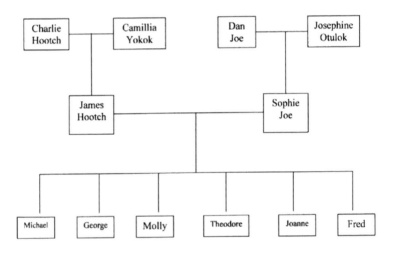

My Family History

My family history has been a real challenge to prepare. Older Eskimos did ¥not use first and last names until the arrival of the missionaries when they were given names. This has made it difficult to trace the generations very far in the past. What is known has been passed down from the previous generations through the spoken word. Little has been written about our ancestors. My effort is the culmination of inquiring from my parents as to what they knew of their ancestors.

Grandparents
Hootch

My grandfather, Charlie Hootch, was born March 17, 1904 and died December 6, 1987 and is buried in Emmonak. My grandmother was Camillia Yokok. I don't know anything about her date of birth or death. Grandpa likely had lived a period of his life at Kwiguk before moving to Emmonak.

Grandpa and Camillia had eight children, which included my Pa. Camillia died long before Pa got married. I do not know where Camillia is buried. Grandpa then married Agnes Prince. I knew Agnes as my Grandma. She had six children from a previous marriage. There are graves at the old settlement of Akulurak containing the remains of a number of the Prince people. We went there to see them while we were in the area of the southern tundra. Grandpa and Grandma Agnes had one child, a girl, named Veronica.

Grandpa and Grandma Agnes lived in a log cabin close by, but farther from the river. I tried to visit them every day. They fed us whenever we came over to their cabin to visit. I enjoyed it a lot. It was one reason I enjoyed going to their cabin to visit. Grandpa made pancakes for me whenever I came to visit. He gave me syrup made from a mixture of sugar and water to put on the pancakes. I liked them very much. Both Grandpa and Grandma were very nice to me and treated me very respectfully.

Grandpa had a dog team and boat. He was a subsistence hunter and fisherman his entire life. I am certain he taught my Pa much of what he knew about subsistence living. I think most of what Pa showed me in what he made and how he lived was handed down to him from Grandpa. When I killed my first rabbit, the tradition was to give it to an elder; so I gave it to Grandpa. Grandma Agnes was a housewife. She did what most Eskimo wives do for the family such as cook, clean fish and care for the kids. I remember when she got her first bra. She showed it to everybody, to the embarrassment of some. She had a real good sense of humor which made her a joy to be around. I don't know the date of her death, but she is buried in Emmonak.

Joe

These were my mother's parents. They both lived in the upriver village of St. Mary's. They are both buried at St. Mary's. They stayed in Alakanuk with my uncle David Joe while fishing during the summer. Sometimes they would come to visit us at Emmonak. I think Grandpa Joe worked with the school in some position at St. Mary's. As a result we rarely saw them. We did not travel to St. Mary's because it was too far to go by boat.

My grandpa, Dan Joe, was raised in the Holy Cross Mission, a village upriver on the Yukon. It is a long way from Emmonak. His parents died when he was very little. That is why he was raised in the mission house at Holy Cross.

I do know that there is a very close relationship to Russia on the Otulok side of my grandmother's family. Josephine Otulok, my grandmother, had a mother who was one half Russian and her mother was full Russian. They lived in a city in Russia before they moved to the island of Little Diomede. From there they moved to St. Michael on the south side of Norton Sound near the north mouth of the Yukon River. Somehow my Grandmother from St. Michael and my Grandpa from Holy Cross met each other. It seems like a great distance between the two villages from which the two met. Maybe that is why they chose to live in St. Mary's, which is between the two villages.

Parents
Sophie Joe

My mom was born March 2, 1931. I am not sure, but I think it was in Stebbins, which is on the south shore of Norton Sound near the north mouth of the Yukon River. She died on December 8, 1999 and is buried in St. Mary's.

It was an arranged marriage between her and Pa. I did not do much with Mom. I spent more time with Pa. She worked as a teacher's aid at the Emmonak elementary school. That was a real financial help to us. It gave us a little money to buy things and food. It was the only source of income for our family. She left us during the late 1960s. She went to Anchorage for a school related meeting and never came back. We did not understand why she never returned to Emmonak to live with us. It really made us wonder what had gone wrong between her and the rest of the family. We were really at a loss to figure it out why this had happened. Her absence created a large void in our family which was difficult to fill.

Mom possessed a wonderful personality. She had a real joy for life and made us laugh with her jokes and casual temperament. She was fun to be around and made all of my siblings promote a love of life which we still respect to this day.

James Hootch

Pa was born October 21, 1927 in the village of Kwiguk. I am not certain about the birthplace being Kwiguk, but it seems to be the most logical location. He died on July 18, 1997 and is buried in Emmonak.

I spent most of my time with Pa. I was a daddy's girl. Almost every part of this book has something to do with my relationship with Pa. He is the one which showed me the Eskimo way of life as I got to experience it with him. If it weren't for the time I spent with Pa, there would be very little for me to write about. I would not have been blessed with these memories which I can share with others. I was likely his favorite because I did things with him and took part in the activities which were important to him.

His personality was very much like my mom's. He enjoyed joking and laughing with us. He always wanted to teach us the Eskimo ways. He was easy going and never let us sense that he ever worried about our welfare. He was a good provider for us. We never went hungry for either food or nurturing love.

Siblings
Michael
Mom and Pa's first child named Michael died in infancy. I don't know where he is buried.

Louise
Their second child named Louise also died in infancy. I also don't know where she is buried.

Michael
Michael was born October 5, 1951 in Emmonak. I rarely played with Michael. He was around five years older than me. We did not do many things together. He was always drawing with colored pencils, crayons or whatever he could find to draw with. He was a very good artist. He went to boarding school with my older brother George. He ended up living in Anchorage. He never returned to Emmonak to settle down.

Michael was a very good artist. His artwork, he called Little Hootch and Friends, was really fun to admire. Many newspapers in Alaska used his drawings. I always looked forward to seeing his latest artwork in the current editions.

Michael died on July 23, 2008 in Anchorage. He is buried in Emmonak. I miss him very much. It is too bad he died so early in life. I am sure he had a lot more drawing to do. It was always a special time at Christmas to see what new artwork he had prepared for my family and me. Now that he is gone, his drawings have much more meaning to me. I know everyone who knew him misses him very much.

George

George was born October 11, 1952 in Emmonak. George was almost four years older than me. He spent most of his time with Michael when we were little. We did not do much together. Whenever I would try to see what they were doing, they would run away from me.

After I left Emmonak in 1978, George became my major lifeline to what was going on in the village. He would share with me via telephone the latest news of Emmonak. He still lives in Emmonak. Whenever I come to Emmonak to visit, I stay at his house. He was a good host during my visits.

Molly

I was born July 12, 1956. I was born between George and Teddy.

Theodore (Teddy)

Teddy was born December 21, 1957. Teddy was younger than me. He spent most of his time with George and Michael. It was a boy thing I think. I didn't spend much time with Teddy. All the boys in the family spent more time running away from me than wanting to play with me. Oddly, I spent more time with Pa than the boys did. Maybe that was why they did not spend more time with me. They knew I was daddy's girl. Teddy now lives in Tuluksak, Alaska.

Joanne

Joanne was born December 24, 1959 in Emmonak. She was my only sister. I could play with her since I could not play with my brothers. We played dolls which we would cut out from the mail order catalogs. We brought them to fish camp with us and played with them there as well as play with them at home. I enjoyed playing dolls with Joanne. We could imagine so much that we could do with the pretend dolls. We also enjoyed playing tea together. The tea sets were bought from the catalogs. They did not cost too much so we could share them between the two of us. We had real tea in the cups and have them with cheese and crackers. Our brothers joined us only if we had real food to eat. As soon as the food was gone, they were gone as well.

While we were at the fish camp Joanne and I played with the Ok-toyok kids. They were the only other kids to play with on the island at fish camp. When we were at Emmonak, we had many more kids to play with. There were lots of cousins to play with in the village. They did not live very far from us. Between Joanne and I we had a lot of other girls to play with in the village. Some of the village games Joanne and I played with the other girls were:

- Hop Scotch
- Tag
- Jacks
- Marbles
- Story Knife

Joanne died on July 16, 1990 in Anchorage. It was with great sadness that I received the news of her death. She was the closest one in the family to me besides my Pa. I miss her much. She died too young. She is buried in Emmonak.

Fred

Fred was born February 9, 1961. He is next to the youngest in the family. He was the baby of the family to me. I treated him like one of my baby dolls. He played tag along with me. In a way I was the babysitter for Fred. I treated him like my older brothers treated me. I tried to run away from Fred if I thought he was intentionally trying to tag along with me. Usually I did not mind it so much. It really depended upon whom I was with at the time Fred wanted to be with me. Joanne and Fred spent more time together since they were closer in age. Fred currently lives in Emmonak in the modern house where I used to live with the rest of the family before I left.

Charles

He was my youngest brother. He became very ill with a sickness and died while he was just one year old. I think he is buried in Emmonak.

Spring

Introduction

The Yupik Eskimo word for spring is Up'nerkaq, which means, To become spring (Time to prepare). It was a time to prepare. The long nights of darkness and cold were giving way to the long days of sunshine and warmth. There was much to be done to prepare for the summer months ahead.

Boats had to be repaired or built for the upcoming fish camp season. The boat was the Eskimo's lifeline to the delta. Without a boat a person was very limited as to what could be done and where you went.

Spring heralded the end of another school season. Teachers would usually leave the village and go to their homes in other parts of Alaska or to the lower forty-eight. It was also a time to prepare for the possible upcoming flood. Everyone kept watch on the river to see when it would run free of ice. As soon as the ice was out it was time to carefully watch for a potential flood. The flood required preparation.

When the flood season ended, then the real activity started in the village. The ships from the southern ports began to arrive for another fishing season. The supply barges made their arrival bringing goods of all kinds to the village for the summer season.

Everyone awaited the arrival of the salmon. This is what the summer was all about. We started to think about fish camp and making preparation toward going there for another summer. The waterfowl would begin migrating north soon. They brought the thoughts of gathering eggs on the tundra islands at fish camp.

The spring season was short in comparison to other times of the year. It was a time for the trees to begin to make leaves. The grass once again turned green. Spring was a wonderful time of transition along the Kwiguk Pass of the lower Yukon River.

Boat Building

Angsaq: Boat

I liked to watch Pa build boats. It was amazing to watch him build without any design or instructions written down. I especially enjoyed the times when the two of us would go in the boat together.

Probably the most important item to an Eskimo is his boat. It allows the Eskimo to fish, hunt, berry pick, gather driftwood and move about during the summertime. It is the only plausible local mode of transportation that can be used to get from place to place after break-up and before freeze-up within the lower Yukon delta. A boat has always been required in order to live the Eskimo subsistence lifestyle.

My Pa was one of the few people in the village who could build boats. He took great pride in his boat building skills. His boats were sought after for their quality in craftsmanship. Because he was so particular about his boat construction, they lasted a long time. He did most of his boat building during the spring in order to have them ready to go by fish camp season. During the spring, he was always busy around boats. He was either building a new boat for someone or he was repairing either his or someone's boat. During the spring it was all about the boat.

Materials

The first step in boat building was to go to the Northern Commercial Company store and buy the materials. He was careful to hand select the very best lumber he could find. He looked at each piece to determine if it qualified for purchase. He needed some dimensional lumber, boards and plywood for the project. He attached most of the boat components with nails. He did use screws wherever they were more appropriate in maintaining structural strength and integrity. The plywood was a marine grade type so it would stand up to the constant moisture and water that it would be subject to throughout its life.

Construction

He started by building the frame of the boat. He used the dimensional lumber to make the struts for the side and bottom. This formed the boat superstructure. It determined its size. The dimensional lumber was cut to form the frame of the boat according to its width, height and length. Some people wanted only a certain boat size. Everybody was different. Each boat was built to suit the particular needs and use of the owner.

After the frame was laid out and nailed together, then the plywood was cut and attached to the frame on the outside. The dimensional lumber and plywood had to be curved and formed to make the bow of the boat. This was a very time consuming part of the construction. It was meticulous work and hard to make the proper curve that was required. The bows had to have an upward tilt so it would plane on the water and not plow into the water when driven at higher speed. That required talent to make all those curves come together at the front point of the bow of the boat. The boat needed to be designed so that when it was operated at the correct speed the front two-thirds of the boat rose out of the water. Only the rear section of the boat was in contact with the water.

Once the plywood has been attached to the frame forming the sides of the boat, then the bottom plywood is nailed to the frame to form the underside. If a keel was desired it was nailed on at this time. The keel helped with steering the boat. Some people desired one to be attached and some did not. It was a personal decision for everyone. Once the sides and bottom of the boat were attached then the transom or rear panel of the boat was built.

The transom had to be built very sturdy and strong. The outboard motor was attached to it and all the heavy forces come together at that point of the boat. It was not to be the weakest part. A structural failure of the transom could be catastrophic. A seat was attached to the transom and both sides of the boat to give it additional structural strength. It also provided a place to sit while operating the outboard motor.

Some people wanted a floor nailed into the bottom of the boat. Some people just wanted it left open and exposed. Many users lined the bottom of the boat with boards as a walkway to get from the front to the rear. Having something in the bottom of the boat was desirable since that was where all the water which entered the boat obviously settled. A coffee can was kept in the bottom of the boat for bailing out the unwanted water collected there.

Sometimes a middle seat was attached if the boat was used often for transporting people. If it was primarily a work and fishing boat, the extra seat just got in the way during fishing. If people wanted to ride in the boat, they just sat on the floor.

Pa built boats during the spring. This was a slow time for him as it occurred between the end of winter and before the trip to fish camp. Another boat builder which I remember was John Charles. He made good boats as well. He was very much like Pa as he was a subsistence hunter and fisherman. He made and sold boats, as people needed them. He lived next to the landing strip on Emmonak slough. That made boat building convenient for him since he was able to drive a boat full of materials right up to his building site. When he finished a boat he was able to push it into the slough and drive it out to the river.

Painting

Once the boats were constructed inside and out, then the process of painting began. Pa always painted his boats gray. When I became old enough to help with painting the boats they began to take on a number of different colors. Pa's boats became dark blue and green in color once I was given the opportunity to paint them and choose the color. I just got tired of all the boats in the village looking the same color. I thought it gave each boat a special character by being a different color from all the rest. I liked being able to choose the color and paint the boat all by myself. I did all the boat painting once I was old enough and Pa approved of my work.

I am not sure what Pa thought about the different colors I chose. I am sure change was difficult for him. He probably thought a generation gap certainly existed once his boats no longer were gray in color. It was inconceivable that a boat could be any other color in Pa's mind. I changed everything. Pa's world had difficulty accepting blue and green as a suitable color for a boat. Over the years Pa came to accept the reality that it wasn't the color that made the boat but how it was constructed. He just smiled and let me choose the color.

Nostalgia

I miss the days of helping Pa build boats. It was fun to watch him work. He did all his work without the aid of any power tools. Everything was cut by hand with hand tools. We did not have any electricity, so power tools were not an option. Each boat was given hands-on construction.

We never owned a store bought boat. Pa never owned an aluminum boat. We just could not afford them. Since Pa could build his own, why buy one? They were very good boats. You could not buy a boat with that level of precision and attention to detail. Eventually more and more fishermen began to purchase the aluminum boats as they had more money to afford them. That was one of the outcomes of the transition from subsistence to commercial fishing. There became fewer boat builders in the village as a result of this transition.

Now it is nearly impossible to find a wooden boat in the village. The only wooden boats you come across are decaying and rotting in the bushes abandoned from days of a long lost era. Now I only have the memories of a time when boat building was an important profession in the village. It was a different time in which to live. If an Eskimo wanted a boat, they had to either build it themselves or have someone build it for them. Commercial fishing has changed almost all aspects of life in Emmonak. More money from fishing means more modern things people can afford. The old ways of doing things are now long gone. The need to be able to build your own items of necessity, such as a boat, is also gone. All the boats my Pa had built have since been taken out of service and no longer used. They have all rotted away and have been replaced by more modern metal boats. His boats may no longer be around, but the memories I have will always remain with me as I think about the days of *Pa's Boat Building*.

Hard work means prosperity;
only fools idle away their time.

Proverbs 12:11

The Flood

Ulerpak: Flood

The flood was just another aspect of our lives. I was amazed at the power of the flood and how we had to respect it when it came.

Almost every year the Yukon River would overflow its banks and flood the entire lower Yukon area, including Emmonak. The entire Lower Yukon delta became an extension of the Bering Sea during the flood. It was simply a part of the cycle of life for us as we adjusted our lives to accept the inevitable event we called the flood. There was no Army Corps of Engineers to provide any flood control in the lower Yukon delta. We had to be prepared for that time when the ice went out and the flood followed. We simply took it as a matter of fact. No big deal. We just had to deal with it. It required patience. Usually it was short and did not last a long time. But, when it was over the next phase of our lives began. In order to get to the fish camp phase of our life, we had to go through the flood. We all anxiously waited for the floodwaters to recede.

On Flood Watch

The flood normally occurred during the last half of May. We watched for rising water while the river was still frozen. When the ice began to break-up we wanted to be careful of the oncoming floodwaters. We listened to the radio all the time to get an idea of the movement of the ice upriver. If an ice jam was occurring upriver, we needed to be concerned about our situation at Emmonak. What happened upriver was likely going to impact what occurred downriver.

As the ice started to move, then we became more vigilant in our watch of the river water level. Watching the ice move was a major event on the river. It had such power. It was quite a sight to watch the ice move and look for the really large icebergs that sometimes came down the river. They carried so much force that they could move anything out of their way if caught in its path.

Flood Preparation

As we saw the water level rising and begin its process of overflowing the banks, we then began to prepare ourselves for the flood that was likely to follow. Everything in the cabin had to be packed into boxes or whatever cartons we had available and made ready to move. The boxes were either put into our two boats or placed on the roof of the cabin. Prior to the approaching flood the boats were pulled close to the cabin. Normally the boats were just pulled up onto the beach a ways to protect them from the winter ice. The impending floodwaters required us to pull the boats closer to the cabin, which was just a little higher above the river level. The boats were placed as close to the cabin as possible and tied to something substantial to keep them from floating away during the flooding. We loaded as much of our belongings as possible into the boats. One of the boats held our personal items such as clothes and mattresses. These were covered by a tarp to keep them dry. The other boat held the dogs and any articles the dogs could not destroy. The dogs would try and destroy anything that would fit into their mouth. The extra items not fitting into the boats were placed on the roof of the cabin. I remember placing the dog sled and fish traps on the roof because they were made of wood and could easily float away in the floodwaters if left on the ground.

Sometimes the floodwaters rose to about three feet above the riverbank. This caused our cabin to be thoroughly flooded. The flood equally affected everybody. Because it was so flat in Emmonak there was no high ground from which to escape. People who lived farther from the river were no more protected than our cabin, which was very close to the river. We were not able to remove the woodstove so it had to stay in the cabin and get completely submerged in the floodwaters.

When I was a little girl our home was built directly on the ground. We had no way to elevate our house off the ground. We did not have the materials or the resources available to elevate our home above the ground. Since the flood was an accepted fact of life we did not try to avoid it. Since we did not have any possessions which could be ruined by the flood, it really did not matter to us. Any flood damage could be easily repaired. It wasn't until the construction of modern homes that stilts or pylons became an integral part of the foundation. It became standard construction technique to elevate the home several feet above the ground. This made a home less susceptible to flooding. This was a wonderful advancement since we no longer had to prepare for or worry about the flood.

As the floodwaters overflowed the banks we all went to the school building for safety from the water. The school buildings were built up on stilts just for the purpose of protecting them from the floods. The school was our place of refuge during the flood. Every family went there to escape the water. Usually by this time of the year school was either out or within a few days of closing for the summer vacation. We kids liked going to the school building during the flood since we were not going there for school. It gave us a chance to use the building for a great game of hide and seek. With all the classrooms and hallways it was ideal for hide and seek play. We were actually oblivious to the situation ongoing on the outside. We did not have to stay at the school building very long. The worst of the flood was over in just a few days. Then we could return to our own homes.

Cleanup

The process of cleaning up after the flood began. Since the stove could not be moved from the cabin it required the most cleaning. The job of moving the items that were kept in the boats and on the rooftops began. First we gave the cabin a complete cleaning. Sometimes the floodwaters brought a lot of dirt that needed to be removed. Some years the floodwater actually performed a real favor by cleaning up the cabin. Each flood year was different that way.

After the cabin was cleaned, we transferred all our belongings back into the cabin from the boats or the rooftop. The boats were then brought back to the beach closer to the river's edge in preparation for the trip to fish camp.

Once the flood was over and the river returned to normal we began our preparations for fish camp. School was certain to be out by the time the flood was over. Families went to fish camp as soon as the ice went out and the river was safe to navigate by boat. If school tried to be in session it was likely to lose all of its kids to fish camp. The parents were not concerned whether school was over or not; it was time to catch fish at fish camp. No one wanted to be late in catching the large, early run of king salmon. School for the kids was a distant second in priority to fish camp.

After the Flood

The floodwaters also brought valuable driftwood to the lower Yukon area. I remember seeing people using hooks or anchors to capture some of the good-looking driftwood that would float by. They stood on the bank and tried to hook the larger driftwood. If the wood was very large then several men were called upon to help in pulling it to the shore. Driftwood was too important a resource to just let it float by without being challenged. The flood actually brought a lot of driftwood to the village.

The flood also had a way of transforming the area. It eroded the cut bank side of the river. This had devastating effects if your village or home stood in its path. Present day Emmonak came into existence through the relocation of the former village of Kwiguk just a short distance upriver then down the south mouth on the opposite bank. Over time the bank of the river was eroded away and cabins built too close to the edge were lost to the river. Eventually only one cabin and a store was all that remained by the time I was a little girl. I think the move from Kwiguk to Emmonak occurred during my father's lifetime. I do remember going by dogsled with our family during the winter to Kwiguk to watch movies. Our first cabin became a victim of the eroding Kwiguk Pass.

The flooding also caused the river to change its channel structure over the years. After the flood, sandbars would appear or disappear as the ice and water left its mark on the course of the river. It usually took years for the incremental changes to occur, but the effects were noticeable over time. When I was a little girl there was just a small sandbar in front of our house in the river. Now the sandbar is a well-developed island which has willows and shrubs growing on it in its place. The flooding has also caused a change in Grandpa's Island at the end of Kwiguk Pass where we went to fish camp. It is more surrounded by mud flats than it used to be. After every spring flood season you had to pay attention to the water when boating even in well-known areas of the river. You could easily find yourself hung-up on a sandbar that did not exist there the year before.

The changing river also has its effects on locations far from the river such as the site of the old village of Akulurak. It was located many miles from the Yukon River, but was greatly affected by the changing river channel. Akulurak Pass used to be able to handle large boats and even small barges to supply the mission located there. Over the decades, in the early to middle 1900s, the Yukon River channel changed so that the water flow into the Pass was diminished. Eventually barge traffic was not possible and the mission buildings had to be relocated upriver to St. Mary's on the Andreafsky River during the early 1950s. Today it is very difficult to get to the old location of Akulurak. That was my favorite berry picking location when I was a little girl.

Cycle of Life

The spring floods were just a part of the cycle of life we had to endure almost every year. We took it in stride. It did not do any good to get angry. We just had to be patient and wait for the river to have its say in the big scheme of things. The flooding did bring good results along with it, so we did appreciate that aspect. It had a cleansing effect on the landscape as it washed away the debris accumulated during the winter. It was proof that nature was the master of the delta. As residents we had great respect for those forces greater than us.

There was something almost biblical about the spring flood. In order to make the transition from winter to summer, we had to go through the flood. Our destination to fish camp could only come by successfully traversing the Yukon flood. Fish camp was our promised land and the flood, like the Red Sea of the Bible, had to be experienced in our quest to get there.

People were always prepared for the flood when it came. It was foolish not to be prepared. It was rare for anyone to suffer due to the flood. Someone drowning was extremely rare. Everyone knew the river had a lot of power when it decided to overflow its banks and everyone respected that power. There are many memories I have of my life as a little girl growing up on the Kwiguk Pass of the lower Yukon River, but some of the most humbling ones were evidenced in the power of the flood.

Pride leads to disgrace, but with humility comes wisdom.

Proverbs 11:2

Spring Arrivals

Tulagtuq – To arrive

Spring was a much awaited time of year for me. Winter can become such a long season of cold, snow and darkness. It felt so good to watch the arrival of spring and say goodbye to winter.

Break-up and ice-out was a long awaited event on the lower Yukon River each year. The winter had become so long by the time we hoped for spring to come. Waiting for the river to become ice-free in late May or early June seemed to take forever. There was so much to be done once the ice was out of the river. Fish camp was not far off. It was a time to anticipate the spring arrivals that transitioned us from the cold grip of winter to the warm sunshine of summer.

Salmon

There was so much to look forward to in the spring. The salmon began their annual migration into and up the Yukon River. The first salmon to enter the river from the Bering Sea were the king salmon. They sure were large fish. The biggest ones could be taller than I. They were also very heavy. It was all I could do just to pick them up. The largest ones were actually too big for me to handle. They were the best eating. After eating dried fish all winter long, it was a real treat to eat some fresh salmon, especially the kings. I think the Yukon River king salmon are the best in the world. Living at the mouth of the Yukon River we were able to catch the salmon when they are the richest in body fat. Their meat was very red and juicy.

Fresh salmon right from the net was delicious. Salmon migrating up the lower Yukon River included:

- King Salmon
- Summer Chum Salmon
- Fall Chum Salmon
- Pink Salmon

We knew that as soon as the river was safe for travel from ice flows we began making preparations to go to fish camp for the summer. Fresh fish from the net would be the normal meal rather than dried fish from the winter smokehouse. That was another reason for the anticipation of going to fish camp. The teachers made certain that school was dismissed for the summer by the time the ice went out.

Fishing season also brought more people from upriver to Emmonak. They were the ones who annually came to the delta just for the king salmon fishing. It was an opportunity to see and visit those friends who we only see during the summer season. The population of Emmonak grew a lot because of the extra fishing families which came during the summer. Emmonak has the reputation of being the best king salmon fishing area of Alaska. It was fun having the extra kids around for play partners.

Pa made sure all the nets were mended and ready for use before we headed to fish camp. Any work or repairs on the boats were done at this time. Everything we did during the wait for spring was in preparation for the trip to fish camp. Dreams of a big catch of salmon were our great motivator.

Waterfowl

Break-up also meant the return of waterfowl to the lower Yukon area. Countless birds came to the delta for nesting. It was an amazing sight to see so many birds in one place at one time. It seemed that every water bird came to our area for the summer. Some of the waterfowl which came to nest along the Yukon River delta were:

- Pintail ducks
- Mallard ducks
- Northern shovelers
- Green-winged teal

- Geese – such as Brant, Canada and Snow
- Whistling swans
- Loons

The warm, long hours of sunshine during the short summer made the tundra blossom with plants of many varieties. The tundra was a haven for many insects. Both the plants and insects provided an ideal rearing area for the migratory birds calling the tundra islands their summer homes.

The birds also brought the thoughts of new food sources. We could treat ourselves to a bird now and again at fish camp. It was possible to get tired of fish everyday at fish camp. Having a change in our diet of all fish was a pleasant surprise when Pa returned to camp with a bird he had shot on the tundra. The eggs of the waterfowl were also a delicacy that was very much appreciated when we were greeted with them. Journeying out onto the tundra in search of bird nests was a lot of fun. The vast open spaces made a little girl seem pretty small on the delta. Wherever there was waterfowl also meant that water, such as a stream, lake or pond was not far away. The water meant another place to play and build things that would float in the stream.

The birds we caught on the tundra also provided not only food for us but also their down feathers were very valuable. We used them as stuffing for our pillows and mattresses. There is nothing like fresh down feathers as replacement for the worn out ones we eventually get tired of sleeping on. It was a real treat to use the new down feathers for sleeping at fish camp.

Constant Daylight

The sun rising higher and higher in the sky also accompanied the transition to spring. During the longest day of the year in mid-June the sun would basically just swing around the horizon. It really did not set for very long. It never got black dark during that time of year.

You could watch the travels of the sun from the treeless tundra island all day long without any obstruction. Since it never really got dark, it was sure hard to sleep. I could find a lot of things to do in the sunshine rather than sleep at night. It was interesting to note that we did not see the stars for a long time. We obviously never saw them while at fish camp.

The most anticipated event of all was the arrival of warmer temperatures. After a winter of cold and blowing snow, it was a wonderful feeling to let the sunshine hit our face and warm us up on the inside. The warmer temperatures though brought with it the prospect of another oncoming horde of mosquitoes and flies of all kinds. They were a real nuisance at fish camp.

Supply Barges

The onset of spring and the river becoming ice-free also gave homage to the annual arrival of the supply barges to the village. As soon as the last of the ice floated away, we waited in eager anticipation for the barges, which carried the replenishing supplies needed for the upcoming year. Supplies in the village always became slim by the late winter months, so the arrival of the supply barges was critical.

The spring barge brought fresh new produce to the local Northern Commercial store. That was highly anticipated by everyone. Fresh fruits sold out fast as soon as the word spread that they were available at the store. When we ran out of those items during the winter they were not restocked because it cost too much to fly them in by plane.

The barge also brought the needed fuel for the summer months. Gasoline that was required for the boat outboard motor was one of the important items brought in on the spring run of the barge. Fuel for the village generator came in on the first barge delivery. Large items which people ordered during the winter were brought on the spring barge too. These were items costing too much in freight to fly in on the plane. You could see all kinds of merchandise being transported to the village by the barge. Most all the barge freight came from the Seattle ports.

It was fun to go down to the unloading area and watch what kind of goods were going to be brought to the village. The barge was one of the main connections we had with the outside world while I was a little girl. After seeing the Yukon so quiet during the winter, it was exciting to experience so much activity during the spring.

When I was little, my family had no money to buy much of anything so it was fun to see what everyone else was getting on the spring barge. Even though there was nothing on the barge for us, I didn't care. Fish camp was coming soon and nothing else was going to matter then. The really fun part of my young life was just about to begin at *Grandpa's Island*.

Freezer Ships

I do not remember when the first freezer ship came to Emmonak. I think it was during the late 1960s or early 70s. The first freezer ship I remember seeing was one called the *Polar Bear*.

The *Polar Bear* was an awesome sight to see. It was the biggest thing I had ever seen in my life. We could see the top of the ship long before we saw the ship's body. The rotating radar antennae and booms could be seen above the treetops upriver as the it came from the south mouth of the Yukon River from the Bering Sea. It had to travel very slowly to keep itself in the river channel and not run into a sandbar. The ship would make a left-hand turn from the Kwikluak Pass of the Yukon to enter the Kwiguk Pass that brought it to Emmonak. I remember watching its every move as it slowly came into view as it turned into Kwiguk Pass. It was hard to believe such a huge ship came to our little village all the way from Seattle. What stories on the high seas it must have been able to tell!

It anchored in front of the Northern Commercial Company store. It also brought supplies that were off-loaded. It would anchor in front of Emmonak until its freezer cargo holds were full of salmon and then return.

It returned to Emmonak every year for many years to come. I remember going to the *Polar Bear* and buying an ice cream cone for five cents. It was a wonderful treat that we were allowed to have occasionally.

The arrival of the *Polar Bear*, and eventually a number of other freezer ships in later years, had a huge impact on salmon fishing. It created the shift from all subsistence fishing for salmon to commercial fishing. It also created an entire industry for our area based on commercial fishing for all species of salmon. This all happened while I grew from a little girl at fish camp, up to my teenage years, and then working full-time at Northern Commercial Company store.

The increase in commercial fishing created the need for *tender boats* that transported the commercial salmon catch from the fishermen's boats to the freezer ships. Fishing for salmon eventually switched from subsistence to commercial purposes. There were still families that fished all subsistence, like ours. Each year there were fewer and fewer of us fishing solely for subsistence.

As a result it changed the economy of Emmonak. More money was now available in the village and caused a change in the lifestyle of the people. Emmonak would begin to evolve into a very different village because of the arrival of the freezer ships and the money that followed their presence.

Bering Sea Fisheries

I do not remember when the cannery barge, *Bering Sea Fisheries,* began its operations. It was an annual spring event to move the cannery barge from its winter anchorage upriver to its operating location along Lamont Slough. Lamont Slough was a waterway that drained from the south side of Kwikluak Pass downriver from the intersection with Kwiguk Pass. A lot of work was required to get it prepared for the start of fishing season. It was a very exciting time as everyone anticipated the upcoming salmon fishing season signaled, by the arrival of the cannery barge in Lamont Slough.

The barge had the capability of canning salmon. That was a novelty among the subsistence fishermen along the river. The shiny cans of salmon had no labels since they had not been sold to buyers in Seattle yet.

Bill Bodey was the manager of the fisheries operation. His operation would buy salmon, then cook it and pack it in cans. Bill had lived in the area since the 1930s. He had worked with salmon his entire life. Since he was a businessman in a very highly regulated industry he had strong opinions about his salmon business and the protection of the salmon resource. He had to balance the need to operate a profitable business as well as preserve the resource for future generations. He knew he could not catch all the fish that migrated up the Yukon River, as that would deplete the salmon run for the next generation of salmon.

These were a few of the signs that spring had arrived on the lower Yukon River delta. It was a quick transition from spring to the busy summer season that was to come. We looked forward to each arrival every year. The spring arrivals ushered in another summer on the delta.

A person who strays from home is like a bird that strays from its nest.

Proverbs 27:8

Summer

Introduction

The Yupik Eskimo word for summer is Kiak, which means, summer. This season was all about fish camp and the many activities that occurred around fish camp. It was a very exciting time of the year. I really enjoyed going to fish camp. I especially looked forward to the preparation and departure for Grandpa's Island, our fish camp destination.

I think it was the thought of going to another place that was so appealing to me. It was so peaceful on the tundra island. The Bering Sea brought so much life to our way of living. It brought us fish, seals and beluga whales that were necessary to our subsistence lifestyle. To stand on the west side of Grandpa's Island and see the greatness of the Pacific Ocean was exhilarating. The sunsets to the west were so majestic and beautiful.

Fish camp was a very busy time of year. It was hard work fishing. It took a lot of physical labor to catch and process the fish for winter storage and it was an endless job. We fished every day of the week. When the salmon were running strong we seemed to work all day long. I always wanted to play in the creek with my friends on the island or just be by myself. It was a wonderful experience to enjoy the waterfowl that nested on the island.

When a seal or beluga whale was sighted, fishing was put on hold for a while. That was a big event on the island. Life came to a stop when they came into the channel. Everybody joined in on the hunt. The promise of having fresh meat was worth all the work that went into the hunting adventure. The summer season certainly centered on fish camp and all the activities associated with it. It was an exciting time of year. Summer at fish camp is what made us Eskimo along the Kwiguk Pass of the lower Yukon River

Fish Camp

Kiagvik: Summer Fish Camp

When I think of fish camp, many memories come to my mind. I loved going to fish camp. It was one of my favorite places to go when I was a little girl. I looked forward to it every summer after school was over for the year. When the ice was out, I knew that fish camp was not far off.

Going to fish camp was an annual ritual almost every family of Emmonak participated. It was an essential aspect of life for us. It was the one event drawing us together as a family. It was a family affair. Every one of the family members had a role to play in its success. The fish we caught became the dogs' and our sustenance for the coming winter. Fishing needed to be successful for our own survival during the following months until the next summer and another trip to fish camp.

Preparation

We usually went to fish camp during the first week of June. Both school and the river ice would be out for the season. My parents did most of the preparation for fish camp. It required us to basically move our home from the village to the island at the end of the Kwiguk Pass near the Bering Sea. We brought a canvas tent which held up to eight people. A little Yukon wood stove was brought as our heat source and also for cooking. Mattresses, usually two, were brought along with blankets and pillows for comfort. It could get quite cold on the island at night, so anything providing extra warmth was welcomed. Our parents packed our clothes for us, since they seemed to know best as to what we should bring. I guess they did not trust us to do our own clothes packing. They knew what was essential. We also brought our pots and pans, dishes, silverware and cups, which were transported in boxes to keep them from breaking during the some-times, rough boat ride.

Pa prepared the fish nets that were used to catch the fish. He made certain they were dried after last year's fishing season, and then placed in the smoke house for storage over the winter. Drying the fishnets was one of the important tasks done during the late summer and early fall. Pa made certain that job was done soon after all the fishing seasons were complete. Along with the nets, he brought the buoys and anchors. Extra floats were brought along just in case some broke or became lost during the fishing season.

We did not bring much food with us, as we did not have the mon-ey to buy any. We relied on the fish we caught and the other foods we gathered on the island. We knew that during the summer at fish camp we were likely to have other foods to eat such as whale and seal meat. The island provided us with eggs from nesting birds and wa-terfowl Pa was able to hunt when he was not fishing and, there were always greens we gathered on the island for eating.

The only foods we bought from the store to bring with us were:

- Sailor Boy® pilot bread crackers
- Tillamook cheese
- Canned butter
- Flour
- Sugar
- Tea for the kids
- Coffee for the parents

Pa made several trips by himself with the boat to bring all the sup-plies to fish camp. It was a very busy time for him, as he wanted to have the camp ready to occupy by the time our entire family arrived at fish camp.

Departure for Fish Camp

Everyone helped in loading the boats with our parents' supervi-sion. We took two boats. One was for the parents, kids and our per-sonal belongings. The second boat was for the dogs and other items that did not fit in the first boat along with us. The dog boat was used to also haul items the dogs could not eat, trample, break or otherwise destroy while going to fish camp. The first boat towed the second boat. The dogs were tied to the side of the boat so they could not jump out into the water during the trip. I don't think they really liked the idea of traveling in the boat as they barked and made noise almost the entire time during the trip to fish camp.

It was about twelve miles to the island where we set up fish camp. We were on watch for driftwood along the way. The driftwood served many purposes at fish camp. It was used as a source of heat for the tent and for the smokehouse fire. Usually there was no sign of human activity along the way. We also watched for waterfowl as a possible source of food.

On the way out to the island we passed the cutoff to the village of Alakanuk. The cutoff to Alakanuk was located on the south side of Kwiguk Pass. It occurred at a point in the river where it narrowed. This narrow section of the river created some very large waves. I liked the big waves. They added some excitement to the trip. The cutoff to Alakanuk was another way to go there. It was a very meandering route, with many turns in the pass. It took longer to get to Alakanuk this way but sometimes we used it for a change of scenery. The chances of seeing waterfowl on the water were better than using the south mouth or Kwikluak Pass. Since we always carried a gun with us in the boat, we were on the lookout for food that might be found on the water such as ducks and geese.

We also had relatives who lived at Alakanuk. David and Marie Joe lived there from my mother's side of the family. The Joseph family resided in the village from Pa's side of the family. We used the boat to visit them in the summer or go by snow machine in the winter. There was also a general store in Alakanuk where we went sometimes to look for goods we might need to purchase. Alakanuk in Yupik Eskimo means mistake or the wrong way. I am not sure why it was given that name. It might be because the early people took that passage in search of the mouth of the Yukon River and realized it was a mistake to go that way.

As we got closer to the Bering Sea the terrain became mostly arctic tundra and very flat, no trees. Even the willows that grew next to the river became smaller and eventually nonexistent. The island that was our destination I called Grandpa's Island, because we went to the same island my grandpa used to set up his fish camp. There may have been a common name for it, but that is what I called it. It was the only island at the end of what people called Kwiguk Pass of the Yukon River. It was triangular shaped with a pointed side to the river

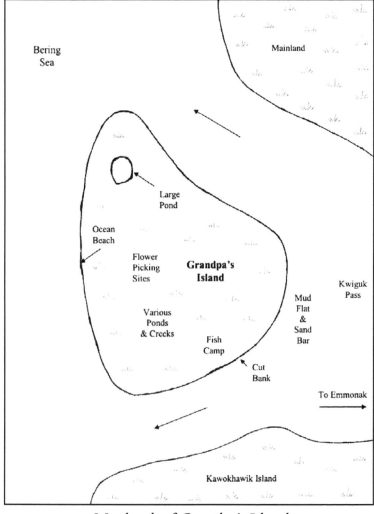

My sketch of Grandpa's Island

and the flat side to the ocean. It was a tundra island with no trees, no brush, just grass or bare clay dirt. The side of the island that faced the river was cut bank. There was also a small mud flat that sheltered Grandpa's Island from the Kwiguk Pass approach. It made the approach to the island a little tricky if you read the water wrong. There was also a sand bar that created an obstacle as we approached the island. Depending on whether the tide was coming in or going out, the sandbar and mud flat made it even more difficult to approach. If the tide was high, you could not see the sandbar as you came near it. You certainly needed to know the water or else you were going to get your boat stuck on the sandbar. The seaside of the island was a more gently sloping beach that was good for walking. As a little girl it was a big island. We could walk around it in about two hours. It had creeks we played in. We picked up rocks, pulled grass and picked flowers for fun and made things with them, or used them as toys. There was lots of ducks and geese on the island. There were ponds on the island, which provided another source of water to play in and provide water used around camp. There was one large pond located in a corner of the island next to Kwiguk Pass and the ocean. It was too deep for safe wading and play. This large pond was a magnet for numerous waterfowl. We found many nests sites around it.

Arrival

Once we landed at Grandpa's Island we had to climb the cut bank in order to get from the boat to the top of the island. Every year it was different because flooding had eroded its surface. We had to cut steps into the vertical bank to make a staircase for walking up to the top. This made getting to the top of the island easier, especially when we had to carry our supplies as well. Pa made the steps during an earlier supply trip to the island.

Pa had erected the living tent during one of his earlier trips and now it was our turn to carry our personal items into the tent to occupy it. The tent was a white canvas-wall tent. It was the same type used by the Klondike gold rush settlers. Each family on the island used one to house the family members. You were able to determine how many families occupied the island by counting the number of white tents. My parents organized the inside of the tent so every item had a place. The tent was going to be our home away from home for the entire summer. The Yukon stove was placed inside the tent near the front door and was used for both heat and cooking. The canvas-wall tent had a hole cut in the roof for venting the stovepipe out the top. The mattresses were organized inside the tent for sleeping near the back wall. We used large coffee cans as a toilet. We emptied them in the river. I think we had a table, but it was usually nothing more than a box turned upside down with the bottom serving as the table-top. Other boxes simply served as storage containers for our food and cooking utensils we brought. More boxes were used to store our clothes. We had no chairs so we sat on the mattresses, dirt floor, or driftwood was cut to serve as a stool. It got a little cramped inside, but it was fun, so we did not mind it at all. There were eight of us inside the tent. We picked up driftwood from the island's beach to use to make fire in the stove.

Other components of the fish campsite included building net dry-ing racks for the fishnets to dry when not in the water catching fish.

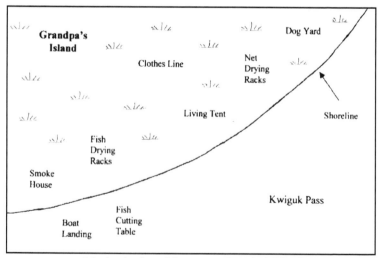

My sketch of our fish camp at Grandpa's Island

Pa drove two stakes into the ground and tied another branch be-tween them to hold the nets above the ground. Another set of similar stakes was driven into the ground a distance away so the net could be hung like a hammock between them. The components of the drying racks were nothing more than driftwood we found on the beach or the island. We built a smokehouse out of corrugated metal with a wood frame surrounding it. The wood frame of the smokehouse was made of driftwood we found lying around. The corrugated metal was hauled from our cabin in Emmonak as it was re-used year after year for just this purpose. It had rows of horizontal poles inside the smokehouse to hold the fish for drying or smoking. We built many rows to hold the fish. For the smoke fire we just used driftwood we found along the beach. Nothing fancy was required. Fish drying racks had to be built. These were used as the first step of the drying process. After the fish were cut into strips they were hung on the drying racks for a while before they were moved to the smokehouse. The drying racks were also made of driftwood we found. Stakes were driven into the ground and horizontal branches were tied to the up-rights on which the fish would hang for drying in the sun. We dried the fish in the sun, then smoked them, or salted the fish for preserving. A clothes line also had to be erected from driftwood poles we found and drove into the ground. Whatever rope or twine we might have was used as the clothesline. A dog yard was setup by driving a wooden stake into the ground to tie up each dog. We had one stake for each dog and made a straight line of the stakes behind the living tent area. That became the dogs' summer home.

The boat was tied up on the beach in front of the cut bank side of the island. We tried to tie up the boat near the steps if we could. The tide determined how much beach area we had between the waterline and the cut bank. We kept the cutting table and the 55-gallon drum as close to the boat as possible to make carrying and cleaning the fish easier. We always had to watch the weather to make certain the boat and any items left on the beach were safe from heavy waves that could occur during bad weather. If the weather became really rough then we anchored the stern of the boat on the beach and faced the bow into the water to keep it from being swamped in the high waves. We also had to be mindful of the tides so we were not caught un-awares during an unusually high tide that could float away anything that was not anchored to the shore.

Flower Picking

I walked around the island and picked flowers. I loved picking flowers from the tundra island when I was young. It was one of my favorite activities while at fish camp when I was not busy helping with the fish. I remember finding and picking the following wild flowers from Grandpa's Island:

- Bluebells
- Wild Iris
- Forget-me-not
- Arctic Lupine
- Fireweed
- Alaska Poppy
- Sitka Burnet
- Horsetail
- Western Buttercup

I remember picking bluebells. When the bluebell flower was picked it left a hole in the middle. I used the hole of the flower and threaded a blade of grass through it. I would then thread more flowers onto the grass blade and make a bracelet or headband. They were pretty when completed. Eventually they dried out and lost their color. I just picked more flowers and made a new one. My favorite flower to pick was the forget-me-not. I loved its blue-colored flower. It seemed to grow everywhere on the tundra. In fact the flowers seemed to grow very large on the island. They received full sunshine almost all day long. There were no trees to shade any of the tundra so I think that made them grow so well. The flowers seemed so brilliant and colorful out there. The island full of colorful blooming flowers was irresistible to a little girl like me. I thought it was one of the most beautiful places on earth.

Our Island Neighbors

Several families used the same island we occupied. I don't remember all of their names. I do remember the Oktoyak family was one of them. Each family had their own site they used from years past. We simply respected each other's territory. Owning space on the island was not important to anyone. It was there for everybody's use, as they desired. There were times when we had to rely on each other for assistance and sharing of goods and food. It was fun having other families around that provided playmates besides my sister and brothers to play with.

I remember the Oktoyak's kids. They had a daughter named Virginia that was my age. She had two younger sisters, Zita and Agatha, and we played games together. It was fun playing with them. It was great having someone my age also living on the island. I enjoyed that part of fish camp a lot. It was one of the reasons I enjoyed going to fish camp as much as I did. Games we played with the other kids on the island were:

- Hop scotch
- Marbles
- Tag
- Kick the can
- Jump rope
- Lap game
- Red rover
- Hide and seek
- Play house
- Play boats
- Slingshot
- Seal hunting

Daily Routine

Usually the parents woke up first. The kids were allowed to sleep later. During the summer the sunlight really never did get dark. We could play all day and night if we wanted to without the use of artificial light. Our parents usually made us go to bed, even when we were not tired and could easily play all night. The sun never really set below the horizon for long, thus the continual daylight we experienced.

Pa made a fire in the stove to warm up the tent and make hot water for us each morning after he woke up. He was usually the first one to wake up each morning. Breakfast consisted of tea, crackers and dried fish for us kids. The grown-ups had coffee, which we were not allowed to have. It was the kids' job to clean up after breakfast. No play was allowed until the dishes were washed, dried, and put away until the next meal. Pa and the older boys then prepared to go fishing for the day. Fishing was a daily event.

Lunch was not at a set time. We simply ate whenever we felt like it. We ate whatever was available and how our appetite suited us. For us little girls we did the chores assigned to us. When the chores were completed then it was serious play around the island that required most of our time in the morning hours. We were hungry by noon for something to eat.

Supper was a time when we all ate together as a family. We made certain that all the family members were present for suppertime. It was a time to share our experiences of the day. We always talked about the fishing. Was it a good day or bad day for catching fish? We all shared what we saw or experienced around the island with each other. It was our main meal of the day. It most always consisted of fish in one form or another. Fried, broiled or dried fish was the main course. Sometimes we had birds, such as ducks or geese, or game found on the island or on the banks of the Yukon River, upriver just a short distance. Making supper was under the direction of Mom. The girls of the family usually were required to assist with the cooking. It was our chance to learn how to prepare the foods we ate. Once the supper meal was finished we went our separate ways. Pa and the boys took the boat to check the fishnets one last time. As usual, we were required to wash the dishes right after supper was done.

The kids then went out to play again. As I said earlier, it really never got dark, but eventually our parents made us go to sleep for bedtime maybe around nine at night. Later in the summer months when it really got black dark we had a lantern in the tent to give us some light. For me the lantern came in handy as a source of light to read by.

We brought our dogs to fish camp. They were staked out individually. I don't remember giving them any names, but I knew them for their color differences and how I treated them uniquely from each other. They had no purpose at fish camp. They could not be left back at the cabin in Emmonak all summer without someone to care for them, so they came along. They had to be fed each day. We fed them fish head soup, which was a mixture of all the fish parts leftover from the gutting and preparation for drying. These leftover parts were kept in a fifty-five gallon drum with water. Whenever the dogs needed feeding, a portion of this fish soup was put in a kettle and heated over a fire. The soup was then transferred to individual bowls and given to each dog. Pa prepared the dog food for cooking. The kids helped if we were around to do so. The dogs were fed before we sat down to eat supper. Everyday all summer long, we ate fish and the dogs ate fish.

Our source of water for drinking or cooking came from either a stream that fed into the Yukon River or from a creek or pond on the island. The water was dirty. We let it settle, carefully poured out the water leaving the dirt in the bottom of the bucket. Chlorox was added to purify the water, before we boiled it. We also swam in the pond for fun. Bathing was not a top priority nor was it a necessity for us at fish camp. We washed our clothes using a washboard placed in a metal tub with water we carried in metal buckets from the creek.

Fishing

Fishing was done everyday. The first fish migrating up the river were the king salmon. They started to migrate the first of June. They were very large fish for me to handle. They were the choice fish to catch. They were the best tasting. Everyone wanted to catch as many kings as possible. The king salmon were kept for human consumption only and were not fed to the dogs. They were too valuable to feed them to the dogs. The next fish to arrive were the summer chum salmon also called dog salmon. The name dog salmon was very appropriate as they were the fish which were almost exclusively fed to the dogs. They were not as large as the kings, but there were a lot more of them. We ended up catching many more summer chums than all the other salmon combined. The last fish to arrive were the fall chum salmon. They were bigger than the summer chum, but not as plentiful. We also called them silver chums because they were so silvery looking. Every other year we caught pink salmon. They were the smallest of the salmon. The quality of the pinks was the poorest of the salmon.

Pa and the older boys went fishing soon after breakfast was over. The fishing was done upriver from the island in an area that offered a good river eddy. Eddies were the best places to set the nets in order to catch the salmon as they migrate upriver. An eddy is formed in that portion of the river where it made a turn. The current of the river formed a cut bank side and an opposite sandbar side as it turned and changed direction. As the river changed direction it caused the water to swirl and move erratically. A net placed in this water had a better chance of catching fish than one placed in straight current. The erratic water movement made the net more difficult to be seen by the salmon as they migrated upriver. We caught the fish in set gill nets. One end of the net was attached to the beach while the other end was anchored in deeper water with a buoy attached to keep it afloat. We used eight-inch mesh nets to catch the king salmon and smaller five-inch mesh nets for the chum salmon. The best fishing occurred when it was raining and windy. That was when the salmon could not see the nets as easily. The worst fishing occurred when the weather was the best with bright sunshine and calm water. Pa and the older boys in the family did the fishing. The girls were not involved in fishing. I was allowed to go with Pa on occasion when the circumstances were just right for him. I enjoyed going fishing, but it sure was hard work and I usually got really wet and slimy from handling the fish.

After the nets were set and ready to catch fish, Pa and the boys returned to fish camp. It was not a good idea to stay in the boat next to the net as it could alarm the fish and they would avoid the net. Setting the net was hard work and the relaxation at fish camp was very much appreciated. The nets were checked periodically depending on the strength of the run. If there were a lot of fish, then the nets had to be checked often. It was important not to allow the nets to get too full of fish or they were nearly impossible to unload into the boat. The early running king salmon were much larger than the latter migrating chums, thus this also had an impact on how often the nets were checked for fish.

When checking the nets the boat was positioned perpendicular to the net. The net was pulled across one side of the boat to the other so the fish could be untangled from the net and dropped into the middle of the boat. The picking process began at the buoy side of the net, which was closest to the middle of the river. As the net was pulled across the middle of the boat, the boat would be naturally pulled toward the shore. When removing the salmon from the net, you had to be careful not to get bitten. The more mature the salmon became because of their individual migration patterns, the easier they could use their hooked snout to bite. I did not like that part of working with the fish. We wore white canvass gloves when checking the nets to protect ourselves from both the net, which could cut our hands, and from the fish that wanted to bite us.

When all the fish were picked from the net, the decision was made whether to leave the net out to catch more fish or bring it in if finished for the day. The trip from the net to fish camp might take longer, especially if the boat was full of fish. The person driving the boat had to be careful if the boat was full. A heavy boat full of fish would ride lower in the water and was more susceptible to swamping under the heavy load. When the boat reached the island it was anchored next to the fish cutting table if the tide allowed. The fish-cutting table was placed on the beach so the boat could be tied up close to it. Some of the fish could be real heavy, especially the larger king salmon. It was all I could do just to hold the big ones, let alone trying to carry them any distance.

Mom cut the fish using an ulu. An ulu was the Eskimo version of a cutting knife. Pa made them for her. They were elliptical shaped and made of metal with a wood handle. Pa cut the oval shape out of a piece of steel with his hacksaw. The oval cutting edge was made sharp with a file. The opposite edge of the ulu was straight. This is where the wood handle was attached. Pa used cut nails to attach the wood handle to the metal piece. It was very strong and very efficient as a foodcutting tool. It worked great for cutting fish or anything around the cabin or fish camp. Because of its oval cutting surface it worked great for cutting anything when laid on a board or flat surface. Mom did not trust us younger kids to assist until we were old enough to be trusted with a knife in our hands. It was my job to carry the fish from the boat to the cutting-table. The fish cutting process included cutting the head off, then slicing the belly and removing the insides of the fish. The heads and entrails were tossed into a fifty-five gallon drum full of water to cure the fish parts to be fed to the dogs. Some Eskimos kept the heads separated in another barrel and consumed them in what was called fish-head soup. We did not eat the fish-heads that way; instead we fed them to the dogs. This was our daily routine at fish camp. It was important that plenty of fish were caught during the summer to provide enough food for our family and the dogs during the winter. This was the whole purpose of life at fish camp and why it was an important ritual for us every year. Once the fish were all unloaded from the boat, another trip to check the nets began if the run were strong. Otherwise the boat was left on shore and the net was taken from the boat and carried to the net rack to be dried until the next fishing day. The net was really heavy. It was saturated with water and fish slime that sure added to its normal weight. It was hard work to carry it up the cut bank steps and then to the net drying racks. It was very important to allow the net to dry when not in the water. The durability of the net was seriously diminished if it was never allowed to dry.

If there were a lot of salmon migrating or running then the fishing continued all day and all night. We had to take advantage of fishing whenever there were lots of fish to be caught. Our lives simply depended on bringing home a lot of fish to hold us over for the winter. If the strong run lasted a long time then there was very little time to do anything other than work on fish all the time. It sure could make a little girl very tired. The worst part of being so busy was that it did not allow for any playtime.

As mom cut the fish into strips, it was my job to carry the strips to the drying racks. The fish were cut so that the tail was used as a handle to hold the two strips of the fish together. This double-sided system then allowed me to hang the strips over a pole of the fish rack. There were many fish racks with a lot of horizontal poles on each to hold as many fish as we could catch. The fish strips stayed on the racks to dry in the sun. As soon as mom thought they had dried in the sun long enough, they were then taken to the smokehouse. The smoking process cured the fish so they could be stored during winter. It also gave them a good taste that I really liked.

The smokehouse also had many horizontal poles for hanging the fish. I helped in carrying the fish strips from the drying racks to the smokehouse. A fire was built in the middle of the smokehouse on the ground. The fire had to be started and maintained in such a way as to give off lots of smoke with little flame. I was not allowed to tend this fire because I either made it with too much flame or it would always go out on me. I guess that is why I was always the one that was in charge of the campfire and not the smokehouse fire. Various stages of smoked salmon were hanging in the smokehouse at any given time. Some were just recently placed on the poles while others were cured and ready to be placed in wooden kegs for storage then hauled home at the end of fishing season.

The weather, of course, controlled every aspect of fish camp life. The rain really did not stop anything, because it resulted in the best fishing. Long periods of rain were not good for drying the fish. We wanted sunny weather for that part of the effort. We could count on catching more fish when the weather was the poorest. The weather ranged from nice and sunny to foggy to heavy rain. When our clothes got wet we dried them over the stove during the night. I don't remember ever getting real sick because of the weather. I think we were just used to it.

Food from the Island

We also picked wild flowers on the island that we consumed. One of them was a flower called Coltsfoot. We ate their leaves by dipping them in sugar. That made for a wonderful snack right from the tundra. I especially liked to pick Labrador Tea, which grew everywhere. We boiled the leaves to make a really good tasting hot drink. That certainly warmed up a person during the cool evenings that were all too common during the summer on the island. Labrador Tea was also used to soothe a stomachache. A flower called Alaska Cotton grew on the island. They made a cottony ball when the flowers matured during June and July. They were white and fuzzy just like cotton balls. The wind blew them all over the landscape when they matured. The lower stems were edible and tasty. The roots grew to the size of small potatoes. We also called them wild potatoes. Mouse nests were a hiding place for wild potatoes. We looked for the nest and took the potatoes that were hidden by the mice. All we had to do was wash them a little and they were ready to eat as they were found. Wild potatoes were also dug up from the ground. They looked something like carrots. We used them in the soups we made. We also picked greens from the ponds. I am not sure what they were actually called, so I just called them greens. They were like lily pads and we waded in the water to pick them off the surface of the water. We boiled them and ate them along with the fish.

The island contained all sorts of birds. We saw swans, geese of many types, and lots of ducks, some ptarmigan and other waterfowl that used the island for summer nesting. We kids were in charge of gathering eggs. I don't know which birds' eggs we gathered. There were so many birds of all kinds and types that I never was able to identify very many of them. When we found a waterfowl nest, we took the eggs. These were eaten as one of the mainstays of our diet while at fish camp. Our favorite way to eat eggs were either fried or hard-boiled.

Pa hunted birds with a gun. The birds he killed were first plucked before we cut them up for eating. The bones and non-meat portions became dog food. The dogs really enjoyed eating the bird by products. We were very careful to keep the down feathers. These were used to stuff our pillows and mattresses. We had to save and use everything we took from the island, as we did not have the money to buy new pillows and mattresses whenever the down wore out.

The Bugs

And then there were the mosquitoes. They were everywhere. They could make life completely miserable. The only good thing about the tundra islands next to the Bering Sea coast was that the winds from the ocean tended to keep the numbers down a little. They affected every aspect of life at fish camp. I don't know how the older people tolerated them before repellent was invented. The mosquito repellent worked very well. We smelled like insect repellent all summer long. On still, calm days they were so thick in the air that you had to be careful in your breathing that you did not swallow too many.

They swarmed so heavy you could see them like clouds just above the tundra. Life on the island was so much better when they ended their life cycle and were gone.

The mosquitoes might be gone but other bugs took their place. The big black biting flies were terrible. They were big enough that you felt them when they landed on you, but if you did not, their bite was painful. Then there were the tiny no-seeums. They landed on you without detection, and were terrible at going up your nose. I guess we had to deal with all kinds of nuisance bugs when I think about it.

Other Fish Camp Cuisine

It was a very special occasion at fish camp when a spotted seal or even a beluga whale was sighted. Everyone joined the hunt. If the hunt was successful and we killed one, it was shared with all the other families that camped on the island. It was a very happy time when we were lucky enough to land a whale. There was enough food in a beluga whale to last several families a long time. The muktuk was rendered to make whale oil, and used in cooking many foods due to its high oil content. Eating the whale flipper was another of those acquired tastes that you had to have to enjoy its value. We found more spotted seals to harvest than beluga whale. The spotted seal became more of our staple food around fish camp, as they followed the salmon into the river. Once in the river channel they were easier to hunt down and capture.

For something different to do we took the boat to the mainland to see if we could find a rabbit. The variety in our diet was a good thing as it got tiresome eating fish for every meal, everyday. We might also find ptarmigan on the mainland as well as rabbits. I also enjoyed the change of scenery. There were other kinds of flowers to be found on the mainland. I would pick a bunch to make a bouquet and bring them back to the island. Looking for more driftwood was another reason to go to the mainland with the boat. We also went out into the ocean to hunt seals and waterfowl on the sandbars that existed far from the coast.

Departure for Home

Eventually the summer fishing came to an end. When the salmon ended their migration, fishing season was over and it was time to go back to Emmonak and our cabin. Typically we left within about one week before school began. The dried and smoked fish were put in wooden barrels and transported back home in the boat. We took down everything that was brought and hauled it back home. The tent, my home away from home, was taken down and loaded into the boat. The nostalgia of life on the island made it difficult to take down the tent and prepare to leave. The tent represented so many of those memories. Nothing was left on the island. The stakes that made up the drying racks, net racks and clothesline were pulled out of the ground and taken home with us. If something were accidentally left on the island it would turn up missing when the spring floods washed it away into the Bering Sea. The dogs were loaded into the second boat and towed back to Emmonak with my family and our personal belongings in the front boat. Pa continued to make several more trips to the island in order to haul everything back to the village.

Summer at fish camp was one of my favorite memories and I will always treasure it. It is what made us Eskimos. The experience taught me how to live without the modern conveniences of today's society. I experienced and saw how a person could easily live off the land and be very content, comfortable, and satisfied. It was an all day job, every day while at camp. It was a part of our cycle of survival every year. I loved every moment at fish camp. Making fire for the family was my job. I took great pride in being the fire keeper at camp. As I grew older and had a regular job at the Emmonak Northern Commercial store, I was not able to spend all summer at fish camp anymore. I would only go there when my Pa or my brothers took me when I was not working. But the wonderful memories are always there in my mind. I will never forget my little girl days at fish camp on Grandpa's Island.

*Work brings profit, but mere talk
leads to poverty!*
Proverbs 14:23

Summary Hunting

Pissurtuq – He is hunting

Hunting was an important activity for Pa. I was proud of Pa's hunting skills. He was a wonderful provider of food for our family.

As we traveled the delta we were always hunting and watching for animals. It was as much a fact of life for us as eating food. During the period of time while the river was open, we were constantly looking for possible food sources.

Whale hunting

When near the ocean, we were always on the lookout for the beluga whale. It is a white whale that grows to about fifteen feet long. While at fish camp it was common to spot a beluga whale near the island. The presence of a whale was indicated by the wake they created or by visual sighting when they surfaced for air. A whale made a very unique wake when traveling under water in the river. A good whale hunter could read the water for the presence of a whale, even if the whale could not be seen at the surface. If a whale's wake were seen, the hunter would wait and watch for the whale to surface to be certain of his suspicion. Beluga whales followed the migrating salmon from the Bering Sea into the Yukon River. They followed the salmon about five to ten miles upriver. It was uncommon to have them go upriver as far as the village of Emmonak. We kept a harpoon in the boat at all times while at fish camp in case we saw a whale. We were always on whale watch.

Pa made his own harpoon. To make the shaft of the harpoon he tried to find a very straight and strong stick from the trees that grew next to the river. He peeled the bark and made it as smooth as possible. He very meticulously used a knife to form the stick to be slender and free of any rough edges. At one end he cut a slit that held the metal spear end. The spear end was filed as sharp as possible and with notches cut in the metal to give it a serrated look and function. This kept the spear from working out of the animal after it was struck. The spear was secured to the stick with twine wrapped around the spear end.

The other end of the harpoon had a hole drilled into it and a rope was attached. The rope had a buoy attached to it. When the harpoon stuck into the whale or seal, the buoy allowed the hunter to follow the path it took.

Once a whale was sighted the hunt commenced. Sometimes a whale was sighted by a lone fisherman traveling the river while going to and from his fish net. He could take the opportunity to go ahead and try to harpoon the whale by himself. Usually the hunt began with a group of people using a number of boats. Hunting a whale as a group was safer than a single hunter trying to capture it alone. The chances of making a clean kill improved when a group worked together.

If we were on the island when a whale was sighted, we were certain to tell everyone that camped on the island. All the families took their boats and went after the whale. Each boat made wide circles as they watched for the whale to come to the surface for air. We always hoped that the whale would sound or surface nearest our boat. The most experienced harpooner in the boat kept himself ready with a harpoon in his hand. When the whale came to the surface, the harpooner tried to strike it in the head. The rope and buoy were let go from the boat and trailed the whale as it swam away. We followed the buoy until it stopped. This usually meant that the whale was either dead or seriously tired from the injury. The buoy was grabbed and the whale was pulled up next to the boat. We headed back to fish camp or Emmonak, whichever was closest to the location we captured it.

The whale was quite heavy and created a drag on the boat, so it was slow going. Once we reached shore the whale was pulled up on the beach. This took several strong men to pull it completely onto the shore where it could be cut up. Everybody came to the beach to assist in butchering the whale. Men and women both assisted in the cutting.

The cutting began at the belly. The insides were taken out, and then the real edible parts of the whale were cut. The whale was cut into sections from the skin down to the bone. There were three parts of the whale that we used for consumption.

Skin

This was a real delicacy to the Eskimo. There are three layers to the skin. The outermost layer was the skin itself. We peeled this layer away and just disposed of it. The middle layer of the skin was the good tasting part. The bottom layer of the skin had a very firm texture.

The skin was boiled and eaten. Some whale or seal oil was added for flavoring. It had a fishy taste. This was a real staple of our diet whenever a whale was brought to the village or fish camp. We looked forward to having whale skin as often as it was provided.

Muktuk

This is the thick layer just below the skin and attached to the muscle. This was the thickest part of the whale. After the muktuk was removed from the whale it was ready to be rendered. It was placed in a bucket and allowed to turn into oil. This was a natural way for us to get the oil that we used for flavoring our food. The heavy texture of the muktuk began to change into an oily consistency as soon as it was removed from the whale. We checked the rendering process often. When it was all converted to oil we transferred the whale oil from the bucket to jars. The jars were for future storage in the cabin. The whale oil was used primarily as a flavoring during our cooking. A popular use of the oil was to add it along with the dried fish.

The whale oil was also used as fuel. It was used as fuel in a wick lamp. I thought it was quite unique that it could be used for food flavoring as well as fuel to burn in our lamps.

Meat

The portion of the whale that was left after removing the skin and muktuk was the meat. Every piece of meat was removed from the bone. No meat was left behind if at all possible. The meat was dried just like we do with the fish strips. It was hung on drying racks to dry in the sun. Unlike the fish we did not smoke the whale meat. After it was dried in the sun, it was transferred to wooden kegs for storage. These were put in the smokehouse.

After all the edible parts were removed from the whale only the bones were left. These were given to the dogs. The dogs really enjoyed the opportunity to chew on the whalebones and pick the bones clean of any meat that could not be removed for human consumption.

The whale was distributed to the families based on need and relationship to the person who killed the whale. The person that killed the whale received the first, choice portions. The people most closely related to him received the next choice. It continued on like this until everyone related to the hunter received some portion of the whale. Everybody received something even if not related to the hunter. No one was left out. We always made certain that everyone got to share in the hunter's success. The Elders were also included in the receipt of the whale food. It did not matter if an Elder was related to the hunter or not, they automatically received some of the whale. It was our way of thanking and showing respect to the Elders of the village or of fish camp.

Anytime a whale was taken, it was a time to celebrate. The parts of the whale were valuable assets to everyone that received them. A hunter that was good at hunting whales was a very valued and highly regarded individual in the village. He carried much prestige and honor. It was his talents that kept food in supply for his family, relatives and village Elders. If a particular family did not have someone that was a good hunter, for whatever reason, we made sure they were provided with food.

Seal hunting

Seals were also widely sought after in the river. Just like the whale, which followed the salmon up the Yukon River, the seals also did the same. Hunting seals was very similar to hunting whales. Unlike the beluga whale, the seal would sometimes be spotted as far upriver as the village of Emmonak. Because they were smaller in size, they were able to go farther upriver. Since they were not as large as a whale, the effort required to haul them and butcher was not as demanding. They did provide us with much the same food value, just in lesser quantity. The seal provided us with muktuk and meat just like the whale did. The seal oil that was rendered from its muktuk was also used as a food flavoring. Seal meat was processed the same way as whale meat, as it was dried on drying racks before being stored in kegs and placed in the smokehouse for the winter.

What made the seal somewhat more valuable was its skin. It had fur and because of that it was used in making a number of clothing items. The sealskin had to be tanned before it could be used. The person using the sealskin required the patience to scrape, stretch and tan the skin to prepare it for use. Sealskins were used in making:

- Boots
- Coats
- Hats
- Mittens
- Eskimo Yo Yo's
- Dolls

The skin was usually given to the person who caught it, right off the seal. It was the responsibility of that person to do the tanning and prepare the skin for use.

I remember Teresa Kameroff, my aunt, was very good at making sealskin clothing. She helped me make one of my rabbit-lined parkas when I was growing up. The ability to use the skin and make clothing items from it was such a gift to possess. It was a talent that was handed down to her from her mother. It was amazing how she was able to take a skin and cut it to just the right size and shape that was required to piece together in order to complete the piece of clothing that she was making. It showed the resourcefulness that many people had toward using the things that nature provided for our benefit. Items made of sealskin were very warm. That made it an excellent choice for the long, cold Yukon days and nights in the winter.

Sealskin also made really good toys. If they were made from sealskin, then you knew they would be very durable. They made very good dolls which any young Eskimo girl simply enjoyed to have. The Eskimo Yo Yo was also a very popular toy that everybody wanted to have. It was an item you desired no matter how young or old you were.

Ocean hunting

Sometimes Pa took the boat and went west into the Bering Sea to hunt. This was an opportunity to search other areas for seal or waterfowl. He took harpoons and guns in anticipation of a successful find. I remember one time just Pa and I went out onto the ocean to hunt.

We went into the Bering Sea via Grandpa's Island with Pa's boat. We headed straight west into the open ocean. We had heard the freezer ship pilots tell us about sand bars that existed in the Bering Sea close to the western coast of Alaska as they came north after leaving the Aleutian Islands. The Bering Sea, we were told, was actually a very shallow body of water with numerous channels and sand bars. A ship had to be careful to stay in the channel to avoid running out of water along the western coast. The existence of these sand bars intrigued us as they might well be isolated homes for seal and waterfowl. Pa knew some were located due west from Kwiguk Pass. He had gone to them before and knew they sometimes contained ocean dwelling sea life. Timing was everything and there was no guarantee that you were going to find game when you arrived. A person had to be very aware of the tide chart so as to maximize your chances of locating the sand bars. If the tide was high there was no reason to go. You wanted to search for them during the lowest possible tide of the season.

After spending what seemed an eternity of driving the boat west we eventually lost sight of land to our east. All around us was water. It was a little unsettling being so far away from land. What if something went wrong with our outboard motor and we were on our own? It was a long way to row the boat back to home. Eventually Pa recognized the change in water that indicated we were getting close to the sand bars. On this trip we saw no wildlife. Pa approached the sand bars slowly and when we were over the top of one he stopped the boat and set out the anchor.

We both got out of the boat and stood on the sand. It was like wading in the small bodies of water back home, but this was the Bering Sea that we were standing in. It was nice to get out of the boat and stretch our legs. An eerie feeling came over me while standing on this submerged sand bar with nothing but water as far as I could see all around me. I sure felt small among the vastness of the Bering Sea. On this particular trip our timing was wrong. We saw nothing that we could catch from the Bering Sea. We were not going to need neither the harpoon nor the guns during this trip. The journey was not all lost as this had to be one of the most interesting and extraordinary trips I ever took with Pa. This was one trip that I would never forget.

There was one small problem that came to his attention while we stood on the sand bar. Pa had failed to bring his compass. If a person did not pay close attention to the time of day we would have had no sense of direction. All that we could see was water. No landmarks were visible from our location. Pa was always aware of the sun's location. We were so far from land that there was nothing from which we could get our bearings. Based on the position of the sun and knowing somewhat the portion of the day it was, Pa knew which direction was east or at least enough to get us back to land. I had every confidence that he knew how to get me back home.

As land came into view we realized that we had gone farther north than we expected. We were going to hit land around the middle mouth of the Yukon River. It was the Kwikpak Pass country that was going to be our landfall. Pa knew the area and followed the system of sloughs to the south that brought us back to Emmonak. It was the trip of a lifetime for me, but I was sure happy to be back home to the safety of our cabin.

We never made such trips in the winter. Going out onto the frozen Bering Sea held too many dangers. It was too white which made it very easy to get lost and disoriented even after going a short distance. The winds could create a whiteout with no advance warning. There were ever-present hazards of pressure ridges and open water that appeared out of nowhere. The Bering Sea was not just a huge flat sheet of smooth ice. It was a forbidden place. I did not want to go there in the wintertime.

Waterfowl Hunting

Life on the island at fish camp required that we hunt the ducks, geese and other waterfowl that used it as their home. The island was not only our home but theirs as well. They used the tundra islands as their northern breeding grounds. There were waterfowl everywhere. It was hard to imagine the number of birds that used it for their summer home. We had to have food, so there they were.

Pa took his gun and went hunting for them whenever we needed additional food. Sometimes it was a matter of eating something different that prompted him to hunt waterfowl. Sometimes Pa used the boat and went to the mainland to hunt waterfowl. Other times he walked to one of the ponds that existed on the island. Pa was a good shot and he usually came back with something to show for his efforts.

I went with Pa whenever he allowed me to tag along during his waterfowl hunts. I have many fond memories of our hunts together. We took a boat to the mainland and walked to a nearby pond. Ponds were everywhere on the delta so it did not take long to find one. He found a dry spot with a good view of the pond. We had to sit extremely quiet and try not to move. We did not make fancy blinds like hunters do today. We simply sat out in the open tundra. Ducks and geese flew all over and around us. They were everywhere. He shot them as they flew overhead. If they happened to fall in the water after being shot then he had to wade into the water to retrieve the bird. Sometimes he shot them sitting on the water. He made certain that they were not in deep water when he shot them.

Hunting was important all year round. There was something special about hunting in the summer. The beluga whales and seals provided many essential foods to our diet. The waterfowl that were everywhere provided not only food but eggs and feathers. The variety in our diet was greatly welcomed. It was a wonderful change from eating fish for every meal everyday. I will never forget the trip to the ocean sand bars. Most important of all are the memories that I have of summer hunting with Pa and all that he taught me.

Plans go wrong for lack of advice;
many counselors bring success.
Proverbs 15:22

Fall

Introduction

The Yupik Eskimo word for fall is Uk'suaq, which means, fall, to become winter. This was another transition period in the life of each villager. The work at fish camp was behind us and the preparation for winter was before us. Fall was a very busy time of year. It was also a time of year that saw the population of Emmonak diminish. The people that came during the summer to fish began to go home.

The freezer ships and supply barges began their trip to their home-ports in the south. This left the village a much quieter place than it was during the summer months. It was a busy time of the year. Preparations for the winter months required everyone's attention. Boats and fishing nets had to be prepared for storage. Mending and repairs to both were done at this time if required.

It was a time of berry picking on the tundra. I really enjoyed the trips to the berry picking fields. It was a wonderful time to be with the family plus, there were so many flowers that needed to be picked while berry picking. Grass had to be harvested in the fall. That required a lot of work. Picking, drying and storing it was just another job that had to be done.

Fall-time meant the return of another school year. There was always the anticipation of seeing the new and returning teachers. For Pa it was the time of year to build and repair dog sleds. He kept very busy with either building new dog sleds or repairing his own or for others. I liked to help Pa with the dog sled work. Everyone awaited the freeze-up of the river. The first snows were not far off. The freezing of the river was the official start of the winter season. When the river froze and the snows came it was time to be ready for another winter along the Kwiguk Pass of the lower Yukon River.

Berry Picking

Atsiyartut: To go berry picking   *I always wanted to go berry picking with my family. It was an opportunity to go to places frequented only during special times of the year.*

Once the days shortened and the temperature dropped the tundra began to turn colors. The tundra, which during the summer was all green, now turned red, orange, brown and various shades of green. It was a beautiful time of year. The ducks and geese were either already heading south or were preparing to head south. School was back in session for another year. All this pointed toward another berry picking season. I liked berry picking because it gave me a chance to go out on the tundra and enjoy all the sights, sounds and smells that made a little girl feel so free. Now that it was fall time, the tundra was drier and easier to walk among its lush carpet of reindeer moss.

We went by boat and Pa always drove because he was the only one that knew the way. There were so many sloughs, side streams, and meandering rivers in which a person could get lost. We would be gone an entire day looking for berries. The best berry sites were the ones deepest into the tundra. It took hours to get to the good ones.

There was a lot of preparation that went into each day trip for berries. The entire family was involved. We had to make certain we always packed a gun, extra gas for the outboard motor, buckets or cartons for holding the berries, and every heavy parka we could find at the cabin was brought along with us. Berry picking usually began in August. That time of year could be quite cold when riding in a boat. If you were not wearing your warmest clothing, it could be a very miserable experience.

The Route

When we went out on the tundra with our boat we usually did not go alone. What if we suffered a mishap or some type of mechanical failure? That could be a real disaster especially if all alone. It was a long ways back to home with only a set of oars to provide the power. Pa would invite his friend, Pius Kassock, to accompany us on our journey to the berry patch. He was not married and one of Pa's good friends from long ago. Having the extra boat provided additional safety just in case something went wrong during the trip. He also liked coming with us while we picked berries. He brought along his buckets and gathered his take of the tundra fruits. He typically followed us in his boat.

We usually took the same route to pick berries. From Emmonak we followed Kwiguk Pass upriver to where the Yukon River splits into the south mouth and upriver. We turned right at this point and followed the south mouth downriver. We went past the old village site of Kwiguk to our right or the west side of the Yukon River. Only a store remained at Kwiguk during my grade school years. There was a lot of history about this now abandoned village site. The people who now live at Emmonak used to inhabit Kwiguk. As we headed downriver we went past the area known as the Big Eddy. The Big Eddy is formed by the intersection of the south mouth of the Yukon River, which is known as the Kwikluak Pass, splitting into the Kwiguk Pass, which leads into Emmonak.

This was a very popular salmon fishing area of the river. The eddy provided numerous good fishing spots to place a set net off the beach and fish into the deeper water. It was also a very tricky part of the river to drive a boat because of the ever present and numerous sand bars existing in the area. Unless you were good at reading the water you would surely hit a sand bar. Going up on a sandbar from upriver was especially difficult because the current tried to push you further up on the sandbar. If we got stuck really hard, then we had to get out of the boat in order to lighten the load and actually push it into the deeper water, being very careful not to step off into the deep water at the edge of the sandbar. The little kids were able to stay in the boat and let the parents and bigger boys do the pushing from outside the

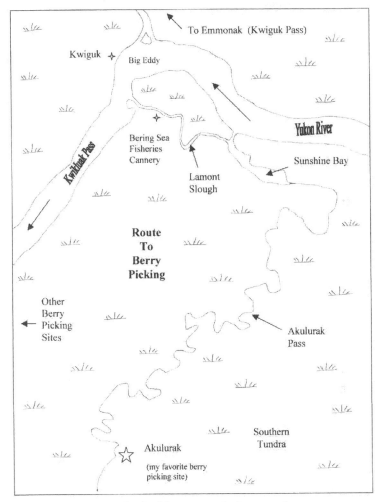

To Emmonak (Kwiguk Pass)

Kwiguk

Big Eddy

Bering Sea
Fisheries
Cannery

Yukon River

Sunshine Bay

Lamont
Slough

Kwikluak Pass

Route
To
Berry
Picking

Other
Berry
Picking
Sites

Akulurak
Pass

Akulurak

(my favorite berry
picking site)

Southern
Tundra

My sketch of the route to the berry patch

boat. The rise and fall of the ocean tides also made it difficult to esti-
mate the depth and location of the submerged sandbars. If you knew
the tide charts and kept track of their cycles that helped to figure out
the navigation of the eddy system.

While in the Big Eddy section we looked for the opening to Lamont
Slough to the left or the south side of the river. Again, unless you
could read the water well or knew by heart where all the sandbars were
located, this was very tricky to navigate. All sections of the riverbank

looked the same in this stretch of the river. Pa knew the river exactly, so he was always able to find the entrance and make his way into Lamont Slough. I think there might have been a few times when he touched a sandbar on the way into the slough. I know, without Pa, I would never find my way into the slough from the main river channel.

Once in the channel of Lamont Slough we went past the Bering Sea fisheries Cannery. This was a floating cannery barge that canned salmon from the local fishermen's catch during the summer. A lot of people worked on the cannery barge when the fish were running strong. It was a nice change to buy some canned salmon from them if we could afford to do so. There was also a little store that sold a variety of food and other items. As a little girl I enjoyed going there with Pa just for the hope of getting a treat while visiting. The canned salmon was then sold to fish markets in the Lower-48. I think most of the canned salmon was sold to Seattle packers. There were also cabins along Lamont Slough that were the homes of Eskimos that lived there all year round. The cannery barge anchored in the slough during the summer commercial salmon fishing season. Before winter freeze up it was moved to a location upriver for safety from the river ice during spring break up.

We continued on down Lamont Slough until we came to an open body of water known as Sunshine Bay. This actually was very close to the Kwikluak Pass of the Yukon River at this point. I think that is why it formed a bay like it did. When we got to the end of the bay it led us to Akulurak Pass. This was the water that would eventually bring us to the berry-picking patch. It took us a long time though before we got there. There were many, many twists, turns and cutbacks to navigate before we reached our destination. A person had to know the area very well or you could easily get lost. This was no territory to lose your way. If you got lost out there on the open tundra, it could be life threatening. How would you ever find your way back? Everything looks the same. It is all flat treeless tundra, except for Akulurak hill as a landmark to the south. But it was so far away, that it could not be used as a landmark to lead you back home. The whole family had great confidence that Pa and Mom knew the way.

We also brought along a net to catch fish for lunch. It was agreeable to take fish from nets which were being fished along the way. No one was going to get upset by taking a small number of fish from someone's net. They knew it went to good use. Just in case we were not lucky enough to catch our own fish or find some fish, we brought along some of our own dried fish for eating. To augment our lunch variety we also brought crackers, cheese and tea or coffee.

The gun was brought along just in case we encountered any bears while on the tundra. Berry picking occurred just before the bears began to hibernate. We always had to be on the look out for them. They could also be wading in the river and sloughs looking for dead salmon. As the salmon completed their life cycle to lay eggs in the upper regions of the rivers, they eventually died. The bears found a big meal awaiting them, as they journeyed to the water after filling up on berries from the southern tundra. Yes, we had to compete with the bears for the same berry patch. The bears did not appreciate being disturbed during a salmon gourmet meal along the river. We had to be on watch at all times. Both while we were traveling the river as well as when we were picking berries on the tundra.

The gun was also used to shoot any ducks or geese we saw along the way. We usually saw them sitting on the water ahead of where we were going. We would turn off the outboard motor and try to float near enough to them to get off a good shot before they took flight from the water. We did not want to shoot from the moving boat because it usually yielded a missed shot. Bullets were expensive and Pa did not want to waste them. I have to admit that Pa was a very good shot. Actually, I was a pretty good shot also. Pa was a good teacher.

We also saw muskrat and owls along the way. The muskrats were right at home in the water. I always wanted to be the first to spot them in the water. Sometimes they were hard to see, and you had to have a keen eye to spot them. Pa always seemed to see them first before me. I felt really special when I spotted them first before anyone else did. For the kids it was a game to see who could spot the most.

The tundra yielded a variety of berries so we had to make several trips to gather all the different varieties because they ripened at various times during the fall. Most of the berry picking was done during the months of August and September.

The berries we picked were:

- Blueberries
- Salmon berries
- High bush cranberries
- Low bush cranberries
- High bush currants
- Blackberries

Mom and Pa knew where the various berry patches were located. The tundra is so flat and devoid of any trees that it made it difficult for me to know where I was. But Pa always knew where he was going, or he let on that he always knew where he was. The only landmark I could see was Akulurak Mountain, which was located a long way from Emmonak on the tundra to the south. It was a magnificent sight to see rising from the flat tundra floor. It was an unmistakable landmark. It did not start to come into view until you got very near the site of the old village of Akulurak.

Akulurak was abandoned in the early 1950s. At one time there was a school and orphanage there. All the buildings have since been moved to the village of St. Mary's. The only landmarks that identify its location are the grave crosses. Even those were becoming fewer with each succeeding year as the permafrost is causing them to sink into the ground. We could still get to Akulurak during my grade school years for berry picking. I don't think you can easily get to it today because of the low water conditions due to the ever-changing Yukon River delta system.

Arrival at the Berry Patch

When we arrived at our destination, Pa anchored the boat on the beach. He was the first one out of the boat and would conduct a bear check of the area. If it was clear of bears then he allowed the rest of us to get out of the boat and stretch our legs for a while on the tundra. The tundra is a very unique place. It is like walking on a deep sponge. You had to be careful that you didn't step into a shallow water pool. This is where a walking stick was very useful. It helped in checking the firmness of the tundra ahead of where you walked. You needed hip boots or waders to keep from getting really wet feet. On the other hand some areas of the tundra were a little drier and you could walk with just tennis shoes. In those areas you could actually run, jump and play like we kids always wanted to do when given the limitless freedom the tundra allowed.

Berry picking was serious business and Mom and Pa made sure we did our part in picking. Each of us found our own spot and picked in that immediate area. That way we avoided each other while picking. It seemed to take an eternity to fill the container we were each given. It was also more tasty to eat the berries fresh off the bush than to put them in my bucket. This made the job of filling my bucket even more time consuming. When salmon berries were ripe they took on the same color as salmon eggs. Ripe salmon berries would appear orange in color. If they did not look like salmon eggs, then you knew they were not ripe enough to pick.

There was not enough patience to get the containers full so that I could go and pick flowers that grew everywhere as far as the eye could see. The flowers seemed to scream at me "please, pick me!" The varicolored flowers that grew on the tundra made such beautiful bouquets. On the tundra surrounding the Akulurak area I remember picking the following flowers:

- Arctic Lupine
- Fireweed
- Alaska Cotton
- Horsetail

A bouquet of these flowers included almost all the colors found on the tundra. The above flowers included blue, red, white and green colors respectively. It made for a beautiful arrangement I could keep for myself or give to Mom. She always enjoyed receiving the flowers from me.

After the berries were all picked and the containers filled we took a break and had a picnic. We started by making a fire. As always, we were on the lookout for driftwood or any wood to make a fire along the way. If we spotted some, we stopped and loaded it into the boat. We could not count on finding driftwood at the berry site. We were very deep into the tundra and the chances of finding any form of wood became unlikely as we continued. Making fire was always my job and I took great pride in making a good one that everyone in the family would enjoy. The fire not only provided us with warmth but also to heat water. Being far from the muddy Yukon River, the tundra river water was very fresh and clean. It was very refreshing to have access to such good quality water. The boiling water was used to make coffee, tea or to boil Labrador tea, which I gathered fresh from the tundra. Labrador tea grew everywhere on the tundra. It was there for the easy picking. We opened the box of Sailor Boy® Pilot Bread crackers and spread either butter or Crisco on them along with some jam. We brought along some dried fish, which we ate at this time. If we caught some fresh fish along the way we cut and gutted the fish and used a stick to skewer it over the fire. It became a very elaborate picnic on the tundra before we had to break with the eating and start on our way back home to Emmonak.

We had to be careful to watch the weather. We did not want to get caught so far from home in an unexpected rainstorm or early snow-fall. The long endless days of summer were long past and the daylight time was getting shorter more quickly each day. It is very difficult and dangerous to try and drive a boat in the dark. There were too many stories of people being capsized and killed from hitting a sub-merged deadhead in the water. A deadhead was a log that floated at an angle in the water. Only the top several inches of it was exposed above the waterline. It was very difficult to see even in the daytime. It could capsize a boat very easily when hit at high speed. The water is not as deep during the fall time, which also made reading the water more difficult. The real hazard to fear most was the cold water. If you fell overboard into the water during the fall-time, your chances of survival were very slim. We were much more careful about the water during this time of year.

Departure for Home

We packed up everything we brought and loaded ourselves into the boat for the long trip home. The same situations presented themselves as we headed back to Emmonak. We kept watch for birds to shoot. Watching the water for any sign of animals that we might be able to catch on the way back. Keeping an eye out for driftwood was on everyone's mind. When we finally got to the Bering Sea fisheries Cannery I knew it would not be long before I was warming up at the cabin with a warm stove beside me. The trip back home was usually much colder than the trip out as the sun was less effective later in the day as a heat source.

When we arrived at home, the unloading of the containers of berries began. Mom oversaw that part of the job. Pa made certain that the boat was pulled up and anchored securely on the beach. Any item that was not related to the berry-picking task was his to tend to. I was usually called upon to carry the containers full of berries to the cabin.

Other Berry Picking Sites

Although Akulurak was our favorite berry-picking site, there were others we frequented during the fall between August and September.

We would go down the south mouth to the village of Sheldon's Point. This area is very close to the Bering Sea where the Yukon empties at its southern-most point. The tundra at Sheldon's Point was very good at growing salmon berries, blueberries and blackberries. Not only was it a good opportunity to pick berries but it was fun to visit the people there. The flat tundra islands that exist at the end of the Yukon River near here are also the best salmon fishing locations on the river. The biggest salmon are caught here as they enter the river from the sea in their most prime condition. Obviously this is a very busy location during the summer fishing season. During berry picking season this area is very quiet.

Along the Yukon River with its many sloughs and passes were other excellent locations for berry picking. Once you got a little ways from the river the area opened into tundra and the berries were numerous. In these spots the best berries for picking were high bush cranberries and high bush currents. But, there is nothing like the boat ride onto the southern tundra near Akulurak for enjoying the wide-open spaces I loved so much.

Underground Storage

Once the berries were brought to our cabin after picking and were unloaded from the boat, they were transferred to wooden kegs. The wooden kegs were the storage containers for the berries during the winter. The wooden kegs full of berries were taken to our underground storage site near the house.

The underground storage site was a hole dug in the permafrost. Permafrost was simply frozen dirt. The underground storage area was about three feet wide on each side and about four to five feet deep. Since we did not have a refrigerator, this acted just as well as one. It was very cold at the bottom of the hole. It was quite a job digging the hole because of the permafrost. You were able to dig about a foot down without a lot of effort, but any deeper took a lot more work. The permafrost was just too hard to dig through. The frozen dirt could not be dug all at once. You had to do it in phases. You dug down a little then let it sit and warm up with the sun for several days or longer depending on the strength of the sun's rays. Then you went back and dug the thawed dirt out and waited a few more days and dug it again. You repeated this process many times for several weeks until you got a hole the right size and depth you desired. The surface of the hole was then covered with boards. It was this underground refrigerator we used to store the berries to keep them from spoiling. The spring flood would ruin the hole each year, so we made sure that everything was removed from it by then. The berries were long consumed before the spring floods came, so that was not a problem making certain the underground storage site was empty. Pa had to dig a new hole each fall to store the berries. It was just another annual ritual around the cabin that had to be done.

Berry Preparation and Consumption

Whenever we wanted berries we went to the underground storage site and took from the kegs however much we needed. This was Mom's job with Joanne and me looking on to learn what she was doing. We used the berries to make two popular items. They were akutaq or Eskimo ice cream, and syrup.

The akutaq was made from:

- Salmon
- Berries (variety of our choosing)
- Crisco
- Vegetable oil (or seal oil)
- Sugar

All the ingredients were mixed together in a bowl and it was ready to eat, just as mixed. It was a favorite food everybody, young and old, loved to eat. It was probably the most popular food made in the village or among Eskimos everywhere along the Bering Sea coast. I liked it very much. There was nothing like using fresh salmon and fresh berries to make for a very tasty treat. It is what Eskimos are famous for making as a family treat enjoyed by everyone. I still make it whenever I can get my hands on all the correct ingredients.

Syrup was another popular way we used the berries. We mashed the berries in a bowl to make a juice out of them. This mixture was then boiled down to a syrup consistency. It was a popular addition to pancakes. We only made enough for immediate consumption, as we did not try to store it for longer periods of time. Mom usually performed this job with us girls looking on to learn how it was done.

Not all the berries were processed into special foods or placed in the underground storage. We simply ate them right after picking. Sometimes we added the berries to various foods we made as a fruity topping. I especially liked them that way. The berries added a new dimension to the common foods we ate. By the time fall came, we were ready for a change from eating fish all the time and everyday. Berries added necessary variety and flavor in our diet that was so much needed for our survival on the Yukon.

I sure enjoyed the flavor and variety that berries added to our diet, but it was the memories I have of berry picking with my family I treasure most of all. The memories of berry picking became an important part of my life as it again demonstrated the necessity of living off the land that our modern society does not require. I miss the openness of the tundra that seemed to stretch forever through my youthful eyes. I miss the opportunity to pick the beautiful flowers that grew on the tundra around the old village site of Akulurak. As I stood and looked upon the old fading crosses that represented the lives of those who tried so hard to work out an existence on the unforgiving tundra, I was awed by the whole idea of living there. The way we live today does not lend itself to experience the simple pleasures that were afforded me while I was a young girl growing up on the tundra of the lower Yukon River delta.

 Some people are so lazy that they won't even lift a finger to feed themselves.
Proverbs 19:24

Fall Hunting

Nukalpiaq: A good hunter

Fall hunting was a much colder experience than when we went during the summer. It was more dangerous hunting in the fall as the weather was less predictable and more stormy.

When I think of hunting, basically it was during the summer that led us to the animals that were our traditional food source. We hunted seals, whales and waterfowl in the summer months. There was some fall hunting done between the return from fish camp and freeze up. During this period of time there was the possibility of hunting the same animals that were our staple during the summer season.

Whales and Seals

After our return from fish camp there was the chance of sighting a beluga whale and seal in Kwiguk Pass between Emmonak and the ocean. If there were still salmon migrating in the river then there was still hopes of finding a beluga whale or seal. It was a wonderful treat to be able to have whale or seal for fall eating. It wasn't the best time of year for drying the meat. Fall was a time of stormy, wet and cool weather. Not the best for drying because of the lack of sunshine. Some of the worst weather occurred during the fall. The river became very dangerous when the storms came through with high winds creating very large waves. The fall-time storms could occur with very little advance warning. You went out on the river only after watching the weather to the west. Depending upon one's cache of meat in the smokehouse, a trip out to the coast may be the only chance of adding to that meat supply. It may be a risk that was justified for simple survival.

Waterfowl

Pa hunted waterfowl up to the time they left for their southern migration. During the fall we took the boat and headed toward the ocean to hunt the ducks and geese on the surrounding lakes to the north of Kwiguk Pass. We hunted the same in the fall as we did during the summer. We looked for a good site to anchor the boat and walked onto the tundra until we found a lake that looked promising for shooting waterfowl.

It was colder this time of year. We had to wear heavier coats, stocking cap, mittens and boots to stay warm while we sat motionless on the tundra waiting for the birds to fly within shooting range. It sure could get cold just sitting motionless on the tundra. Not only was the air temperature colder than in the summer, but also the sun was lower in the sky and provided less warmth. Despite the cold and uncomfortable conditions, the wait was worth it because the waterfowl were in prime eating condition in the fall. Their bodies are more plump and fattened from their eating frenzy as they prepared for their migration. They were much better eating in the fall than during the summer when they are thinner. The birds are more uniform in size this time of year as compared to the summer when the birds ranged from large adults to juveniles to small fledglings.

Big Game Animals

For the most part big game animals were non-existent on the lower Yukon River delta. The western arctic tundra simply doesn't provide enough food to support large animals. If we desired to hunt large animals we had to go far upriver to find them. Pa did not hunt upriver because it cost too much to make the journey.

Bears

The only place we found bears was out on the southern tundra when we went berry picking in the fall. We never encountered bears while berry picking because Pa made certain we kept our distance from them. He made the first watch after docking the boat to make certain no bears were in the area. If he saw a bear or was suspicious of one's presence then he got back into the boat and we would continue to look for another site to dock. I never saw a bear on the tundra because Pa protected us from any encounters with them.

The bears came onto the tundra to eat berries that were plentiful. The tundra south of the Yukon River was not the home territory for bears. Their home was in the forested area that existed to the east. It was easy to see the western extension of the tree line while flying between Bethel and Emmonak. It was amazing how the edge of the tree line met the arctic tundra. It was such a distinct and well-defined line. The dense forest of trees abruptly terminated and treeless tundra began. It was quite a contrast. It was easy to see where the bears came from while they went on their berry eating forays. Once the berries were past ripening and dried up, the bears returned to the forest to prepare for their winter's hibernation.

Pa never went bear hunting. The chances of success were very low. It was not worth the effort it took. You had to be at the right place at the right time in order to see one that was within shooting range. Rather than going out on the tundra for hunting bear, we went berry picking. We actually wanted to avoid them when we ventured out onto the southern tundra while berry picking.

Moose
Moose were never seen in the Emmonak area. I think we were much too far out on the tundra. There were no trees or vegetation that moose desired this far west. If hunters wanted to find them they had to go far upriver. Pa did not go moose hunting because it took a lot of time and money to make the journey. There was no guarantee you would return with a catch.

Caribou
There were no caribou herds that existed in the lower Yukon River delta area. We were too far south for them to exist.

Reindeer Herding
In the old days the mission at Akulurak kept a reindeer herd. I remember Pa telling me stories about him helping with the herd during his youth. The residents at Akulurak used the reindeer as an addi-

tional food source. He mentioned that the herd had grown to several thousand at its peak. My Pa's parents helped with the reindeer herding. He talked about living in a tent when they resided at Akulurak while working with the reindeer. Herding reindeer was a white man's idea. Pa told me about a law that prevented management of reindeer herds by anybody other than Natives. The mission herd was turned over to the Eskimos after the law's passage. The Natives did not have any interest in managing the herd and it began to dwindle. Reindeer herding at Akulurak ceased during the early 1940s I am told.

There were many stories regarding life at Akulurak and its many exploits. I find it nostalgic mentioning my Pa's involvement of this historic venture by the missionaries. These events explain my grandma Agnes' connection to Akulurak and the population of a number of her relatives' graves that have since vanished into its permafrost.

Hunting in the fall was a much different experience. There was more urgency while hunting in the fall. It was our last chance to find food that helped us replenish our smokehouse for the upcoming winter. Hunting required more vigilance of the weather around us as the days became shorter and the temperatures colder. Any mistake while fall hunting could lead to disastrous results. It was more dangerous hunting during the fall but success made the effort worthwhile.

 Look straight ahead, and fix your eyes on what lies before you.
Proverbs 4:25

Grass Harvest

Canegtar: to gather grass

Harvesting grass was my job when I was growing up. It was an activity that provided an important resource that we needed for both my family and the dogs.

It might sound peculiar talking about grass and the lower Yukon delta, but the two are very deeply connected in time and by the people. Grass was used for a wide variety of purposes. It was harvested, stored and used as an important part of village Eskimo life. I remember my fall time being spent working with grass. As a young girl on the lower Yukon I remember spending a lot of time working during the period of the grass harvest.

Once early fall came to the Lower Yukon area, it was a signal that the task of grass harvest was close at hand. Usually grass was harvested just before and after the start of school. As the days grew shorter and cooler, the grass started to turn yellow. Once it turned yellow that was the signal that the grass was dry enough to cut and begin harvest. Before the first snows fell, the grass had to be harvested. It was too difficult to work on the grass after very many snows had fallen.

My Job

Cutting and harvesting the grass was primarily my job. I learned how to cut and harvest grass by watching Pa. I followed him to the grass field when I was very young. I wasn't able to really help him with the work. I was too small to handle the grass bundles and I was not allowed to use the cutting scythe by myself. I would probably end up cutting myself without parental supervision. While Pa cut the grass I played in a selected corner of the field. I helped however

89

I could. I was able to help move the smaller grass bundles from the field to the pile of bundles at the field's edge. The grass was cut in the afternoon when the dew was gone. A person got very wet and completely soaked if they tried to cut while the dew was still on the grass. Since the grass grew as high as I was tall, I was certain to become wet from head to toe. Obviously that was also the hottest part of the day.

When I became old enough to handle the task by myself, it became my job. My younger brother and sister, Freddie and Joanne, also assisted with the work. Sometimes they just came along to play. The grass grew to about four feet in height. A little person could easily play hide and seek in the grass. We went to the west end of Emmonak because it was the best area for finding the kind of grass we wanted to use. It grew best in the open areas where the sun shone on it all the time. The best areas were also the places where it was very moist. Similar to bog or marsh areas it must have a constant supply of water. It grew best next to the river. The grass we desired would ultimately be used as dog bedding and boot lining. Other people in the village made grass baskets, but a different kind of grass was required for that purpose.

I used a hand scythe to cut the grass. Gloves were required to keep my hands from wearing out. I used the same white canvas gloves that were used during fishing season. Those white gloves were used for almost every job that required my hands to be protected. They were the cheapest ones we could buy at the store. The scythes were bought from the N.C. Store. Pa kept them sharp for me. He kept them very sharp to the point where I had to be very careful not to cut myself accidentally. That was his contribution toward grass harvest.

I looked for a good stand of grass and began cutting it with long swings of the scythe. I grabbed a hand full and used the scythe to cut it near the ground so as to keep as much grass as possible in the bundle. After I grabbed a few handfuls, then I laid the grass on the ground and used a few nice long blades of grass and tied the bundle together. The tied up bundle was laid on the ground and the process of gathering another handful and cutting it with the scythe was repeated again and again. It got boring after a while, but the job had to be done. We needed the grass for our winter use. I sure got tired also. I thought it was pretty hard work. I was very worn out when the job was done.

For a break in the work monotony, we gathered up the tied bundles and hand carried them to the cabin. This was also hard work because we had to climb up the riverbank and walk the grass bundles in our arms back to the cabin. The bundles were stored in the smokehouse. This kept them from getting wet and not weather so bad. It was important to keep it as dry as possible for the purpose of making good dog bedding. I am sure the dogs did not appreciate wet, musty grass to lie on during the cold winter nights.

The work continued until we had what we thought was enough grass to last the winter. When the first few snows came, the work of cutting grass had to stop for the year. It was important to cut only dry grass. Cutting the grass when wet caused it to mold and become black after being placed into storage. We made certain that we provided plenty of space in the smokehouse for the grass. The smokehouse was already full of dried fish, nets and any other items that could not be exposed to the weather outside or placed in the cabin.

Dried Grass Uses

The harvested grass had many purposes depending upon the family that harvested it and its intended use by the family or family members.

Dog Bedding

The primary use of our grass was for our dogs as winter bedding to protect them from the frozen and snowy ground. All of our dogs were Malamutes, thus they were by nature acclimated to the cold. From a little girl's vantage they were very large dogs. Their fur was thick and long. They were excellent dogs suited for the lower Yukon River winters. We felt sorry for them and let them lay on the grass to protect their bodies from the cold snow. Whenever we saw that the grass was becoming worn out in their bedding place we replaced it with a new bunch of grass. The task of watching out for worn grass bedding was everybody's job. If someone in the family thought new grass needed to be added they did so. Each dog had a shallow place to lie in and that was where the grass was placed.

Boot Lining

Another use of the grass was as a lining for our boots before the days of boots with liners. We grabbed a handful and crunched it up and put it in the bottom of our boots. This added a little insulation value and actually made the boots more comfortable for walking. Eventually the grass wore out and needed to be replaced with a new batch of grass. When we were able to purchase boots with liners, the grass was no longer needed for that purpose.

Fish Braiding

Some people used the same type of grass we harvested and used it for braiding fish. This was a process of binding the smaller fish into a string of fish. Braiding fish was used with smaller fish such as smelt. A number of fish were braided together and then hung on the drying racks to air dry in the sun. We did not engage in smelt fishing, so we did not braid any fish. The larger fish we caught were too large for grass braiding to be of any benefit.

Grass Weaving

The most economical use of grass was to weave it. There were Eskimos from Emmonak who made very good grass baskets and other items made from grass from the surrounding area. I know Catherine Moore was a very good grass weaver. She could make very nice things out of grass. She used it to make such items as:

- Baskets
- Mats
- Dance fans
- Dolls

The grass used for making baskets and other objects was different than the kind I cut for our use primarily for the dogs. Baskets and mats made from grass could bring a very high price when sold commercially. If you were able to sell them in the big cities of Anchorage, Fairbanks or Juneau then you could do very well financially. This was especially true of doll making. When I was a little girl the idea of selling what you made was not even considered. People made what was important to have around the cabin.

Every Eskimo dancer was expected to have a pair of dance fans. The women's dance fans usually used a lot of grass to make them. The men's dance fans did not use as much grass in their construction. The men's dance fans were made more of branches and feathers than grass.

Because of our subsistence lifestyle, it was critical that we made what was needed instead of buying from a store. Most people simply did not have the money to buy anything. Mom did not weave grass so I never learned the art of grass weaving while I was growing up.

Nostalgia

Picking, cutting, drying and storing grass were very important aspects of our life when I was little. It was another event that was required to get us through the winter with a little more comfort than if we did not work with the grass. I must admit that a grass-lined boot sure was more comfortable and warmer than one that did not have grass in it. I know the dogs appreciated the grass that lined their bedding area. Some families did not use grass for dog bedding and just let the dogs lay in the snow. Everyone did not consider grass a necessity. We did it for our dogs. I remember Grandpa did not harvest grass for his dogs.

I took on the job of cutting grass. Pa did not tell me to do it. I simply wanted to make sure the dogs were well cared for during the winter. I felt sorry for them if they did not have grass to lie on during the cold winter nights. I cut grass for the comfort of the dogs and for the comfort of my feet.

You never knew how important something that grew everywhere, and was taken for granted, could become. Harvesting grass was just another aspect of life on the lower Yukon River delta. It was something we did because it was another important aspect of survival. It required a lot of physical labor working with the grass. I know I harvested grass because I had an interest in keeping my feet and the dogs' warm during our cold winters. It was another memory I have of my younger days when it was very important to make preparations for the grass harvest along Kwiguk Pass.

We can gather our thoughts, but the LORD gives the right answer.
Proverbs 16:1

Winter Preparation

Uksugu: This coming winter.

Preparing for the upcoming winter was a major activity that involved every member of the family. We had to be ready for the long winter days ahead.

A family that was not ready for the first snows and cold temperatures did so at their own risk. Winter was a time of year that deserved respect. There was no option but to make the necessary preparations as we felt the end of the fall season descend upon us.

As the long, warm days of summer gave way to the short, cool days of fall we knew our lifestyle required changes that prepared us for winter. It was a look to the future. It was time to repeat the rituals of winter preparation that the generations before had to cope with. I remember watching and helping Pa as he focused his attention toward making those preparations. The following are some of those preparations for winter.

Fish Net Repair and Maintenance

After fishing season was over the task of getting the fishnets prepared for the next season began during the fall. The nets were unloaded from the boats that came from fish camp and carried up the beach and laid on the drying racks that were built for the purpose of sun-drying them. It was a mistake to store the nets while they were wet. They would mold and not dry properly. The nets were too expensive to replace every year. The wear and tear the nets endured during the summer of fishing required repairs to be made to them.

Pa used twine to repair and mend the tears the fish made in the nets. The really big king salmon could do the most damage to the nets. Other non-salmon species could also do a lot of damage to the nets when in the water. Those other animals could be seals and beluga whales that followed the migrating salmon into the river channel from the Bering Sea. If they got any of their body parts wrapped up in the nets they could cause a lot of damage. They could create very large tears in the net. If these large tears were not repaired, fish could easily swim through the holes. That defeated the whole purpose of using the nets.

I watched Pa perform his magic of transforming a worn and torn net into something that was as good as new. It was like sewing, except on a much bigger scale. He was carrying on the traditions taught him by his father. As always, it was these necessities of life that played a huge part in the life of the Eskimo on the lower Yukon River. A net was a valuable piece of equipment to the people of Emmonak. It was to be used over and over for many years. A good, well maintained net caught more fish than a poorly maintained one.

I remember as a little girl walking along the sea shore of Grandpa's Island at fish camp finding glass floats that washed ashore from the Bering Sea. They did not come from the Eskimo fishing nets, but from the Japanese high seas fishing fleet. In the old days we used whatever would float on our salmon nets. I also remember using a whale's gut as a marker buoy on the subsistence fishing nets that Pa used. The stomach of a beluga whale was very tough and when inflated worked great as a buoy. It lasted a long time. When commercial fishing became more common as a fishing industry, a subsistence fisherman was not allowed to use a number-marked buoy while fishing. A whale gut buoy was the perfect choice as a replacement on Pa's fishing nets. He was never a commercial fisherman by trade, only a subsistence fisherman by necessity.

After Pa repaired the nets he made certain they were dried completely before taking them up to the smokehouse for winter storage. He either hung them up on the drying racks or placed them neatly folded on the floor of the smokehouse depending on the space available within the smokehouse. They needed to dry completely so they did not mold. Pa was also hired by Northern Commercial Company to repair and maintain their nets. This provided our family with some economic means during the fall. The company either paid for his work or applied it as a credit on purchases my family made at the store. The company was in the business of renting fishing nets to those people that did not have nets of their own. We were fortunate to have our own nets. The nets the company rented out during the summer required repair. They knew Pa was good at mending nets, so they hired him for that job.

There were two kinds of nets used for salmon fishing. The king net was an eight-inch net. Each mesh was 8 inches measured diagonally. When using this net, only the larger kings could get caught in the mesh. The smaller chum salmon were not migrating during the peak king salmon fishing season. The smaller chum salmon could get caught in the king net if it was large enough. The chum salmon began their migration toward the end of the king salmon migration season. There was some overlap between the chum and king season.

During the commercial fishing season, the Alaska Department of Fish and Game placed a ban on the use of the king nets once they concluded that the season for king salmon fishing was over. The only nets that could be used after that point in time were the smaller chum nets. These nets had a mesh size of 5½ inches measured diagonally. When using these nets only the smaller fish (chum salmon) could be caught. This was a natural selection for the larger king salmon, as they were too large to get caught in the smaller mesh size. The larger king salmon were able to avoid the nets. The kings were not caught in the chum nets and were allowed to migrate unharmed to their spawning grounds upriver. That was the purpose of switching the required mesh size for the commercial fishermen. This ability to control the number and type of fish caught and allowed to migrate upriver was called escapement, and was an important tool for salmon population control.

Boat Repair and Maintenance

After fishing season ended the boats were pulled out of the water and stored farther up the beach. When to pull our boat out of the water was always an uncertain proposition. You wanted to leave it in the water and available to be used for river travel as long as possible.

You also did not want to leave it in the water too long and become frozen in the river ice at freeze up. It was always a best guess as to when to take the boat out of the water.

The fall-time was also a period where Northern Commercial Company needed boat repairs. They hired Pa to paint the boats and patch holes that occurred during the summer fishing season. The company had a large fleet of tender boats that were used during the commercial fishing season to gather the salmon caught by the river fishermen and transferred them to the fish processors. Not all the boats got repaired or painted during the fall. Those that did not make the fall schedule were held over and completed in the spring. Pa did most of his own boat repair and maintenance during the spring.

Gathering Driftwood

Wood, especially driftwood, was a very precious commodity on the lower Yukon River. Since we did not have any real trees that grew along the banks of the river, we had to depend upon wood that floated down the river from upriver. Once you got away from the river just a little bit you found yourself on treeless arctic tundra in the Emmonak area.

Wood was used for heating and cooking within our cabin. It was used for making smoke in the smokehouse. Wood was the source of heat in the sauna for those families that had one. It made the fire that cooked the dog food outside in kettles. We made journeys, especially during the fall-time, to the coast or go upriver in search of driftwood. We went about every week in the fall in hopes of finding a lot of wood. The Yukon River was always a dependable source of driftwood. It provided an ample supply for the village.

I cannot underestimate the importance of finding an adequate supply of wood to run us for the winter months ahead. It was so important to all of us. I would rather be warm than cold in the winter. It was a real find when a large tree was spotted floating down the river in front of the village. It was a sure thing that someone in the village would spot it and make certain it was captured for village use. If you found a large tree floating in the river while in a boat you made every effort to rope it and tow it back home.

No matter where we were or what we were doing, we were always on the lookout for driftwood. That necessity was always on our mind. It is hard to describe how driftwood affected our lifestyle day in and day out.

The logs were hauled up onto the beach and placed in stacks. Some of the stacks were very large. A person gathered as much as possible. There was no such thing as having too much driftwood. The large logs were cut by hand into smaller pieces. We did not have a chainsaw when I was little. It had to be cut by hand. It involved a lot of physical labor. The kind of saw Pa used was too big for me to operate. I was no help when it came to cutting the logs. The logs were cut into even smaller pieces and then split into smaller useable pieces. The split pieces were carried up to the cabin and stacked next to the entrance door for convenience. The final haul from the split woodpile to the stove was a short distance. Obviously we did not want to carry the wood very far in the cold from the outside. We kept a small pile of split wood next to the stove in the cabin. This allowed it to be dry when we used it for cooking or as heat.

The period of time that elapsed while the river was freezing up was a vulnerable one. We were not able to go out and look for wood. We had to make certain there was enough wood in storage to get us through that time period. If we ran low or out of wood during that time, then we cut some of the brush that grew around our cabin. Desperate times required desperate measures. Nobody wanted to be cold. I sure wanted to avoid it at all costs.

To conserve on our wood supply, we intentionally let the fire go out during the night at the cabin. It could sure get cold by morning. We, especially me, made sure we went to bed with lots of blankets next to us at bedside. As the fire went out, obviously the colder it got inside the cabin. I started adding blankets as the night got colder. I have a lot of memories waking up many mornings very cold. Again, it was a fact of life. There was no getting around the reality that the winter nights were going to get cold. You just lived with it.

Pa was the first one to wake up and make a fire for the dawning of a new day. It did not take long to warm up our two room cabin. All eight of us bundled as close together as we could to keep each other warm. Before long the cabin was warm and the water was getting hot for drinking purposes. Feeling the warmth from the stove made one appreciate all the hard work involved in gathering driftwood.

I never knew when winter would make its presence known. The first snows were always a lot of fun to anticipate when I was a little girl. I had to quickly switch from cool jackets to the winter parkas as the cold winds began to blow. The short, thin tennis shoes had to be exchanged for the tall, thick winter boots. I had to hunt for my mittens and stocking hat every year. Which box did I last place them in a few months earlier? It was a fun transition knowing that the winter months would bring new experiences and places to go with Pa and the dogs. The world of the lower Yukon River was about to change from the browns of the fall to the white of winter.

The wise inherit honor, but fools are put to shame!
Proverbs 3:35

Back to School

Skuulaq: School

It was exciting to look forward to another school year. I enjoyed meeting the new teachers and welcoming back the returning ones.

I always looked forward to the beginning of another school year. I enjoyed the learning of new things. The teachers were almost always new each year and that added extra excitement to the first day of going back to school.

The teachers came back to the village a few weeks prior to the start of the school year. When the planes arrived during the fall, many kids went to the airstrip to meet the people as they got off. We wanted to be the first to meet the new or returning teachers. We always wanted to know who was coming back to teach us again for another year. We were anxious to see who the new teachers were that came for the first time. It was a highlight of our day to meet each plane as it arrived.

I don't remember all the teachers because some of them came for a year and did not return. Some of the teachers I remember were:

Mr. and Mrs. Lind
Lois Lind taught at Emmonak during the 1960s. Her husband, Marshall Lind was also a teacher at Emmonak. They had two girls, which were much younger than me. They paid me to wash their dishes. Marshall became the Commissioner of Education for the state of Alaska. He also became one of the defendants during the Molly Hootch Case.

Mr. and Mrs. Henry
They both spent quite a few years teaching in Emmonak. I went to

101

their house and played with their daughter Karen. She was my age. They had two other children named Blaine and Kathy. They eventually moved to Mountain Village. I went there to visit them at Easter or Christmas when my parents allowed.

Miss Moore

I remember her as one of my grade school teachers. She was a tall lady. She taught at Emmonak for about two to three years

Mrs. Early

She was short and skinny. I think she taught at Emmonak for about two to three years. According to her she was always early for everything.

Mr. and Mrs. Evans

I think they taught at Emmonak for about two to three years. They had a daughter named Aurelia. She was much younger than me. I remember Mr. Evans liked to take naps during his class. He taught me the mathematics' tables.

We kids walked the new teachers to their home away from home. We had lots of fun walking with them from the airstrip to the school. We felt in our little hearts it was our duty to make their welcome a good one. For every new teacher it was probably a nice thing that we made them feel very welcome. I am sure they felt a little homesick at first and we tried our best to help them overcome their anxieties as well as ours. It was not uncommon for teachers to only stay for one year and never return. It must have been a real challenge in their lives to make the journey all the way to the end of the Yukon River to teach us little ones. Those teachers that stayed for more than one year were certainly the exception. We got to know them like family. They were going to be with us for almost nine months out of the year. Thus, they were a big and influential part of our young lives.

The school at Emmonak only held grades one to eight. There was no allowance made for the high school grades. If we wanted to continue our education beyond the eighth grade we had to leave the village and go to a boarding school a long distance away. We had to leave the village for the entire school year.

One nice thing about the school year was that we got a good lunch every school day. I really liked that idea. I remember they had a flavored peanut butter that we spread on pilot crackers. It was really good. We could not afford peanut butter at the cabin so it was a real treat to have it at school. We also got a milk break before lunch. Sometimes for fun we tried to drink our eight-glass per day allowance all at once. Most of the families in the village were not able to provide us with the nice and nutritious meals the school gave us to eat. At the cabin, we did not have the opportunity to get three complete meals a day. We were lucky to get just one complete meal a day. The teachers were also very concerned about our hygiene. They made us wash after every meal. That was different. We were not used to that. We also did not have access back home at the cabin to the good quality water the school provided. The teachers also required each of us have a toothbrush at school. We had to brush after every meal we ate at the school building.

I especially enjoyed the recess periods at school. That was our opportunity to play. When the weather was nice we played lap game or tag outside. During the winter months when the river was frozen we played on the ice with our skates during the recess period. There was always something for us to play during recess period, regardless of the weather or time of year. During my grade school years I remember the following classmates that attended with me:

- Juanita Lamont
- John Lamont
- Joyce Johnson
- Nita Johnson
- Virginia Oktoyak
- Waska Charles
- Lorena Kameroff
- Wilbur Hootch
- Angela Kamkoff
- Amelia Tucker
- Karen and Blaine Henry
- Elias Keyes

They were my close friends at school as well as at home. We played all the time together whenever we got the chance. I no longer have any real connection with any of them today.

Mom worked at the school as a helper's aid. That was a very good thing as it gave us some money in the household. Pa was a subsistence person, so he hunted and fished to provide food for all of us.

Before I began my grade school years some of the teachers did not allow kids to speak Eskimo. My older brothers Michael and George told me stories about how they were not allowed to speak Eskimo at school. They were reprimanded for speaking a language other than English. That was difficult for them to understand the reason for that rule. It was really confusing to them because we always spoke Eskimo before we started going to school. By the time I started grade school that rule no longer was enforced. I spoke English all the time when I was around my friends. There was no reason to speak Eskimo at school. We were all English speaking kids by the time I started grade school.

As I look back on my grade school years I find myself thinking about what the future would have been like if the Molly Hootch Case had never occurred. Without any hope of attending high school in the village, many students, just like me, were likely to never continue on in school and never receive a high school diploma. That had such an adverse effect on every student in the village. Growing up as a young person in the villages would be completely different than the situation today. The villages would have fewer high school graduates. I am happy that high school age kids do not have to go through the hardships I had to endure just to get a high school education. Again I want to thank all the people who became teachers and sacrificed a portion of their lives to teach us in the villages as I remember going back to school.

Don't be impressed with your own wisdom. Instead, fear the LORD and turn your back on evil.
Proverbs 3:7

Sled Building

Ikamraq: Dogsled

Many of my fondest memories are of watching Pa build sleds. It was magical to observe his skills of turning a pile of lumber into a beautiful dog sled.

Of the many memories I have of my Pa, one of the most fascinating was to observe his talent at sled building. It was important to have dogs and a sled. They were crucial for survival on the lower Yukon River delta. It was the only way to travel before the introduction of the snowmobile. Every family had a team of dogs and a sled. The dogs required a lot of work. You were not only fishing for your own food but for the dogs as well. They had to be cared for all year-round. They required attention everyday. Eventually the snowmobile replaced the dog team. There were fewer dog teams as the years went by. This resulted in fewer sleds for my Pa to build for others. Subsistence fishing for the dogs soon became unnecessary. There are no dog teams in Emmonak today.

It amazed me how he could take wood and make it into a piece of art such as a dog sled. He could cut, smooth and shape wood into pieces that were breathtakingly beautiful. It was an art form I think must have been handed down to him from his Pa. As a little girl looking into his concentrating eyes as he worked, I thought it was magical. His craftsmanship was awesome. I simply looked at his work and asked, "How did he do that?"

Materials

A new sled began with a trip to the Emmonak Northern Commercial Store. There he bought hickory wood. It was sold in a number of sizes and lengths. Pa went through the pile of hickory and examined each and every piece looking for just the perfect ones. He felt the grain. He looked at it length-ways and examined the contour of its structure. He gave it the smell test to determine if it was at its proper seasoning. Was it too dry or too wet? Did it have too many knots and how were they spaced? You could see his mind building that sled as he analyzed each prospective piece to figure out if it would work. After careful evaluation of each piece, he either placed it back on the pile as a reject, or put it among the other pieces that qualified to be bought and taken home. I helped him carry the smaller pieces to the sales counter where he would pay for them. The two of us, or with the help of my brothers, carried them to our home where they were carefully stored and racked in the corner of our cabin.

We did not have a shed or extra out building for the purpose of storing the wood or tools. Everything had to be done in the same cabin we lived in. The log cabin served multiple purposes. It was not just a home for us but also served as the shop for building dog sleds.

Sizing

The next phase of the building process was to cut the larger dimensional wood pieces into smaller ones that were going to be used to make the sled. We did not have any power tools to accomplish that task, since we had no electricity in the village or at least not to our cabin. If it was available, we were not able to afford it. Pa used his handsaw to rip then cut the larger wood into smaller dimensional sizes. This also aided in the drying process of the wood. He was very careful not to allow the wood strips to warp or twist in such a way that hindered the bending that was required later.

Sled building occurred during the fall and winter months. The sleds needed to be built by the first snowfall. That first accumulating snow always came by early October at the latest. After we concluded our summer at fish camp, sled building began. Pa built sleds for the people of Emmonak or within the surrounding area of the lower Yukon River. Very few people built sleds and Pa was very good at what he did. His sleds were highly valued for their tough construction and craftsmanship. Each sled took lots of time. Patience was required. I did not have much of that when I was a little girl helping him whenever I could without getting in the way and causing a nuisance of myself. But I also wanted to help especially if it was our sled he was building. I knew I would get lots of chances to go on the trap line with him and the dogs. It was also a way to make money for Pa. The large freight type sleds sold for about $800 to $1,000. As a result, he took great pride in his work and made certain each sled was built just perfect to his demanding and rigorous specifications. Pa's sleds had his own signature design demanding sled users looked for when comparing quality to other sleds they could buy.

Steaming and Bending

The sled building process began with building a steamer container that was used to heat the hickory pieces in order to bend them to the required shape. A couple of empty 5-gallon kerosene cans were joined together with their ends cut out. He laid this joined set of cans on the cook stove and partially filled them with water. Once the water inside began to boil and became steamy he placed the hickory pieces into the cans and left them until they were steamed to just the right saturation point for bending. This is where his experience showed how good he really was at working the wood to make it shape just as he desired. Once the piece was just right, he took it out of the steamer and placed it on specially built and curved wooden frames. This is where the hickory pieces began to take the desired shape he wanted. It was as if the wood became alive and acted just the way he wanted. It seemed like magic to me, to watch him work on every piece; one piece at a time. It sure took patience. The bending frames I mentioned before were also a piece of art.

The bending frames were how the hickory wood was forced to take the desired shape. Each piece was different. Each bend had to be different than the one before or after. The length of bend was never the same as the one before or after. I was always amazed at how Pa knew how each individual hickory piece needed to be made to arrive at its pre-designed shape, curve, bend and length. Each hickory piece was brought from the steamer and placed on the bending frame. C-clamps were used to force the hickory to conform to the desired shape. The C-clamps held the hickory piece to the bending frame. The hickory piece stayed clamped until the shape required was permanent and would not straighten out when removed from the bending frame.

Not every attempt to make the hickory piece conform to the proper shape was successful. If the wood cooled down too soon, it would not work. There seemed to be more potential problems than correct ones. It was an effort that required several attempts to get each one right. If it did not curve the way Pa wanted it to, he placed the hickory piece back in the steamer and started the process over again. He sometimes did this many times before it was just right. Each piece had it own unique shape, size, curve and length to make the sled complete as one unit. Each piece played a very important and integral part in the construction of the whole sled.

Pa was a perfectionist when it came to building his sleds. That meant each piece had to be perfectly formed so they fit precisely together as one very strong unit that would last many years and be able to resist breaking under the severe conditions they endured in the lower Yukon River area. In order to accomplish that goal, it took him between two to three months to build each sled. I suppose you could say patience pays dividends in a quality product you want to stand behind. That was Pa and his approach to building sleds.

Before each hickory piece was fastened into place, it had to be planed and smoothed to remove any rough spots on the wood. Pa used a hand plane for that purpose. Once it was planed down to the proper size and feel, then it was hand sanded to the exact smoothness that was desired. Some pieces could be left rough, while others had to be very smooth on the surface, depending on where it was located within the sled. If the hickory was exposed to handling then it had to be very smooth without any splinters exposed. All edges had to be sanded to a lustrous smooth finish so the user would not get cut or splintered when handling the sled. It seemed weird to me that with the roughness of the lower Yukon area, that it required all this attention to avoid a few splinters in a dog sled. Every detail was taken into account when building the sled.

Construction

The hickory pieces were fastened together with screws. This required that each position where a screw was to be used needed a hole to be drilled. Pa would use his hand drill for that purpose. Again, no electric drill was available, so each hole had to be made by hand. The holes of each contiguous piece were lined up and a screw was inserted to fasten each piece together. On the big sleds there were lots of screws, thus a lot of hand drilling. A lot of screws had to be tightened. I got so tired from tightening what seemed to be hundreds of screws. It was probably the most important part of the sled's construction. Pa certainly did not want one of his sleds to come apart because he shorted himself on the number of screws he used.

He used a combination of flat head and round head wood screws depending on the location and function of the screws. He used round head screws for most of the fastening. In certain areas of the sled he used flat head screws. These were used in the bottom of the basket area where people were likely to sit. No one wants to sit on round head screws during a rough sled ride. This required Pa to go to the extra effort of counter-sinking each flat head screw. This was tedious work because he had to create a counter-sink around each screw hole. He used his smallest wood chisel for this purpose. When the flat head screw was tightened down, the head of the screw was perfectly flush with the surface of the wood. A very smooth sitting surface was then provided for whoever had to sit in the basket compartment of the sled. Because the screw to wood surface was flush smooth, there was no chance of tearing one's clothing on an exposed screw when going in and out of the sled. Also, too many sleeping bags and blankets were ripped because they got caught on a screw head that was not countersunk properly.

Certain points of the sled parts could not be fastened with screws. These areas had to be tied together with heavy weight twine. The twine had to be wound very tight around both pieces of the wood to keep them from coming loose. Once the twine was wound tightly in place, linseed oil was used to act as an adhesive to keep the twine together as a unit. In certain positions of the sled, related pieces of wood had to be tied together with twine. Screws did not work be-cause they made the points too rigid, which caused the connection to break rather than flex as pressure was applied to these sections of the sled during hard use. Each sled was a masterpiece of physics as well as of wood. Wrapping twine around the sled's handle bar made grabbing the sled easier on the hands rather than keeping that area as bare wood. Pa also wanted to avoid any sharp edges or potential splintering around the handle bar area. Safety was always first prior-ity when he designed and built his sleds.

Strips of metal were attached to the bottom of the runner hicko-ry strips. Without the metal runner strips attached, the wood run-ners wore out too fast. Wood only runners were subject to breaking too easily. Adding the metal runners made the sleds last for a long time. At the very back end of the runner, Pa would use Teflon plas-tic runner pieces. These were placed directly under where the sled driver stood. Since most of the weight was located at this point of the runner, Teflon was smoother than metal, thus less friction at that point. Snow was also less apt to stick to the Teflon. The sled could go faster because of this little modification to the bottom of the wood runner system.

A foot brake was added to the underside of the rear of the sled. A piece of hickory was attached by heavy weight twine at the front with a metal tooth-shaped point attached to the end of the hickory for digging into the snow to stop the sled. The rear end of the hickory wood was held up with a spring attached to the handlebar when not depressed by the sled driver's foot.

Once all the parts of the sled were completed and attached, then the entire sled was finished with linseed oil. The linseed oil was ap-plied to all the wood parts as well as to the twine. Several coats were applied until a nice sheen was achieved. Not only did the linseed oil make for a nice finish, but it also helped preserve the wood and twine and protect it from the weather.

The basket

A trademark of Pa's sleds was its unique circular construction that acted as a backer for the basket. He took two hickory strips about one quarter inch thick and bent them together to make a circle. He held them together using heavy weight twine at six equidistant points around the circle. This served to hold the two sides of the rear of the sled together and made a very comfortable backrest for anyone sitting in the basket of the sled. I again was always amazed at how he could bend the wood and hold it together and make the circle all at once. It actually made the sled very strong at the rear of the sled. The circular configuration made the sled very flexible and less apt to break under the extra stresses placed on the sled at that point. It was a picture of wonderful engineering that was unique to only Pa's sleds. No one else used that design. His sleds were always easy to spot because of that construction technique. This construction technique was handed down to Pa from Grandpa.

Repairs and Maintenance

Eventually, any sled wore out or just needed maintenance performed on them. Pa brought them into the house because he did most of that work during the late fall or winter when it was too cold to work outside. We kids really enjoyed that part because we could play in the sled while it was being worked on. In our mind it was just another toy for us to play with. Of course Pa would have to tell us to leave it alone if we got a little too carried away with our play, while he was trying to repair a sensitive part of the sled.

I enjoyed helping with the sled building or repair. This is a talent that has since vanished over the last several decades. Sleds, especially dog sleds, are no longer needed on the lower Yukon. They have been replaced with snowmobiles. The wooden, hand made, dog sleds Pa made have been replaced with heavy-duty plastic sleds purchased from the store. They have a metal hitch that allows them to be pulled by a snowmobile. Dog teams have become a thing of the past. No dog teams exist in Emmonak today. That aspect of the subsistence lifestyle is now gone. The era of living with dogs has given way to modern means. The tie that bound us to the land through our dogs has been eliminated. It has been replaced by the modern conveniences afforded through the use of snowmobiles. I only have the memories of those days gone by that was such an important part of my life growing up as a little girl in Emmonak watching Pa build his dog sleds.

*Good planning and hard work lead
to prosperity, but hasty shortcuts lead
to poverty.*
                    Proverbs 21:5

Freeze-Up

Cikunerraq: Newly formed ice

The onset of winter was a time to watch the land and river change from green to white. An almost magical transformation came over the entire landscape. The cold and snow had a quieting effect on everything.

The time between the end of fishing season and the beginning of winter snows and cold weather was a time of preparation. We had to be prepared for the onset of the first snow, which we were for certain guaranteed by Halloween. We had snow on the ground by that holiday every year. The temperatures dropped to zero by then. Every aspect of our lives during this transitional period was focused on being ready for winter. You simply did not want to be caught without the important preparatory work not done. It could lead to a dangerous situation or cause one a great deal of unnecessary extra work if not prepared. When the days grew short, the temperature fell and the ice began to form on the river. We knew it was not long before freeze-up came upon us.

Once the fishing season ended the activities of the village transformed. In the old days traffic on the river really did not change. People just went about their lives as usual. That all changed once the freezer ships came to buy salmon on the lower Yukon River. These ships mostly came from the Seattle, Washington area. The prospect of a generous catch of Pacific salmon from the lower Yukon was seen as an economic paradise that was too lucrative to pass up. Eventually the Japanese became involved in the fishing process with their salmon roe industry.

As soon as the commercial fishing season ended, the ships began, one by one, to depart their anchorage from Kwiguk Pass and head down the Yukon River to their eventual home in the Seattle area. Finally all the ships were gone. The river was quiet once again.

The cannery barge anchored in Lamont Slough, called the *Bering Sea Fisheries*, was moved to the safety of a river tributary along the Yukon River. It was tied up for the winter somewhere upriver. It was towed to a location that was more protected from the Yukon ice both during freeze-up and at flooding time in the spring. This had to be done before the first ice began to form on the river.

As the freezer ships departed, the last supply barge of the season arrived at Emmonak. The last barge tried to arrive in late September. It would offload the goods that were ordered for the winter. The last supply barge was an important one because it contained the essential items required to take us through the long winter ahead.

There were years when the Bering Sea froze unusually early and the last supply barge was not able to enter the Yukon River. There was no last barge shipment to Emmonak when that happened. The supplies that were expected did not arrive during those years. That caused real problems for the village. Without the supplies from the last barge, shortages could create a very serious situation in the village during the long winter months.

It was the last chance to receive any large items that people required. It was too expensive to order large items by plane, or impossible if they were too large to fit into the small planes that could land at the Emmonak airstrip. The last barge also brought the village its winter supply of heating oil, blazo fuel, diesel fuel and gasoline. Those items were required once the village had a number of snow machines, vehicles and a generating plant to provide electricity. The local school always required a substantial supply of heating oil to cover its needs during the long winter months. The barge would depart just before the river began to freeze. The barge operators did not want to become trapped in the river because of an early freezeup. With the last supply barge gone, it was time for the long winter quiet to descend upon the lower Yukon River.

The waterfowl, that was so plentiful on the delta, began to migrate to their southern homes. The geese started flying around and forming their signature V-shape formations. The lakes and rivers that were so full of birds during the summer, now became empty. By mid-October almost all of the waterfowl had gone. They began their journey to such distant locations as California, Mexico, the Hawaiian Islands and Australia. Some of the small birds, I was told, flew as far as the Antarctic seas. Not all the birds left for the winter. The raven, ptarmigan and snowy owl remained to live throughout the winter. I guess they did not want to go where the weather was warmer.

Freeze Up

Watching the river for signs of freeze-up began. It started as a thin layer of ice that formed in unconnected sheets we could see along the edge of the riverbank. Over time the thin sheets of ice protruded further and further into the main channel of the river. The sheets of ice thickened and in what appeared as an overnight phenomenon the river became completely iced over from one bank to the other. It took a little time before anyone ventured out onto the ice to check its thickness and strength to hold up a person.

Usually by Thanksgiving Day there was enough thick ice to walk on. Some one went out with a stick and pounded on the ice with it to determine if it was safe enough to walk on. We waited until the ice was thick enough to hold up a snowmobile before we ventured out onto it. There were too many stories of people falling through the ice and drowning for us to risk ourselves. We waited until we were absolutely certain of the safety of the ice thickness.

We kids played ice skates on the portion of the frozen river that was smooth and devoid of snow. Those areas made for good ice-skating. We went skating during recess at school and after school. After school was the best time because we could stay out on the ice for as long as we wanted or until it got too dark to see. I shared a pair of ice skates with my sister. Not every family could afford ice skates for every child in the family or if at all. We gladly shared the skates we had with those who did not have any.

I remember we liked to play games on the ice with the other kids who joined in. Some of the games we played as a group were:

- Hockey
- Snake
- Tag

What can I say? Kids would be kids and the river ice just added to our enjoyment of the winter. It was going to be a long and cold time of the year, so why not try to enjoy it the best we could?

Walking Stick

I mentioned earlier how a person walked out onto the ice and used a stick to test the depth and sturdiness of the ice after freeze-up. This was to determine whether it was safe to go out onto the ice. This was one function of the walking stick or Ayaruq in Yupik Eskimo. This stick was most important to any Eskimo when going out in the wilderness or any place that had unknown footing.

A walking stick was similar to *wise words* spoken by the elders as both gave our life guidance. A person would not be without their walking stick when uncertain about the conditions they were going to enter. A walking stick was vital. It could mean the difference between life and death. It was a necessary survival tool. It gave guidance to our lives when we did not know which way to go. The Ayaruq was used to check:

- Ice thickness after freeze-up
- Ice sturdiness during the spring break-up
- Walking conditions on the tundra
- Water depth when traveling unknown rivers and sloughs

It was used to check the surroundings before you. It gave you guidance so you would not walk down the wrong path. According to the elders a properly used walking stick would lead you in the right path. Its virtue is similar to wise words in that both keep you on the right path. You ignore wise words and the use of a walking stick and you will go down the wrong path.

It showed the safe and the dangerous options on a person's path. The walking stick only worked if the user followed it according to traditional teachings. A person would not be helped by a walking stick if he didn't know how to use it properly. A walking stick gave you inferences as to the two paths in life: the right one and the wrong one. It was up to the user of the Ayaruq to choose wisely.

Winter Tundra Travel

Freeze-up allowed for more mobility in the lower Yukon River area. There were places we could go during the winter that could not be reached during any other time of the year. Once the tundra was frozen, it was friendlier to mobility. When it was not frozen it was just like trying to walk on wet, mushy organic matter. It was difficult to walk on. You had to wear hip waders just to keep your lower body dry. There were always the unexpected steps that could lead to nothing but water it seemed. You had to be very careful. Even the arrival of fourwheeler machines was no match for the arctic tundra when it was not frozen.

Once the tundra was frozen, we could travel it by dog team. Later the snow machine was introduced and the tundra was then completely navigable. If we wanted to go to a nearby location, we could travel a direct line to get there in the winter. In the summer we had to follow the river and sloughs to get to our desired destination. That was not always the most direct or shortest route. The snow-covered tundra allowed us to go almost anywhere we wanted by either dog team (which our family owned) or by snow machine.

The most important concern regarding travel on the snow-covered tundra was its whiteness. The landscape was devoid of any trees. There was nothing from one horizon to the other. The lack of trees made for no shadows to sight against. It could actually blind a person on a bright, sunny day. Pa made a mask-like device out of a piece of wood he put over his face to cover his eyes. It had tiny slits cut horizontally where each eye could see out. This helped greatly. Actually it was impossible to go out on the tundra during the daytime in the winter without some form of eye protection. You could really get sunburned if you did not protect the exposed parts of the body. It was usually really cold traveling on the tundra. The open areas were simply wide open for the wind to pick up speed and blow hard. Your face could get frostbite in no time if not protected. It seemed there were more ways to get hurt on the tundra in the winter than by traveling the river during the summer. It was a wonderful place to be though when it was quiet and no wind. The vastness of the never-ending terrain of the arctic tundra was stunning as well as humbling.

It was also very easy to get lost. That could be another of the most dreaded fears of traveling on the tundra in the wintertime. Since everywhere you looked, it appeared the same, it was easy to get turned around. Pa was very good at knowing where he was at all times. He would use the sun's position as a compass and timepiece. I know he always kept in mind where he was and how far he had gone. He traveled the land his entire life and learned the way from his father. Everything looked exactly the same to the untrained eye like mine. It was all flat white in every direction you looked. When a compass became available to the Eskimo people that helped greatly in reducing the number of people that became lost while on the tundra. It was a serious situation if a person became lost. If you had to spend the night out there, you had better be prepared to handle anything that came up against you. Making an igloo was a talent to which you made good use. We played making igloo when we were young. It could prove to be useful when stranded. Hopefully you remembered to bring a handsaw in order to cut the ice blocks to make an igloo. The igloo was going to be your only hope of survival if you had to overnight on the tundra.

Winter River Travel

Traveling the river during the winter also had its potential dangers. The river did not freeze completely smooth. It could also freeze with ice jams and pressure ridges forming. These tall chunks of ice were to be avoided while traveling the river. If you accidentally hit one of those, it could cause great damage. A person could be critically injured from the impact. Because of the whiteness of the river surface landscape, a person was required to wear some type of eye protection. The mask Pa made for tundra travel worked well also. Without the eye mask, a person runs the risk of permanently blinding their eyes. This also made watching the river ice surface for hidden dangers even greater. It only got worse if you found yourself traveling the river ice in the dark of night. At least a snow machine had a headlight that helped quite a bit. A dog team knew enough to go around the dangerous spots on the river. The dogs had that certain sense about the river ice and what to watch for. They were not about to risk their lives running into an unknown and potentially dangerous situation.

The river ice was also ever changing. The ice structure and character never stayed the same for any length of time. You could not depend upon the course to be the same way the next time you traveled it. Pressure ridges and overflows were always changing during the winter. The overflows were places where the river ice would overlap and allow water to form on the surface of the ice. Once you saw the water you could avoid it. It was the overflow that had only partially froze over with thin skim-ice that posed a hidden danger to the traveler. You simply had to know how to *read the ice* in the winter just as you had to know how to *read the water* in the summer.

The river always had its dangers, no matter whether you traveled it during the winter or the summer. Just because it was frozen did not make it any safer from injury. Nighttime travel in the dark was simply asking for trouble. Traveling faster than you could see with the snowmobile headlights added to the danger. If you did not know what you were doing, you were probably going to come back with some story of a near miss, or an averted tragedy at the end of your journey. If a person was not confident in their read the ice skills then they probably should not be traveling on the ice during the winter. As a result, I never tried to travel the frozen river by myself. I thought it was too dangerous for me to travel by myself without expert advice or assistance. I think because of that I am still here today to write about those memories I have of freeze-up during my days as a little girl growing up on the lower Yukon River.

It is safer to meet a bear robbed of her cubs than to confront a fool caught in folly.
Proverbs 17:12

Winter

Introduction

The Yupik Eskimo word for winter is Uksuq. When people think of Alaska they seem to think of snow, cold and lots of darkness. I think that would describe the lower Yukon Delta during the winter very well. It is a season that has to be appreciated for the grip it has on the people that live within its confines. There is a certain toughness required to get through this season of the year.

Among the wonderful memories I have of winter came from my experiences of riding in the sled while Pa ran the trap line. I really enjoyed the time I spent with him on those journeys. I discovered a very deep appreciation of the natural world that existed around me.

Fishing never stopped just because the river froze over. Winter fishing with nets under the ice was just another opportunity to catch different fish than what was available during the summer. Fishing the lakes was another opportunity that was the vastness of the Yukon delta tundra. The dog team was used to take us to the old village of Kwiguk during the winter months to see movies that were shown at the store located there. Those trips along the Yukon River at night in the winter offered some of the most beautiful views of the northern lights. They would fill the entire nighttime sky from one horizon to the other. Living without the modern conveniences that we have today creates a sense of wonder as to how we made it through the winter months.

Winter also drew people together. The potlatches, between the villages, were an opportunity to share and fellowship together. It brought us closer together as Yupik Eskimos. It showed us that we are all in this life together and we don't have to bear it alone. Once understood, the winter was a beautiful time along the Kwiguk Pass of the lower Yukon River.

Running the Trap Line

Melqulegcurtuq:
He is trapping

Going with Pa as he checked the trap line was one of my most wonderful memories. I really loved the times I spent with pa on the trap line and with the dogs.

Among the many fond memories that I have of growing up on the lower Yukon River, and one of the most enjoyable was the relationship I had with the dogs, especially while running the trap line. I loved being around the dogs. I played with them whenever I had the chance. Although they could be quite annoying when they all began to bark at once, especially at night when we tried to sleep. I still liked having them around and the friendship they afforded. Dog sled teams played a very important role in the lives of the Yukon River Eskimo. It was our primary means of transportation in the wintertime. Almost every family had a team of dogs. A lot of work went into caring for the team. We had to make certain we not only had enough food for ourselves, but for the dog team as well.

I especially enjoyed going with Pa on the trap line. I would tell Pa before I went to school for the day that I wanted him to wait for me after school so I could go on one of his trap line runs. As soon as school was out on that day I ran home as fast as I could go. I quickly changed into warmer clothes. It was wintertime so I had to wear my heaviest parka, mittens and pack boots in order to keep warm while I sat in the basket of the sled. I was so happy that Pa waited for me.

He had the dog team ready to go when I arrived at the sled. The dogs were harnessed and attached to the towrope ready to pull the sled. The sled was tied to a metal rod sunk deep into the ground to hold the dogs from going until we were ready. The dogs, once hitched to the sled, were so full of energy that it required a large amount of immovable force to keep them from taking off with the sled. I quickly jumped into the sled and off we went when Pa released the anchor towrope. The dogs took off as fast as they could go at first. Eventually they settled into a pace they held for the next two to three hours.

Malamutes

We typically used about eight to ten dogs for pulling the sled when we went on the trap line. We had about fifteen dogs in the kennel. Some were left behind to rest for the next journey. Those that were left behind barked and pulled hard at their stakeout rope trying to get loose so they could come along. You could tell that they were really upset to be left behind.

Our sled dogs were all Malamutes. They were large and powerful. Their fur was very thick and long. They were perfect for our Yukon winters. They made great sled dogs and they became very good pets. We did not give them names. They were just dogs and we did not think they required individual attention with a unique name. The kennel of dogs we had was handed down to Pa from his father. They were very much like family to us, and they were treated as such. Some of the dogs would have grown up with Pa or would have been within a generation of Pa while he was a young man. Pa learned his sled dog skills from his father. His father must have been a very good teacher because he sure knew a lot about how to handle the dogs. I admired him so much for his knowledge of dogs.

There was no selective breeding of the dogs. They had pups the natural way without any regard for which male should breed with any particular female. The female dogs would just breed whenever they came into heat. The pups were saved for Pa or given away to others who needed some dogs. Everybody in the village knew everyone's dog kennel. If someone needed a dog, one was provided. I especially enjoyed the pups. They were always fun to play with while they were little.

Each dog was individual as to their personality, talent for sledding and intelligence. Pa placed them among the dog sled team based on each one's individual characteristics. The superior dogs, the leader of the pack, occupied the front of the team at the leader position. They were also the most experienced dogs at pulling the sled and leading it through the trails that were used along the trap line. The most powerful dogs were placed nearest the sled. They provided the power to pull hard on the sled and push the other dogs to the pace Pa desired. The dogs in the middle of the team were just ordinary dogs without any particular talents. They simply provided extra dog power. They were needed to assist when making turns so the entire team turned as a unit and not get all tangled together.

They responded to certain commands Pa yelled to them. It was amazing how he made them know the words he used and how to translate those words into the appropriate action the dogs were to undertake. It must have been one of those musher-to-dog relationships that were always the great mystery. A few of the commands he used were:

Hike - go
Gee - turn left
Haw - turn right

There was no word to make the dogs stop. A few colorful metaphors were tried to see if they had any effect. Those usually did not work very well. To stop the team, the sled brake was pushed hard into the snow, and if that did not make them slow, a sled anchor would be thrown to make the sled come to a stop. That always worked as a last resort. If the dogs could not be stopped then a very dangerous situation could result. A run away sled without a driver could leave a person stranded very far from home. The dogs were very likely to get the sled wrapped around some tree that would capture them. Unless they could be found, both the driver and the team were in serious danger of exposure during the cold winter night.

On the Trap Line
Pa managed two trap lines. One was located to the north and the other to the sought of Emmonak. Two trap lines were better than one because

the population of animals that were trapped always changed. If one was a poor producer then the chances increased in getting animals if we had a second one. The animals that we trapped were always migrating and having two trap lines increased our chances for success. We didn't want to depend on only one trap line in case it became a poor producer. Our subsistence needs required a certain level of good trapping results.

Northern Trap Line

To get to the northern trap line required a long trip by dog sled across the tundra to the north of Emmonak. Pa had to find a good forest of trees in order to set his traps and snares. This is where the animals lived. The journey took us north to where we crossed the Emmonak slough then to the upper shore of a very large and unnamed lake. From there we turned right and headed north and east to where the trees were located. This trip led us deeper into the mainland to the east and away from the arctic tundra of the ocean. The sloughs and river passes were larger there and as a result more trees grew around them. This environment made for better trapping conditions. The trip across the open tundra to get to this trap line was a very cold and windy experience. The lack of trees allowed the wind to blow unobstructed. The wind chill could really hurt a person's exposed skin. I was very happy to be covered under the canvass in the sled basket. It was much farther to travel to the northern trap line, but it was important to have as many traps and snares set out as practical.

Southern Trap line

To get to the southern trap line required only a short ride across the Kwiguk Pass river ice to its south bank. After crossing the river we headed south and west to get to our destination. As soon as we reached the south bank, we were already among the trees. We went further south and west to keep our distance from the riverbank, as that was not a good site to place traps and snares. The animals did not want to live close to the village. The area across the river opposite Emmonak was a very large land area that was uninhabited and wide open for setting a good trap line. It consisted of dense willow trees primarily. Nothing grew very large anywhere on the delta.

A few other trappers used these areas as well. Each trapper was always aware of the other trapper's territory and trap line layout. I do not ever remember having disputes over each other's trap line. We simply respected each one's traps and lines. We never considered intruding on another person's trap line. There was plenty of land to be shared by everyone. There was no such thing as land ownership during the time of my youth. That would change with the Native Claims Settlement Act about twenty years later.

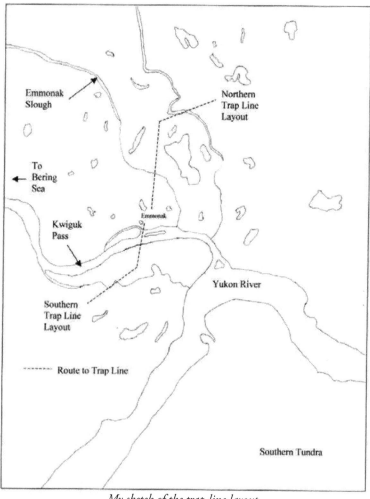

My sketch of the trap line layout.

Pa did not go on the trap line everyday. He alternated every other day to check the line. I did not go with him every time. School sometimes interfered and I also had other little girl activities to do. The trap line was a combination of snares and traps.

The snares were used to catch rabbits. Along the lower Yukon River we found both the Snowshoe Hare and the Tundra Hare. Both species were brown in color during the summer and turned all white in the winter. The snares were made of wire. The wire was formed into a loop for the rabbit to try and run or hop through and then tighten so that it could not get away. After finding a rabbit track that appeared to be regularly used, Pa would find a low hanging branch from which to hang the snare right above the rabbit trail. He was extremely careful not to disturb the snare site. The rabbits could sense any disturbance that was unnatural and thus avoid the snare. As usual, Pa was good at placing snares.

The leg hold type traps were used to catch red foxes, lynx and weasels. Pa looked for the tracks and well used trails and set the trap in the trail. He covered the trap with snow and made it look like a part of the trail. He was careful not to disturb the immediate area and spook the animal into going around the trap. He used a chain or heavy-duty wire to attach the trap to a stake so the animal caught in the trap could not carry it away and get lost among the brush.

If a trap or snare was successful and caught an animal it could be either dead or alive by the time we checked it. The dead ones were removed and put into the sled. If the animal were still alive, then Pa had to kill it before it was placed in the sled. He carried either a wooden club or used his 22-caliber rifle to kill the catch. If it were a rabbit then he simply broke the rabbit's neck with a quick twist with his hands.

We were also on the watch for firewood. We always tried to come home with a sled full of wood. We tried to never return home empty of wood.

Snowshoes and Guns

Pa also brought his guns and snowshoes with him at all times. The snowshoes were kept in the sled during heavy snow conditions. It was a tremendous workout trying to walk in the deep snow without the use of the snowshoes. A person became so tired, hot and sweaty from the physical exertion of walking over the snow without them. They made walking over deep snow much easier. Once a visual trail was made from the use of the snowshoes over the same path, then the walking was much easier.

Pa made his own snowshoes. It goes without saying that he was a good snowshoe maker. He took the same pride in making his snowshoes as he did with the sleds he built. One difference being that he used birch for the snowshoe frame while he used hickory for the sleds. He found the birch wood from the birch trees that grew near the river around Emmonak or slightly upriver. They grew larger a little ways just upriver. He peeled the bark so the soft wood was exposed. He cut the wood down to size with his handsaw. He did the bending of the wood by using his steamer container that was also used for hickory bending during sled building. After he removed the wood from the steamer he bent it into shape and tied the two free ends together. These formed the tail, or rear, of the snowshoe. Once the wood had cooled and conformed to the shape he desired he drilled holes in the frame through which he threaded rope to make the mesh of the snowshoe. The holes had to be made with a hand drill since we did not have electricity to operate an electric drill. We did not have the money to buy rawhide for the webbing so Pa used rope. It worked well. You had to make certain the rope was tight at all times. It required constant maintenance to keep the rope webbing tight within the frame. He attached a rope assembly to the top deck of the snowshoe into which his boot was secured. He tried to keep a couple pair of snowshoes available at all times. One was for immediate use and another was kept as a backup.

The guns were not necessarily for protection as much as for shooting ptarmigan and rabbits we might see along the way. We were never guaranteed of catching animals in the snares or traps so the gun was for extra assurance of getting game. He brought his shotgun and a 22-caliber rifle. Pa was exceptional at seeing and or finding game. When he spotted or sensed that there was game around, he stopped the sled, got off, put on his snowshoes, took his rifle or shotgun and searched for the food he was after. I stayed with the sled and played in the snow while he hunted. I always had the dogs to keep me company while he was gone. I don't remember getting cold while waiting for Pa to return. You might think that it could get really cold just sitting and waiting for him to return. When I heard the gunshot I knew he had found what he was searching for. He returned shortly to the sled with his catch of the day. He placed his kill in the sled. Before we departed for the next leg he made sure I was secured in the basket, unhitched the brake and off we went to work the rest of the trap line. He had that extra sense about him that made him so aware of the wilderness that surrounded him. He could spot the white rabbits and white ptarmigan against the white snow long before I could. Both the rabbit and ptarmigan turned all white during the winter months. To spot either of them against the snow you had to know how and where to look. All that identified them were their dark eyes against the white background. He was almost always successful at finding animals during the time we were out on the trap line.

My First Catch

I caught a rabbit once. Well, I mean I killed a rabbit once. I always said catch or caught to people and they looked at me funny. "How did you catch it?" they asked. I had to explain that I killed it, is what I meant. Pa was the one who saw the rabbit first. He showed me where it was and asked me if I wanted to shoot it myself. I was happy that he gave me the opportunity to shoot it. If I missed, then it was one less rabbit for the dinner table. I shot it with his 22-caliber rifle. I retrieved it and put it in the sled with the rest of the catch. I made certain that it was separate from the others so I could identify it when we unloaded the sled when we returned to the cabin. Since it was my first kill, I was required to give it to one of the elders. This was according to Eskimo tradition. I could not keep it for myself. I gave it to grandpa. He was very happy to receive it from me, and congratulated me for a fine job well done. Actually, that was the only time I was fortunate enough to catch anything. I never caught anything else for the rest of my life. That was it. Period.

The Trapping Routine

I really enjoyed riding in the basket of the sled. Most of the time the ride was smooth. We never did have any accidents with the dogs or sled. Pa was always very careful. I think he was extra careful when I was in the sled. He did not want anything to happen to me. I never got cold riding in the sled. He used the tarp that he always carried in his sled to cover me and keep me warm. I made certain that I brought along and wore more than enough winter clothes to keep warm. The weather varied from day to day and especially winter to winter. Sometimes the sledding was warm and sometimes it was very cold outside. I especially enjoyed the sled rides when it snowed. There was something magical about being out on the trap line with a snowfall coming down. It made everything around us so quiet. The fresh snow diminished the noise of the sled and the dogs seemed to make less noise. The whiteness of the wilderness was hard to put to words or express the feelings one got. The new snow covered all the old animal tracks and wiped them clean in preparation of another round of tracks to be discovered. How fortunate I was to have those memories to carry with me forever.

The dogs could go at a steady pace forever it seemed. The sound of their paws patting the snow and the sled sliding over the snow was serene. We were very quiet so we could sneak up on an animal we might be able to shoot with one of our guns. The dogs had such an amazing endurance. They could go for miles without requiring a stop or break. The dogs got a break with every stop to check the snare or trap. With every stop, there was the anticipation of finding something in the snare or trap. Each time we would catch something, it was an occasion to celebrate. This was important for us. The rabbits we snared became our supper to eat and the fur we used for other purposes such as parka linings. It was simply the cycle of life we lived in harmony with. All of nature surrounded us all the time.

The process of stopping at each snare and trap and checking it for its bounty, then returning to the sled and going to the next check point was repeated more times than I could remember. We tried to be back home by dark. We did not bring a light with us so darkness could be a real problem if we were to get caught out in it. Unlike berry picking, we did not stop for a picnic or snack break. It was important to get the trap line checked and back home before darkness descended upon us.

Back Home

When we arrived back at the cabin we began the job of unloading everything and getting the dogs settled in. We started the process of removing the harnesses from each dog. The dogs were not as energetic and hard to handle as they were at the start. This job went much easier. After we took the harness off, then we tied each dog up to its respective post. We also had to remove the booties from the paw of each dog. The chore of feeding the dogs began. Depending upon whether it was warm or cold determined what we fed them.

If it was warm we gave them dried fish or fresh sheefish that was caught from ice fishing from the river under the ice. It was important to feed them the right food so that there internal temperature was correct. We did not want to make them too cold or too hot on the inside.

If it was cold then we started a fire and cooked up a batch of dried fish or sheefish. We used a kettle and filled it full of water and fish. This way, we were able to give them a meal to warm up the dogs on the inside.

After they were fed, we treated them to extra dried grass for them to lie on while they slept at night. We laid the dried grass on the snow in a shallow spot by each stake that each dog made for sleeping in at night. These were malamutes, so they had no problem with the cold and sleeping on the snow covered ground without the need of a doghouse. Once these chores were done we were ready to treat ourselves to supper in the house. The dogs were not allowed to be in the house with us at any time. They were forced to be outdoor dogs. After the sled run the dogs were very tired. Once they had some good food in their stomachs, they were ready to bed down and sleep for the night. They had little desire to bark after a long run and a full stomach.

Pa made his own dog harness sets. He used a special type of nylon webbing he bought at the Northern Commercial store. Just like making the dog sleds I was amazed at how easy he made the assembly of the dog harnesses look. He just knew how long to cut each piece, stitch it together and before you knew it, it came to life as a perfectly fitting harness set for each dog. We had to make our own harness sets because they were too expensive to buy from the store.

He also made the booties for each dog's paws. I can't remember of what material he used to make them. The booties had to be either repaired often or new ones made from scratch. The dogs wore out the booties quickly. He used the booties on the dogs during those really cold days when he felt sorry for the dog's feet. It was important to keep their paws protected.

The obvious purpose of running the trap line was to check the snares and traps for any animals caught in them. The snares were primarily used to catch rabbits as I described earlier. The rabbits we snared provided two needs for us. We ate them. They became the main ingredient of rabbit stew. Or, we ate them in a cooked or fried form with gravy. Either way I enjoyed them very much. The fur of the rabbit was either used as a part of the parka linings that were made by Mom, or were sold to the fur buyers for money. A rabbit fur lined parka was very warm and comfortable. Its soft fur felt so good on the really cold winter days. In either case the skins had to be tanned or prepared for their final intended use. That preparation stage was Pa's job.

The Furs

Pa always had a variety of stretch frames he used for stretching and cleaning the skins. He made his own stretch frames that were of many different shapes and sizes, depending on what animal he was tanning. Since Pa was so good at working with wood, making the stretch frames was easy work for him. They usually took an oval shape and had a number of holes drilled around the circumference to attach the edge of the animal skin to the frame with twine. The more points that the skin was attached to the frame, the tighter and more even the skin dried without wrinkles. This improved the quality of the fur and brought a higher price with the buyers.

The fox, lynx and weasel caught in the traps were usually prepared so they could be sold to the fur buyers. We did eat lynx on occasion. Once the animal was skinned the fur was attached to the stretch frames. Pa had a favorite knife he used for skinning. He always kept it very sharp. I remember him spending much time sharpening his skinning knife during the winter evenings. After the skin was removed the rest of the animal parts were tossed into a kettle and boiled as a soup for the dogs. As usual the dogs got to eat the leftovers. The skin was then regularly scraped, using the ulu, to remove the fat from the skin. This process took about two to three weeks. I was called upon to help with that job. It was tedious work. You did not want to scrape too hard or with the wrong angle of the ulu or the skin would tear. That ruined or seriously damaged the quality of the fur, thus a lower price for it could result. When the skins were cleaned, they were taken from the stretch frames and placed with the other furs. The furs while on the stretch frames were kept in the cabin. This kept them away from any animals that might try to eat them if kept outside. There were always a number of skins in the cabin during the winter in various stages of cleaning. Piles of skins were kept in the cabin waiting to be brought to the fur buyer.

We brought the furs to the Northern Commercial Company store. It was the center of activity during the winter fur-buying season. Pa loaded the furs into the sled and took them to the store where the buyers were located. There was always a lot of activity surrounding the buyers.

As the furs were handed over to the buyers, all I could think of was the hard work that went into each fur before it was sold. When I think of all the effort that went into this aspect of our lives, it was amazing how it all worked out. It seemed that no part of our existence was without a lot of work. Nothing came easy, but Pa had a way of making it all look as though that was the way it was. No problem. It was just another season of our lives that revolved around running the trap line.

I became a fur buyer after I worked for Northern Commercial a few years. You could say I came full circle as I grew up. From a little girl tagging along with Pa to sell his furs to one day becoming the company fur buyer. I became the person I used to look up to as one who had so much power in buying the furs the local Eskimos delivered to be sold to me.

Boss

My favorite dog was one I called Boss. He was a male malamute. He followed me everywhere I went. He was my protector. When he walked next to me nobody could get very close to me without Boss allowing his permission. He was my pet during grade school, until I had to leave for boarding school in Anchorage. He was also a part of the dog sled team. Pa used him when he hitched up the dogs to run the trap line. I have a lot of memories of our time we spent together. There is something special about the bond a person makes with their dog. They seem to be almost human in their affection for their master. I was fortunate to have had that experience in my life. I remember the frolicking Boss and I experienced together. I was sad when I learned about his death. I had grown up and so had Boss. When I left for high school I never had that special companionship with him that was so special while I was younger. I still miss the days we were together especially the memories of the times we spent together running the trap line.

I loved going with Pa on the trap line. Riding in the sled with Pa afforded me some of the most wonderful memories I have of my youth. It was great to leave the village behind and have my special personal time with Pa and the dogs. I learned so much about the struggle for life as lived on the delta's tundra. Today we are so far removed from the reality of life and our relationship with nature. With Pa, I was able to experience it first hand. The lessons I learned from running the trap line profoundly influenced every aspect of my life. I was so blessed to have had them as a part of my life while growing up a little girl on the Kwiguk Pass of the lower Yukon River.

People with integrity have firm footing, but those who follow crooked paths will slip and fall.
Proverbs 10:9

Winter Fishing

Kuvyatuq: Catch fish with nets

Winter fishing required a completely different set of skills as compared to summer fishing. Besides the cold, winter fishing required much more physical effort. Pa made it look so easy.

Once the waters of the Lower Yukon delta froze for the season, fishing took on a different look and purpose. Fishing did not stop just because the river froze over. Another method of fishing took the place of summer fishing. There were still fish to be caught below the ice. It was a whole different experience to go winter fishing and catch the fish that lived beneath the ice.

Net Fishing

When the Yukon River froze enough so we could travel it with dog sled or snow machine, we took the smaller, chum salmon nets with us and used them under the ice. We traveled upriver to where the Kwiguk Pass and the Kwikluak Pass met. From there we traveled downriver to find the area of the river where it was at it widest. It was a location near the Big Eddy. This is where we set our nets under the ice. Pa generally had at least two nets fishing most of the winter in the river.

It took a lot of work to set the nets under the ice for the first time. Once the nets were positioned under the ice then it was just a matter of reopening the holes and retrieving the nets to see if any fish were caught. If the nets were catching fish then we left them at that location all winter. Pa usually knew where the good spot to fish the nets were. His own experience at fishing the river along with what his father taught him usually made for a successful selection site for using the nets.

The first time a net was set under the ice required a lot of work. Pa did not have access to powered ice augers or chain saws to cut the holes in the ice. He had to rely on using an ice pick to make each hole. It was hard work digging a hole in the ice large enough to feed the net into the water. He started on one side of the river and dug the first hole. The hole was about one foot wide and the ice was about three to four feet thick. The top of the hole had to be quite large in order to make the hole large enough at the bottom to handle the fish net. Because he only had an ice pick, it was a physically hard and time-consuming task. I helped him with the job. It took a long time making the hole large enough. We had to constantly dip out the ice chunks that would build up and impede our progress. As a little girl, it required a lot of patience. It seemed to take forever to chip the ice with the pick and get to the bottom. If we weren't working so hard it would surely have left us both really cold. The river was very wide where we fished and the wind could really blow in that section. It was a wonderful feeling to make that last effort and break through the ice to the water below. But the hole had to be large enough to handle the net so there was still a lot of chipping to do before we were finished. There were still several more holes to be made.

The next hole was positioned further out into the river. The series of holes ran perpendicular to the riverbank. The distance to the next hole depended upon the length of the pole that was used to thread the net from one hole to the next under the water. I am not really sure how long the poles were that Pa used. I think they were about eight to ten feet long. They were cut from the strongest and straightest trees he could find along the riverbank. They could not be too long or thick. A big, long heavy pole was too hard to work under the ice. It had to be thin enough to feed through the hole and float at the bottom of the ice to be hooked when found at the next hole. After the second hole was made the real magic of net fishing under the ice began.

The shore end of the net was attached to a stake driven into the ice next to the hole just made. This kept it from disappearing down the hole and slipping away under the ice. Pa tied the other end of the net to one end of the pole. The end of the pole that did not have the net attached was pushed down the first hole and positioned so that it was pointing to the second hole. A hook was lowered down the second hole to grab the free end of the pole. As the hook caught the free end of the pole it was pulled up through the hole. With the leading end of the net attached to the pole, it was also pulled up through the hole. When all the net was pulled through the hole it was laid on the ice. Now the process of cutting the third hole began. More holes were cut until the entire length of the net was stretched out under the ice.

After the third hole was cut we went back to the second hole and feed the free end of the pole under the ice and pointed it to the third hole. A hook grabbed the pole under the water and was pulled up through the ice bringing another section of the net along with it. This process was repeated until the entire net was under water. When we were finished we had the net completely under the ice. The net then extended from the shore to the middle of the river. We tied the rope ends of the net together on top of the ice and left it on the ice. A stake was driven into the ice near the outside of each outermost hole. We used a short section of rope to connect the stake and net rope together. This rope kept the net from moving between the holes under the water. The stakes also gave us a bearing as to where the net was located if a heavy snow or blowing snow covered the net rope left on the ice. When we were done the rope laid on the top of the ice and the net was positioned under the water. It was now ready to catch fish. We gathered up the equipment and headed back to the village or to another net that needed checking.

The net was checked about every other day. The holes were frozen over by the time we returned, so the job of chipping the ice began all over again. We started at the middle of the riverside of the net. That hole was reopened. Then we proceeded to the hole nearest the shore and reopened it. The middle holes that were used to set the net were no longer required, so we did not reopen them. They just froze over and remained that way all winter. Only the holes at the end of the net were required to be open when checking the nets. These holes also had the rope end of the net exposed. Although the holes had been open once while putting the net in the water, it was still a hard job chipping the ice out of the hole and making it large enough to pull the net through. Pulling the rope from one hole and walking to the other hole accomplished the process of pulling the net out of the water and checking for fish. This pulled the net out of one hole and eventually was stretched out on the top of the ice between the two holes. We simply inverted the rope and net configuration. Now the net was on top of the ice and the rope was under the ice. While the net was being pulled through the hole in the ice we picked the fish from the net. We used rubberized gloves to keep our hands as dry as possible. It was quite a messy job as the fish slime froze on the gloves and made picking the fish from the nets a very cold task. It was difficult to stay dry and warm. I usually managed to get wet and cold. As the fish were picked from the net they were tossed on the ice. Later we put them in gunnysacks to be hauled back to the village. We continued to pull the net through the hole and pick fish until all the net was on the ice.

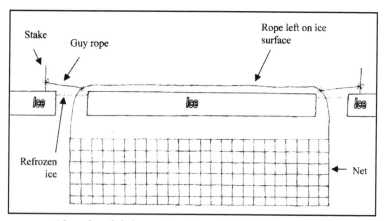

Sketch of fish net in the river under the ice.

To replace the net under the ice we grabbed one end of the net and start walking to the other hole. This brought the rope back on top of the ice through one hole and the net was pulled back under the ice into the water at the opposite hole. It was quite an ingenious system that had been developed by the Eskimos to fish under the ice. When we were finished the net was back in the water and the rope was left on top of the ice. It was such hard work net fishing under the ice. It

had to be done though if we wanted food for ourselves. Our liveli-
hoods depended on it. The dogs also needed fish to eat.

Using the nets to fish under the ice in the wintertime allowed us to
catch the following fish on the Yukon River:

- Sheefish
- Whitefish
- Pike
- Burbot

The fish we caught fed our family and the dogs. The sheefish especially were used for both our own family consumption and for the
welfare of the dogs. If we had too many then the extra was given to
the dogs.

If we caught too many and other family relatives were low on fish,
then we gave them some of our catch. Winter was a time when some
families did not have enough fish to go around. If they exhausted
their summer catch then we shared our fish with them. We made
certain that we took care of each other. The older villagers could be
most vulnerable. We watched them and continually asked if they had
enough food. It was our duty to always pay attention to our elders
in the village and see that they had enough food at all times during
the winter. If someone was hungry they let others know of their need
and fish was given to them. A community network was established
to avoid anyone going hungry.

Trap Fishing

We also caught fish using fish traps. Fish traps were used under the
ice on the surrounding lakes. He used both wood and metal fish traps.

Pa made his own fish traps. Since he was good at working with
wood and making things from wood, it was natural that he made his
own wooden fish traps. He first looked for long, straight sapling trees
he cut. He peeled the bark to expose the white wood underneath.
This was the best wood because it was soft and very bendable without
having to heat it first. After peeling the bark then he cut the wood
into dimensional pieces he made into the frame of the trap. The

longest pieces of wood ran the entire length of the trap. This gave it a continuous construction that made it less likely to break in the middle. Shorter pieces of wood were wrapped around the long pieces making a circular looking trap with a funnel shape. The overlapping pieces of wood were held together with rope or heavy-duty twine. There were up to three sections to each trap. The outside section was the widest which allowed the fish to first enter the trap. The next section became smaller, while finally the innermost section was the smallest. Between each section there were funnel shaped sticks that guided the fish into the trap. Once the fish entered the innermost section of the trap it was unable to escape. This was accomplished by using sticks that were pointed and sharp at the small end. These sticks were arranged so a funnel shape was formed. The pointed stick ends would not allow the fish to swim back through the trap to get to the entrance and escape. This trap worked very well at catching fish that lived in the lakes. I was always amazed at the ease at which Pa could make the traps. He made it look so easy. He had about three to four of the wooden traps that he used regularly.

Pa also made and used wire mesh basket traps. He used heavy gauge wire to form the outside frame of the trap. The shape of the trap was very important to its ability to catch fish. He learned this trade through his father. I am sure that his father also told him what worked and did not work in the design that best caught fish. Grandpa would have shared all his secrets with my Pa. Someday grandpa would have to rely on Pa to catch fish for him. Once he had the outside frame made and tied securely together, then he covered the frame with chicken wire. He made a trap door assembly to provide for removing the fish when they were caught in the trap. This trap was very successful at catching fish. It was more difficult to be seen by the fish than the wooden traps he used. I am sure the fish had an equally difficult time recognizing it sitting on the lake bottom. This was all due to the fact that Pa put so much pride in the construction of each trap. He was always careful to make certain that every detail was meticulously cared for. He made sure that every trap was not a hindrance to catching fish, but actually aided the fish in seeking out his trap. The construction of each one was created with the blackfish in mind. He probably asked himself the question, "If I were a black-fish would I go into this trap?" Pa kept several of these metal mesh fish traps available for use when he went to the lake.

The traps were used for fishing in the lakes. He went inland to find the lake. I don't remember going with him to trap fish on the lakes. He said that he usually stayed close to the shore and cut the hole in the ice with his ice pick. The hole had to be large enough to handle the trap and lower it to the bottom of the lake. I don't remember him using any bait for catching the fish. A piece of rope was tied to the trap so it could be lowered and raised when required. The rope was the only sign used in finding the location of the trap under the ice.

The traps were not checked every day. I think Pa only went to the lake for checking the trap about twice a week. Since they were under water and the fish could live in the trap, there was no rush to check them everyday. Checking the traps required the use of the ice pick again, to chip out the hole in order to retrieve the trap.

Fish traps were used to catch blackfish when used in the inland lakes. Pa traveled to and from the lakes using his dog team. The blackfish were transferred from the fish trap to gunnysacks for transport back to the village. The fish were removed from the wooden trap by removing the innermost section of the trap from the remainder of the trap. No door was required to be made because of this arrangement. The two sections of the trap could be separated thus allowing the fish that were trapped inside the innermost section to be removed. Once the fish were removed from the trap it was reconnected, usually with wire ties, and ready to be used again as one complete unit.

We prepared the blackfish by pouring hot water over them and bringing the water containing the fish to a boil. The blackfish were about three to seven inches long. There was not much meat available for eating from each fish. The meat of the blackfish did taste really good. It had a sweet taste as compared to other fish we ate. The parts of the blackfish we could not eat were given to the dogs. They sure appreciated that snack on a cold winter day.

Fishing for blackfish was a winter long activity. Grandpa showed Pa the lakes to use. As usual that is how he learned everything that he knew about making the traps and using the traps for fishing. Once he found a good producing lake, he continued to use it all winter long. If it was not a good producer then he went to another lake and tried it. The blackfish were pretty small compared to the salmon we caught in the summer. It took a lot of work to get so little meat from the blackfish. It was very tasty though, which made up for its small size.

————·————

Fishing did not stop just because the river was frozen. Fish were required to be caught for family consumption during the winter months. It could become very cold standing on the ice while preparing the nets and baskets. A lot of hard work went into fishing in the winter. That is what made it such a special time for us, as the fish that were caught while winter fishing became an important food in our wintertime diet.

 Lazy people don't even cook the game they catch, but the diligent make use of everything they find.
Proverbs 12:27

Christmas

Alussistuaq: Christmas

Christmas was my favorite holiday. I enjoyed it as much as the other kids in the village. It wasn't just receiving gifts that mattered, but the love that was shared by those giving them that really counted.

This was a white man's or kass'aq holiday. It was just another day during a long winter in the life of the Eskimo. Christmas was an unknown holiday. To the old Eskimo there was no Jesus, thus no reason to celebrate. That all changed with the arrival of the missionaries. They taught us about God. They told us about the existence of a Son of God, called Jesus. The missionaries explained the Bible stories of the birth of Jesus to us. The Eskimos were already aware of a supreme power: we just had no name associated with it. The efforts of the missionaries told us about Jesus, his birth, and how it led to the celebration of a day called Christmas. Historically Christmas did not come to the Eskimos of the Lower Yukon until the early 1900s.

It was a favorite time of the year for me. By the time Christmas came around, we had snow on the ground since Halloween. It could really be very cold by this time of the year. There was always a lot of snow on the ground. The days were at their shortest during Christmas. There was not much sunshine to enjoy. It never got completely dark on the shorter days because the sunlight reflecting off the ice pack kept it brighter than you might expect. Although we might not see the sun, it had an impact on the white surroundings. It was always fun to anticipate what may come for Christmas.

We did not celebrate Christmas with a tree. There were no evergreen trees on the lower Yukon River delta. No trees of any significant size grew on the delta. We did not decorate our cabin with anything. We could not afford it anyway. There was no electricity to our cabin to power Christmas lights.

On Christmas Eve all the families of the village went to the Community Center. There was an artificial Christmas tree at the Community Center. It was provided by some of the teachers I think. Each family brought one gift for each of their children in the family and placed it under the tree.

The parents sat and visited like parents do, while the kids played like kids do. This was all in anticipation of the arrival of Santa Claus.

When Santa Claus made his appearance, he distributed all the presents that were placed under the tree. Children were certain to get a present even if their parents could not afford one. Everyone in the village made certain that if it was known that a child would go without a gift that one was made available some way somehow. Each gift had a child's name on it, which Santa read out loud and gave it to the recipient. We knew the gifts really did not come from Santa but was placed under the tree by our parents. That did not matter to us. Receiving one gift at Christmas was all that we ever desired anyway. Santa also distributed candy to all the kids that were present. No child was left out.

As I look back on the Christmases we had when I was a little girl, they were very special. Living on the lower Yukon River was a tough life. We did not have very many things. Most of the toys we had were hand made for us. That made them very special. When we received a gift from Santa, that was extra special and something to be very thankful for. Although we did not decorate with the Christmas lights that are used today, we had our own outdoor lights, the natural ones.

The northern lights, or aurora borealis, were especially beautiful on the cold, clear nights that usually occurred during Christmas and into the following winter months of the New Year. The displays were magnificent on the very cold nights. They consisted of almost every color of the rainbow. They extended from horizon to horizon and were very active. They could be so beautiful and vibrant. It was awesome to watch them when they were really active. It is almost impossible to describe in words their breathtaking beauty. The northern lights danced like rough ocean waves of color across the black nighttime sky. Their movements so violent you almost thought you could hear them making noise. The colder the night the more active the northern lights became. In other words the more unbearable the cold, the more active was the display. They danced in the sky in vast waves of color. Sometimes, when they seemed to vigorously dance in the sky, they were almost too scary for a little girl. They made one's imagination run wild. No man-made lights could compare to the natural ones of the northern lights. They made Christmas a very special time of the year.

Christmas was always a special time for me. I loved the joy of receiving that special gift from Santa Clause. There was a similarity I thought in the giving of the gifts brought by the Magi to the Christ child and to the giving that was shared by our parents. The gifts given by the Magi represented the finest and most expensive gifts they could offer. The gifts given to us by our parents represented the finest that our parents could afford. It represented the love shown to me by those that loved me very much. I especially enjoyed the opportunity it gave to the entire village as each family came together to share with each other and with their neighbors. The same sharing spirit was demonstrated by the Magi to Christ was also shown to the children of the village by our parents. It was a wonderful time of the year for sharing, especially the giving.

Giving a gift works wonders, it may bring you before important people!
Proverbs 18:16

Kwiguk Movies

Suuliyartuq: Going to a movie

There was something very special about going to Kwiguk as a family to see movies. Going to a movie allowed us to get away from the hard reality of living that we faced each day in our subsistence lifestyle.

The village of Kwiguk had a very colorful history for its part of the lower Yukon River. It was located just downriver from the intersection of the upper Kwikluak Pass and the Kwiguk Pass of the Yukon River. It was about three miles by river from the village of Emmonak. The fond memories I have of Kwiguk were the Saturday night dog sled rides to watch Kwiguk movies with my family.

Village of Kwiguk

The stories I heard of the early people who lived at Kwiguk were ones of migration. Some of the people who first inhabited Kwiguk were from the Black River area along the Bering Sea coast south of the drainage of the Yukon River. Some of those families moved to Kwiguk because they were required to send their children to school. The Black River was too shallow to support supply barges for a school or church to be located. As a result they had to move and some of them found a good location at what would become Kwiguk.

Other inhabitants of Kwiguk came from settlements upriver. Some of the people who lived in the upriver villages of Hamilton, New Hamilton and Fish Village came to Kwiguk to settle. Those who did not move to Kwiguk chose to move to Kotlik. The people who lived at Bill Moore Slough, for example, decided to move to Kotlik instead of Kwiguk. They were all required to enroll their children in school, thus the need to move. As a result there are still remnants of old settlements now abandoned along the upriver portion of what is known as the North mouth of the Yukon River. It is common to travel some of the sloughs of the Yukon River and find old abandoned log houses. Some of them were still used as summer fish camps during my grade school days. These upriver people also chose the site of Kwiguk as their place to live.

Actually the location of Kwiguk was a very good one for fishing. It is located next to one of the best upriver fishing sites. The Big Eddy was right next to Kwiguk or possibly downriver just a little. The Big Eddy was ideal for salmon fishing in the summer and was a favorite site for winter net fishing. Although we used Grandpa's Island as our summer fishing site, it was Pa's choice for net fishing in the winter.

The Big Eddy is created by the westward flow of the Yukon River (Kwikluak Pass) becoming slightly constricted at the entrance of Kwiguk Pass before it turned southwest. The turn to the south and west is what we called the South Mouth. This conjunction of the river with the abrupt turn in direction caused a very pronounced cut bank feature on the west side of the river. There was an associated large sandbar that developed on the opposite or east side of the river. The water would actually eddy, or twist and turn, as it made this change in direction. The sandbar side of the river was excellent for set gill net fishing into the river's eddy. The water current was more turbulent, thus the salmon could not see the nets as well and would get caught in them.

The Big Eddy was tricky to navigate. You had to know how to read the water and be very aware of the rise and fall of the tides. The water might look deep, but on the east side of the river there were sandbars everywhere to ground any unwitting boater who might run upon them. It was especially frustrating to run aground on a sandbar going downriver. The current simply pushed you further onto the sandbar.

It was a very desirable fishing site and many fishermen still use it today as a prime location for in-the-river fishing. It was a prime location for which the immigrants from upriver selected Kwiguk as the site to which they moved. It was also a location, which would not last long. Because of the flow of the river it would slowly erode away at the cut bank, which is where Kwiguk was located. The village was right in the path of the Yukon's full force of water flow. The river wanted to cut the bank away toward the west. Eventually the annual floods took their toll and eroded away the land upon which the village was established.

The eroding riverbank eventually began to consume the buildings who were built on the site. One by one the cabins, who were peoples' homes, were washed away in the Yukon River. The people who had migrated to this location had to face the fact that they had to move again. All the settlers moved to another location on Kwiguk Pass. It took them away from the water hazard of the mighty Yukon River. They could hopefully live in safer water along the north bank of Kwiguk Pass. Basically everyone moved from Kwiguk except for Cyril Okitkun who owned the village store. He remained the only holdout to stay behind. The people moved to the north side of Kwiguk Pass. It was later called Emmonak, which means blackfish in the Upik Eskimo language.

Emmonak was not completely uninhabited at the time the people moved from Kwiguk. The move from Kwiguk to Emmonak occurred before I was born. I have no recollection of the village of Kwiguk with very many people. My relatives told me that some of our family already lived at the site called Emmonak along the blackfish slough. A few other families had already settled in Emmonak prior to the move by the people of Kwiguk. The Redfox family lived in Emmonak before the move from Kwiguk. Prior to the move, Kwiguk was more populated than Emmonak.

The only memory I have of Kwiguk centers around the movies we went to watch almost every Saturday night during the winter months. Since Cyril Okitkin remained with his store, he would show movies once a week there. It was a real treat to go by dog sled on the river just for that purpose. During my grade school years it was a nice change of pace to watch the movies at his store.

Going to the Movies
The whole family (eight of us) would load ourselves onto the sled and let the dogs take us to the movies with Pa driving the team. It was so much fun. The trips to the movies are memories I will never

forget. I loved the close family time we spent together in the sled. We all had to bundle up tight and wear everything we could find to keep us warm during the ride. Pa covered all of us in the sled with his canvass before setting the dog sled out on the trail to the river.

I loved traveling by dog sled with my Pa. It was even more exciting when we went as an entire family. It was about a three-mile trip to Kwiguk from Emmonak by the river. There is something very special about traveling the river at night by the moonlight to guide us. We had to be very aware of the dangers of traveling on the river at night. There were always the dangers of overflows and pressure ridges that were more difficult to see in the dark. It was always dark when we left for the movies. The crisp, cold, and humid air of the winter nights made for very cold rides if not dressed for the trip. On the clear nights, the stars were so bright and numerous. Sometimes we were treated with a show of the northern lights in the sky.

We arrived at the store and all of us got out of the sled and walked in. The area in the front of the store was full of dog teams with sleds. Each sled was anchored with either the sled's brake or with a heavy rope tied to a nearby tree if one could be found. The dogs remained hitched to the sled while the family went into the store. Upon arrival the dogs were very noisy and barking loudly. After a while they realized they were going to be tied up for a while and quieted down. Each dog made a shallow depression in the snow and went to sleep. I am sure they were tired from the run to Kwiguk.

I remember the excitement of walking into the store from the cold outside. I met friends who came from other villages such as Alakanuk and Lamont Slough. This was the only time I was able to see them. There was so much to talk about when we met.

It sure felt good to get warmed up with the store's stove. We had the opportunity to drink something hot to warm us up on the inside. The parents usually had coffee while the kids drank hot chocolate. Other families came to the store to watch the movie. It was a social event for everyone who came. It was a time for the parents and older ones to talk about whatever parents talk about. We kids played before the movie started. I especially enjoyed being able to play games outside with the other kids. We also asked our parents if we could have candy before it began. I remember he sold candy for a quantity of eight pieces for one dollar. The choices were, as I remember:

- Snickers
- Zero
- Hershey
- 7-Up candy bar
- Almond Bar

Cyril used a reel-to-reel movie projector and showed the film on the wall of his store. The movies were almost always about Westerns. I can't remember seeing anything other than Western movies. It really did not matter what the movie was about. Just being able to go, be with friends, and watch a movie was just fine. It was these little things we did which I enjoyed so much when I was growing up. When I grew up, I never did go to a movie just to watch a Western.

I can't remember what the movie cost. If it had a price, I don't think it was very much. I think Cyril actually wanted us to come and spend money in his store buying snacks and whatever else we kids might try to talk out of our parents to buy for us. It was very kind of Mr. Okitkun to offer us the opportunity to watch the movies on his store wall.

We only went to the movies during the wintertime. There were some movies to watch during summer but we were too busy with the fish that we normally didn't go to the movies. Most of the time everybody was too busy fishing to have time to go to Kwiguk and watch movies. We would have had a problem with the long sunny days also. The windows would have to be covered to make it dark enough inside to watch them.

The Return Home

When the movie was finished we went to our sled and unhooked the sled from its anchor which kept the dogs and sled in place. The dogs which appeared to be too tired to even get out of their hollow in the snow would quickly come to life. The barking and jumping that preceded each sled journey started again. Pa checked each dog to make certain that each was securely fastened to the harness assembly and to the sled's tow rope. When he was assured that all was ready to go, then we set off on our journey back to Emmonak. Several family dog teams arranged themselves in a single file line as we followed the river back to the village.

It was colder and darker on the way back. The Northern Lights were sure to be out by then. We were all tired by the time the movie was over. It was usually a quiet trip back to the village. There is something very soothing about travel over the snow and ice on the river. The dogs found their pace and just pulled the sled. They were always quiet unless another team came too close. Pa would see to it that we kept our distance from other teams. The quiet sound of dog paws and sled runners on the Yukon snow always put me to sleep before we reached Emmonak. It was almost a magical experience to see the shadows of each dog team traveling across the Yukon River. If it was a full moon then the river was so bright as the moonlight reflected off the river ice and snow. The snow cover and clear air gave it an almost daylight effect while we traveled the river.

When we arrived at the cabin, Mom and Pa always had to carry one or more of us kids to the cabin because we were fast asleep. I was ready to go to sleep as soon as we were all arranged on our sleeping mattresses. There is something about the cold that makes a person very sleepy. Once my body got snuggled under the covers with a warm blanket over me, it was lights out and fast asleep. What a wonderful time that was growing up on the lower Yukon River with memories of the Kwiguk Movies.

———

It was only a matter of time before Cyril Okitkun had to move from Kwiguk to Emmonak. I can't remember if the store eroded into the river or if he had to close the store due to lack of business. By that time there were at least two stores that competed for his business not far away. The Bering Sea Fisheries was located along Lamont Slough just downriver from Kwiguk. There was a complete store located there that sold the same items that Okitkun's store sold. The Northern Commercial Company store located in Emmonak would have proven very difficult competition for his store as well. In either case the building that was his store no longer exists at the site we call Kwiguk. I am sure the riverbank erosion had a lot to do with the decision to close the store. The Yukon River always has the last word.

If the godly compromise with the wicked, it is like polluting a fountain or muddying a spring.
Proverbs 25:25

Potlatch

Curukaq: Villages feast together   *Potlatch was a very special event in my life. I really enjoyed seeing people from other villages that I would see only during potlatch. I especially liked watching the dancers and drummers that came to perform at each potlatch.*

One of the most important events in the lives of the lower Yukon River Yupik Eskimo was the potlatch. It was held once a year usually during the month of March. The event created much anticipation for the host village. The population of the village grew, as people from all around came to take part in the celebration. It was a winter event that took advantage of the ability to get around the delta, which was easier that time of year. It was also a slow month in the annual rhythm of the Yupik lifestyle. It was a time for the host village to show its pride in its Eskimo heritage to the villagers who came from afar.

The Event

The potlatch was held in the communal house during my grade school years. In my later years it was held in the community center. That was the logical place to host the large event. It was normally the largest building in the village. It was already the focal point of village activity. It was the usual meeting place for the villagers to gather. The communal house was designed with dancing as a part of its function and one of the primary reasons for hosting a potlatch was to observe the dancing by the host village residents and those visiting from other villages.

A potlatch was a weekend long event. Emmonak hosted one and it brought in lots of people. There were dog sled teams everywhere in the village. It was an exciting time to see so many people and dogs in the village. The visiting people were housed either by their relatives who lived in the village or by families who volunteered to open their cabin to those visiting. The potlatch was an event that was rotated between the three villages of Emmonak, Alakanuk and Kotlik.

Emmonak

This was my home village. It was located on the Kwiguk Pass of the Yukon River. In Yupik Eskimo it meant blackfish. My village was located between Alakanuk to the south and west while Kotlik was located to the north and east.

Alakanuk

A village located on the south mouth or Kwikluak Pass of the Yukon River. In Yupik Eskimo it meant mistake (the wrong turn). We had a couple of related families who lived in Alakanuk that would come to the Emmonak potlatch.

Kotlik

A village located on the north mouth or Apoon Pass of the Yukon River. In Yupik Eskimo it meant river, like a pair of pants. The potlatch was not held more than once a year nor in the same village more than one year in a row. It took so much in food resources to host one that the burden to host a potlatch was spread out between the villages and between the years. Food preparation for a potlatch was a large effort for the host village. Every effort was made during the summer and winter fishing to catch enough fish to feed all the people that came to the potlatch. The following foods made up the majority of the needs during a potlatch:

- Dried fish
- Fish strips
- Akutaq - as a dessert
- Seal oil for seasoning
- Tea and coffee

Pa did not go to the potlatches. He did not even go to the ones hosted by Emmonak. He told us that he had more important work to do than go to them. I really did not understand why he felt that way. I can only guess that he did not believe in the dancing performances and some of the other spiritual manifestations that were a part of the potlatch. He was not convinced that this was appropriate for an Eskimo. Mom would go to all of them all the time. She was very active in the potlatch activities. She was always ready to go to them. She liked them very much. It was a happy time for her as she attended them. She had a lot of fun being a part of the activities. Me and my brothers and sister would usually go. Pa would not prohibit us from going. He likely thought that we should judge for ourselves if we wanted to be involved in them or not. We were more curious than anything else to observe the festivities. We only went to the potlatches that were held in Emmonak. We did not travel to the ones in the other villages.

First Time Dancers

At each potlatch there were first time dancers ready to perform. This was a very special time for the individual that was going to dance for the first time at a potlatch. It was a turning point in the life of any Yupik Eskimo. It was a time of maturing as a young girl or boy. The individual practiced a long time and got very nervous as the day of the potlatch approached. The parents were equally nervous. The family of the first time dancer gave gifts to all the families attending the performance at the potlatch. The family spent all fall and winter preparing the gifts that were given during the potlatch. An example of some of the gifts given included:

- Gloves
- Hats
- Scarves
- Candy
- Pop
- Cigarettes
- Snuff

It was a time to be proud of the individual dancing for the first time and for the family. This was seen as a succession of a very important aspect of Eskimo life. It guaranteed the continuation of a very colorful and important legacy of the village life. For the first time dancer it was an important first step in becoming a recognized member of the village.

Coming Together

What I remember most about the potlatch was how it brought together not only the members of each individual village but the villages as well. It was a beautiful time to share each other's hospitality and of course the food that was shared. The potlatch brought together the entire lower Yukon River delta. I was able to catch up on friends that I rarely saw except during the Emmonak potlatch. We had so much fun playing together when they came. I especially enjoyed the dog teams that came to the village from outside Emmonak. There were lots of dog teams tied-up all around the communal house during the potlatch. It seemed the village had literally gone to the dogs.

Today the potlatch is held in the community center. It is very modern and designed just for the performances that are still an important part of the event. People do not come by dog team anymore. They come by snow machine or fly into the village. The warmth and hospitality is still as prevalent at a potlatch today as it was almost fifty years ago during my youth. That aspect of the event has not changed.

Dance Fans

Since my Pa never became involved in the potlatch dancing, he made me a pair of men's Eskimo dance fans. Every dancer had a pair of these. We did not dance so we never had a pair that we called our own. I think Pa felt sorry for us because we missed out on that in our life. So he made me a pair of men's dance fans. Mom provided me with a pair of women's dance fans that I could call my own. I treasure the ones they made for me very much. They are a constant reminder of my connection with Pa and Mom. The women's dance fans are made of wolf hair surrounding a grass woven mat. There is a finger hold at one end for holding onto it while a person dances with them. The men's dance fans are made of waterfowl feathers surrounding two circular willow branches. The point where you hold onto the dance fan is woven with grass to make handling them easier on the hands. The dance fans are used to act out the story being told by the dancers. They are a very important part of the dance routine.

The dance fans are what make the dances we perform very uniquely Yupik. In the home of every dancer you will find a pair or several pairs of dance fans hanging on the wall prominently displayed. Once you see them you know a dancer lives at that home.

Prohibition

There was a time in the past when the missionaries did not approve of the potlatch. They thought they were a worship of gods other than our god. In some villages they were not allowed. It had to do I think with the great disagreement between the missionaries and the shaman. It was not looked at in the light that the dancing during a potlatch was a Christian thing to do. Eventually the missionaries realized that they were in the wrong. The potlatches were providing a very positive attitude for the Eskimos. The fellowship, love and friendship that occurred during a potlatch was a very good thing. The missionaries admitted they should not have stopped the practice. After the change in heart occurred, the missionaries even supported potlatch events and even encouraged other missionaries to join in and participate. It actually was no more than a misunderstanding of the social function of the potlatch.

Dancing and Drumming

Potlatch was a time to demonstrate each village skills for drumming and dancing. The men played the drums while other men, women and children danced. The village became the potlatch. Good drummers and dancers translated into strong villages. It wasn't at a competitive level between villages. It was a time for sharing those skills between villages. It was an opportunity to recognize, emphasize and encourage villagers to drum and dance. The strength of a village was a testament to the talent demonstrated by its drummers and dancers.

Each dance told a story, either real or fictional. Sometimes it was of an actual event that happened long ago. This was one way of keeping our history alive. Other dances were fictional, merely to entertain everyone. The men used hand-held drums that they beat to the melody of the song they sang. The men and women dancers danced the story in front of the drummers facing the audience. The women dancers stood in the front row while the men dancers sat behind the women dancers while they performed. It was a time to remember the old as well as encourage the new. Since a potlatch was a time of sharing, it promoted a sense of togetherness. If people had differences, a potlatch brought them together.

Potlatch events are still a very thriving part of the village community life. It is still a time of sharing and fellowshipping between villages. The shamans no longer play a major role in the event. It is no longer a priority for teaching and listening by the young people as it used to be. Dancing is still the center of attention. It will always be the glue that holds the potlatch together. It is still the glue that holds the village together. A family that dances together is a stronger family unit. An individual that dances is a stronger Eskimo in the village community. Dancing is what makes us Yupik Eskimo. Dance: Is the essence of being Yupik. As long as there are dancers, there will be potlatch.

Fear of the LORD is the beginning of wisdom.
Proverbs 9:10

Miscellaneous

Introduction

Some of the stories that I wanted to share did not lend themselves to be associated with a particular season. I placed these stories in the Miscellaneous section of my book.

I felt that some of the stories of my youth I wanted to share were not applicable to any particular season yet were important to the culture of the Lower Yukon Delta. Each story represents one aspect of my life as I grew up as a little girl along the lower Yukon River.

I wanted to include my home and the life my family and I lived within our modest means. The size and simple layout of our first cabin made for a close and loving home.

Although I don't remember the arrival of the first missionaries, their efforts had profound influences on the lives of my generation and me. The native culture certainly was affected by their presence.

I mention the communal house because it was the center of activity for every villager of Emmonak. The fact that it no longer exists today is testament to a changing and evolving native culture. The lives of the lower Yukon River Eskimo is not the same today because of its absence.

I saw and experienced my share of firsts while growing up in Emmonak. These are the stories that represent the significant advances that took place during my lifetime. These firsts would have a major impact on the lives of everyone in the village.

The last subject involves the games we played. We played for the fun of the games involved. We did not realize it at the time but the games we played also helped in the development of our bodies physically, our minds mentally and for our culture's legacy.

Home

I have been blessed to have grown up during a time when we had so little yet we were rich beyond our dreams. The home is where love begins for the family.

The first home that I remember was a two-room log cabin. I think Pa built it before I was born. I do not remember seeing it built while I was a young girl. I know it was a big cabin when I was little. As I grew older it started to feel smaller. It was a very modest cabin even by Emmonak standards back in the 1950s and 60s. One thing for sure, it was my *home* and I loved growing up in it with my parents and siblings.

I was born in the cabin on July 12, 1956. I was named after Molly Alstrom. It was a tradition to name a newborn after someone who had recently passed away. That way the memory of the deceased person was kept alive. My middle name of Agnes was given to me, as it was my Grandma's first name. It was during fishing season when I was born. I think everyone in the family except for Mom had gone to fish camp for the summer. Since she was pregnant with me she was left behind at the cabin in Emmonak. She told me that when she was ready to give birth to me she asked for Pearlie Johnson, the postmaster in the village, to come and assist with the delivery. She acted as a midwife for my Mom. I am told that Pearlie was cutting fish at her home when she was summoned to help Mom give birth to me. The cabin had a very special attachment for me. It truly was my home from birth.

The First Cabin
Pa built the cabin from driftwood that he had gathered from the

river. It consisted of logs on the outside and inside. He built the cabin close to the river. The cabins were built in parallel rows. Our cabin was in the row closest to the river. Grandpa's cabin was located in the second row but close to us. The cabins were built in locations with no particular organization as to family or property ownership. No one *owned* the land where his or her cabin was built back in the time of my youth. That all changed with the introduction of the Alaska Native Claims Settlement Act in the mid 1970s. That act gave all Eskimos a piece of property on which they could call their own. During my grade school days a cabin was built wherever the person or family thought was a good location.

Cabin layout

There was no finished interior wall in the cabin. The roof was built of logs. It had three windows. There was one on each side and one on the backside of the cabin. There was a front door on one end that opened into the cooking/living area. The door was made of plywood with a typical lockset as a doorknob. I don't remember what was used to caulk the gaps in the logs to keep the wind, cold and bugs out.

On the inside was a partition wall that divided the cabin into two rooms. The cooking/living area was the larger of the two rooms. The other room was for sleeping where the beds were located. The opening between the two rooms was covered with a curtain.

The cooking/living area had a wood cook stove situated in one corner of the room. Wood was piled next to it to keep it dry and easily accessible. We tried to keep a large supply of wood inside so that it was always dry for burning and so that we did not run out at an inopportune time. The stove was used for both heat and cooking. The stove had numerous purposes besides serving as a heat source. We always kept a kettle full of water on it to make coffee or tea whenever we desired or when people stopped by and visited. The stove also provided the heat for Pa when he worked with wood bending. The stove was made out of cast iron so it was very heavy. During the flood it was left in the cabin. It was just too heavy to carry out. Even if we did carry it out of the cabin there was no place to store it away from the flood. After the floodwaters had gone down we cleaned it out for use again. It had a front door for loading the wood into it from the front or you could pull out the heat plates in the top of the stove and put wood in from the top. We used a stick as a poker to arrange the burning wood and ashes on the inside of the stove. The ashes were removed periodically when they filled up the inside of the stove to the point that we could not load enough wood inside it. The ashes were then carried to the river, since it was close, and deposited there. The stove was the center of attention at the cabin. It was used for baking bread as well as for cooking meals. A lot of family time was spent around the stove. During the winter we let the fire go out in the stove. It used too much wood to keep it going all night long. As the fire died down and eventually went out I had to put more blankets on me to keep warm until Pa restarted the fire in the morning. Pa usually started the fire in the morning. It was all of our responsibility to see that it kept going throughout the day. When it got really cold during the winter the heat from the cook stove was very important to us. We made certain that it received everyone's attention.

The rest of the living/cooking area had a table with chairs for each of us. We stored most of our things in cardboard boxes. I remember we hung the pots and pans from nails on the log walls. We tried to keep this area clear as Pa was always working on something and needed plenty of open space. He built and repaired sleds, traps, frames and all types of other items in this area of the cabin. In the winter it was his indoor workshop. We did not have another outdoor building that he could use for this work. Whatever he brought inside the cabin became a new toy for us to play on. We were always told to be careful around his work items. I especially enjoyed playing on the sleds he brought inside to work on. He was always busy working on something inside the cabin during the winter.

We did not use the cabin during the summer as we lived at fish camp instead. The cabin was primarily used only for three seasons of the year. Since we lived in it only during the spring, fall and winter months we really did not have to deal with the bugs getting into the cabin. Any open spaces in the door, windows or between the logs really did not bother us much. Obviously the cold winter winds could bring a lot of discomfort due to any holes in the cabin. An effort was made to caulk the gaps with whatever material we could find.

It wasn't until late summer or early fall that it became completely dark in the cabin during the nighttime. For a light source we used a gas lantern. It was Pa's responsibility he took upon himself to start and extinguish the lantern light. The white gasoline that it used was expensive. We purchased it in five-gallon cans from the Northern Commercial Company store. This limited how long it was lit during the night. It was our only light source, as we did not have electricity to the cabin. It was noisy as it made that hissing sound while it was lit. It also made the cabin smell like white gas smoke while it was running. We just put up with it. We had no choice. It was much better than the alternative of just sitting in the dark until bedtime came. I found my favorite corner of the bed and read with a flashlight. I can't remember if the batteries for the flashlight were supposed to be used by me or not. I used them for reading anyway. I do remember I was told to turn off the flashlight sometimes by Pa.

Flower Picking

During the fall-time I went flower picking around the immediate Emmonak area. There were many varieties of flowers that grew within a short walking distance from our cabin. The mixture of wild flowers that grew on the soil next to Kwiguk Pass was much more diverse than on the tundra. The flowers I remember picking near the cabin were:

- Bluebells
- Monkshood
- Common Hairbell
- Arctic Lupine
- Alaska Poppy
- Sitka Burnet
- Arctic Daisy
- Horsetail
- Wild Iris
- Siberian Aster
- Forget-me-not
- Fireweed
- Western Buttercup
- Alaska Cotton
- Coltsfoot

Not all flowers I picked were just for showing off their beauty.

Some of the wild flowers I picked had other uses. Among the other wild flowers was wild celery we cut up and then ate with salt and seal oil. Labrador tea leaves were boiled into a tea as a drink. Arctic dock was eaten for their leaves, but they had a sour taste.

Family Time

Wintertime was very long in Emmonak. The dark nights also lasted a long time. I sometimes forget what all eight of us did on those long, cold nights. We each had our own little space in the cabin that we used as we desired. We had no television at that time in my life. No video games to play. We listened to our battery-powered radio. Our favorite radio station was KNOM radio from Nome, Alaska. It played songs and was a link to many of the villages in the lower Yukon area. It was our only source for news events. It was a means of communicating with other people from the surrounding villages. It was our primary source of village news. People left messages to each other by way of the radio. We always listened to the village chatter program to find out what was going on with others around us.

The language we spoke as a family was determined by who was speaking and to who was the center of the conversation. If we were speaking to Pa or required Pa to be involved in the conversation then we all spoke Eskimo exclusively. This was because Pa could only speak and understand Eskimo. If the conversation included just Mom or was directed to Mom then we spoke mostly English with some Eskimo whenever we felt like doing so. If the conversation included everyone in the family, but Pa wasn't really involved then we spoke about half and half. When I was speaking to my siblings then it was mostly English unless we felt the need to speak occasional Eskimo. Generally speaking I would say that I spoke mostly Eskimo when I was young, but began to speak more English and less Eskimo as I grew older. When I was around Pa I would speak only Eskimo. I really don't know if it was an actual Eskimo dialogue we spoke to each other, but we understood what we were trying to say.

We played outside as much as we could. Usually we went out before suppertime. It could get very cold outside but we kids got tired of being cooped-up in the cabin for very long. Going outside to play with our friends was worth any discomfort we might have to experience. Our cousins who lived nearby came over and we had a lot of fun playing together. I especially liked to play with Linda, Gail, Wilbur, Herman, Irene and Rudy Hootch when they visited our cabin. My favorite play was making snow forts in the winter. Our parents would call us for supper and that ended our outdoor play.

When supper was over and the dishes were cleaned and put away, it was our individual time to do what we wanted.

Me

I read books from the grade school library. I found my own personal space in the corner of the bedroom where I did my reading. I really enjoyed reading. I think I would have been very bored if it wasn't for the opportunity to read the books from the school library.

Joanne

She usually was playing with her dolls. We were not able to buy real toy dolls so we cut them out of the catalogs. We found a Sears or JC Penny catalog and cut the model pictures out of the pages. This gave my sister and I an almost unlimited supply of doll material. Together we played with our cutout dolls. Time sure went fast when I played dolls with my sister.

Michael

He usually drew in his spare time. He was sure a good artist. He could draw some very nice pictures. He eventually used his talent and created a set of characters he called little Hootch and friends.

George, Teddy and Fred

I can't remember what they did in their spare time in the cabin. I think they would rather be outside. There was always the radio to listen to when there was nothing else to do.

Mom

She was busy sewing and mending clothes. She liked to knit mittens and hats from yarn she bought from the Northern Commercial store. In the winter there was the constant need to mend our parkas and boots. She did all the cooking. Joanne and I watched and tried to help if we could. It was my job, as the oldest daughter, to wash and clean the dishes after supper.

Pa

He used the cabin to build and repair sleds. He made wooden and metal fish traps. They required constant maintenance. He used the cabin to tan the hides and furs. He also made dog booties and harnesses. The living/cooking area of the cabin was kept empty for him to work in. He always had some building or repair project that required the cabin space.

Soon after our individual free time was over it was time to go to bed. It always came too soon for me. I tried to use my flashlight and keep reading under the bed sheets while everyone else went to sleep. Eventually Mom or Pa caught me reading and made me turn the flashlight off and go to sleep. Bedtime was nine PM for us kids during the school year.

Bedtime

The kids (six of us) slept on one or two beds. Since we were all small we could fit ourselves on one or two beds. We must have been seen like sleeping sardines in such a small space. It was just a fact of life. We did not need our own individual sleeping space. We were so happy to be able to share the bed with each other.

Mom and Pa slept in their own bed separate from us. We all slept in the same room. We kept the sleeping room separate from the living/cooking room with a curtain over the doorway. This allowed the heat from the stove to warm the sleeping space during the winter night.

We each had our own cardboard box for storing our clothes. It was nice to have a place to put our own things to keep them separate from the rest of the family belongings. After a while though all the clothes found a way to form one large pile that eventually had to be sorted and washed. Using a washboard in a tub of water we washed our clothes. Washing was done by Mom with me helping as I could. We hung the clothes inside the cabin if there were not very many of them. If we were washing a lot of clothes then we hung them outside. We hung the clothes outside even in the winter. The cold froze them solid. You could actually stand them up in the snow. They would freeze dry in the sun eventually and then be transferred to the cabin to be folded and put in their respective cardboard box.

No Running Water

We got our water from the river. During winter we had to dig a hole in the ice first. That was always a hard job. It seemed we were always cutting holes in the ice for one reason or another. It is hard to imagine how much work went into just getting water to drink and use during the winter. We filled as many buckets as we could carry. The water buckets were stored inside the cabin near the cook stove. If we left them outside in the winter they were frozen solid before we had a chance to use it. The quality of the water was much better in the winter under the ice than during the summer. We still boiled it before we used it for cooking and drinking purposes.

The cabin did not provide for any means of bathing ourselves. It did not have a shower or bathtub. Since we did not have any running water it was our responsibility to perform that task however we could. Actually, bathing ourselves was not an important issue. We bathed only when we felt a strong urge to do so. It was not a priority in our life. No one cared, nor was it ever an issue in our subsistence existence. Pa went to the community sauna along with the other men and boys of the village. There was a time for the males to go to sauna and a separate time for the females. I was never allowed to go to sauna with Pa or any of my brothers. It was segregated between males and females. Going to sauna was a very special occasion. It was a time for the elders to teach the young men the Eskimo ways and culture. After the men were finished, it was the women's opportunity to go. I went with Mom and my sister Joanne. It could get really hot inside. That was the whole purpose of going to sauna, to get hot and sweaty and then wash up. We did not have the luxury of indoor plumbing. We did not have a flush toilet available in the cabin. We used, what is called a honey bucket as our toilet. It was located in one corner of the cabin. There was a curtain that provided the user some privacy. It was not always emptied after every use so we used Pine Sol to help keep the smell to a minimum. It was another fact of life that we just tolerated the smell.

Nostalgia

The cabin where I grew up as a little girl with my family was another of many wonderful memories I have. I was certainly blessed to have such a loving family to grow up in. I think back to the days in the cabin and wonder how we all lived in such a tiny space. How did we all get along during those long winter nights? It was a cozy existence inside the cabin. We just knew no different. That was the way it was living in the village. The simplicity had its good side. No utility bills to pay. It just took a lot more hard work to keep life comfortable for all of us. I am so happy I had the opportunity to grow up in such a simple environment. I appreciate the modern conveniences we have today while I look back on what we did not have during my youth. The first cabin where I was born and grew up no longer exists today. Only the memories I have of growing up there remain. Over time the river started to erode the north bank of Kwiguk Pass. The river encroached on our cabin with every succeeding flood and seasonal storm that occurred. For this reason Pa had to build another cabin. Eventually the first cabin was washed into the river. Kwiguk Pass had claimed the home of my birth.

The Second Cabin

It was during my high school years that Pa built the next log cabin. I called this the second cabin. This one was built further west and away from the river in the village. It still had only two rooms, but had a loft, which gave us a lot more space. It was a big cabin compared to the first one. It is located on the same property where my brother George built a modern home. The second cabin is still standing today, but is quite run-down since it is no longer used and maintained.

The Modern Home

Eventually, Pa built a modern home and we moved into it during the middle 1970s. It was much larger than even the second cabin. It had more rooms. It is located on the extreme west side of Emmonak.

My brother Fred and his wife, Gertie, and their kids live in it today. I call it a modern home as it had electricity run to it. That was a huge advancement for my family. Electricity allowed us to have access to modern appliances such as a stove, not run on wood, and a refrigerator. We did not have to rely on the permafrost storage site as our only way to keep food items refrigerated. The modern home was built of plywood siding rather than driftwood logs. The homes were elevated on pylons driven deep into the permafrost. This allowed them to no longer be overcome by the spring floodwaters. That was a real advancement in how we prepared for the flood season. Electricity brought so many changes to our lives. It allowed us to have a television and eventually telephone service when it finally came to the village. Eventually a sewage system was introduced to the village and our home was hooked up to it after I left in 1978. The days of the honey bucket came to an end.

The modern home changed every aspect of our lives. By that time we were more financially on our own. We were able to afford the things we wanted to buy. The modern conveniences were slowly changing our lives from completely subsistence to more commercial activities. The money we were making, simply made the subsistence needs of our life less important as time went on. If we needed food, we were more apt to go to the store and buy it rather than rely on the river or the land to provide for us. This effected Pa's subsistence lifestyle. Because I was working and earning money, he was not required to go out and fish, hunt and trap as often. Our family's changing economy influenced Pa's attitude toward subsistence. His importance as the food gatherer became less important over time.

At the site of the modern home Pa built a sauna. He also built a shop where he could work on his projects rather than use the house for that purpose. I think he was very pleased to finally have a building he could use exclusively for his work. He could keep all his tools and construction materials in it rather than having to depend on the house for storage.

Certainly the modern home was no comparison to the first log cabin where I grew up. The modern home represented many changes that had occurred in all of our lives. Mom was no longer a part of the family as she had left for Anchorage. Michael had also left Emmonak for his venture into the life he had chosen. It was just not the same living in the modern home as it had been when I was little. Our family was no longer a complete unit. Time had caused changes and it was never the same as when I was younger. I would undergo changes in my life also. I left the village and pursued the life God had sent me. Although I am far removed from the home in Emmonak, I still have vivid memories of my young life at home.

*It is better to be poor and godly
than rich and dishonest.*
Proverbs 16:8

Missionaries

Ayagcetaaq: Missionary   *I had mixed feelings about the missionary effort while growing up a little girl. It was a time of struggle between the existence of an Eskimo deity and God. It is obvious that God won the struggle of wills.*

I do not remember the coming of the missionaries. They arrived in the Lower Yukon area long before I was born. I remember some of the stories about their arrival, as told to me by my Pa and Grandpa. They certainly changed the character of the people and their lifestyles with their conversion of the Eskimos to Christianity. The Eskimos were willing to adopt the religion of the missionaries, as their subsistence lives were a testament to a very strong belief system endeared them by their parents and grandparents. The Eskimos had always believed in a higher power that controlled the world around them. They knew that someone or something controlled the environment and the animals that affected their lives so intimately. They had a God. He just wasn't worshipped in the same way as the missionaries' Christian God.

The missionaries would have easily converted Pa. He already believed there was a higher being that was responsible for creation and all the things he experienced around him. He knew there was an intelligent designer capable of creation. When the missionaries brought their Christianity to the Yupik people he would have accepted it readily. Since the early missionaries were Catholic that was the religion to which he became associated. Thus Pa became a Catholic and remained true to that faith his entire life. I would not be so readily inclined to adopt it as a lifelong religion. I wanted to check out the other faiths to which I was introduced before I chose it as my life's religion. I think in Pa's heart he accepted that fact for me and let me choose for myself which faith I would eventually follow. The village of Emmonak was certainly affected by the arrival of the missionaries. They had built a base of believing Eskimos within the village. Eventually that led to the introduction of at least two churches within the village during the time of my youth. Each had their very own independent religious denominations and congregational following.

Sacred Heart Catholic Church

This was the first church in Emmonak. It came into existence before I was born. It was located near the old grade school. When I was a little girl I remember going there every Sunday for Mass. We went as an entire family. We had no choice but to go since our parents went. It was all right with me. I remember that the men and boys all sat on the right side of the church, while the women and girls sat on the left side. I really did not question the reason behind that. It was just the way it was.

We sang from song books written in English. The Mass was spoken in English. The priests were white people from the outside. I am certain they did not know any of the Yupik language. We sang and followed the Mass in books that were written for Catholic churches. They were not written any differently just for us that spoke Eskimo. I am really not sure what Pa got out of it as he could not speak or understand English. He could only speak and understand the Yupik Eskimo language. I am not certain whether it was Pa or Mom that was the guiding force behind the church attendance. My mom was able to speak and understand English. Since we kids were taught it during school, it was easy for us to follow along during Mass.

We did miss Sunday Mass while at fish camp. We could not afford to come to the village just for the purpose of attending Mass. Sunday was just another day at fish camp. It was really no different than any other day. It was too important to catch fish during the summer. We could not take time out of our lives to drive the boat back to Emmonak for Mass.

As a result, I grew up a Catholic kid when I was young. I, like all my other friends that attended the Catholic Church, went through the catechism program classes during my grade school years. It was a matter of learning a lot about the church and related important information. Graduating from catechism was a big event. We dressed up in our finest dresses for the occasion. Taking our first communion was a giant step in our young lives. All the family members attended the service to witness the event. My grandpa and grandma and many relatives came as well.

I remember that eventually a new Catholic Church building was built. It was located nearer to the Northern Commercial Company store. It was much larger compared to the small one room building that was used while I was very little. The old church building was eventually converted to our first one room high school. I attended my eleventh grade of high school in that building. It was different going there again as a high school student and not as a church member.

Baptist Church

The Baptist church came later in time. I do not remember exactly when it was established. It had a much smaller congregation than the Catholic Church. I remember that it was the newer of the two when I was young.

The Baptist church was located very close to our cabin. I went there and checked it out during the Sunday evening services and during the Friday evening activities they hosted. I especially enjoyed the Friday evening youth activities they held. They had games and movies for us to attend. I brought my sister and brothers with me when they agreed to come. It was a fun experience whenever I went. I have a lot of fond memories going to their evening activities.

The pastor was an Inupiat Eskimo. His name was Willie Johnson. I liked him very much. He made the evening activities a lot of fun. The fact that he was an Eskimo like us made a lot of difference to me. He could relate to us very well.

It was not the accepted thing to attend the Baptist Church services. Since we were regular attendees of the Catholic Church, it was frowned upon to go there. Some of my friends told me I should not go to the Baptist Church activities or bad things would happen to me. I did not believe them, so I continued to go whenever I found the opportunity. My parents never went there. It was all right for us to go since my grandpa agreed. He said that we would be good kids even if we went. I knew that grandpa knew what he was talking about. I thought it was a lot more fun to go there since they had activities for us kids. It was a very short walk to the building. It was much closer to our cabin than the Catholic Church. That was another reason I wanted to go.

I will admit that attending the Baptist Church had an effect on my life. I really did not follow the Catholic Church doctrine very much. I preferred the Baptist Church teaching. As a result I was not really interested in becoming a life long member of the Catholic Church, as I am sure my parents desired. It opened my mind to the fact that there are other religions. Not just the one that I was born into.

As I became a woman and more independent I was willing to follow my heart where ever it took me within the religious realm. Once I left the village and became engaged to my fiancé I adopted his religion and was baptized into the Christian Church. I know that I have found what my heart has always longed for in my relationship with my husband, my children and God. I am very thankful that I had parents who were faithful to God and taught me the value of having Christ's influence in my life. Without the influence of the churches in Emmonak that might not have been possible. I am thankful to them for their caring for us in the village. It was a hardship for them to come and shepherd us so far from their home. I am encouraged through their sacrifice of being separated from their loved ones that good things were allowed to happen to us in Emmonak.

Akulurak

I am told that one of the earliest settlements that were started by the missionaries was at Kanelik. It was located off the south mouth of the Yukon River. It was set up on the tundra along what is known as Kanelik Pass. The missionaries soon learned that Kanelik was a poor site because of its lowlands and relocated further south on higher ground. The new location was called Akulurak as it was situated on the waterway known as Akulurak Pass. A school and orphanage was established at Akulurak in the very late 1890s. I had some aunts and uncles who attended the school there. It had to be moved from its location along Akulurak Pass around the early 1950s. The school and orphanage was relocated at St. Mary's, which was upriver on the Andreafsky River, a tributary of the Yukon River.

As the Yukon River changed its course and caused the water level to drop along the tundra sloughs to the south, barge traffic came to a stop. The larger boats and supply barges could no longer navigate the lowering water levels. I am certain that life on the tundra in that area was very difficult. The permafrost could not support the large, heated buildings that were required for the school and adjacent buildings. Eventually the tundra reclaims what man tries to build.

Neither my grandpa nor Pa has any recollections of spending time at the school there. They did talk about their experiences of reindeer herding with the missionaries. I know stories of diseases breaking out because of the missionaries' presence caused the local Eskimos not to associate with them. There were many Eskimo people and families who were lost to disease outbreak. As a result the orphanage became home to many homeless Eskimo children who lost their parents to disease.

When the school and orphanage was moved to St. Mary's, all that remained were pieces of wood and the graveyard. When we went berry picking onto the southern tundra we stopped at the site and visited the graveyard. Grandma Agnes had relatives buried there. The crosses are slowly sinking into the permafrost. I remember one trip to the site in the mid to late 1970s and the only remnant of the settlement were a few crosses. It is hard to believe that once it was a thriving and bustling missionary settlement. A person could stand on the tundra from there and see Mt. Akulurak to the south. It was not a very tall hill, but it was a most unique landmark that rose out of the flat and barren tundra to the south.

Shamans

It cannot be disputed that one of the most noticeable influences of the missionary effort was its effect on the shamans. These were the medicine men of the lower Yukon River Eskimos. They were also the elders of the village and as such were given much respect. Before the missionaries came, they were the most influential men in the village. They had powers and capabilities that ordinary individuals did not possess. They received their power from sources that were not available to regular people. According to the shaman, they could fly like birds and swim like fish. There are stories told about the shamans during the older days whereby their bodies became possessed by supernatural powers that gave them strength to do what ordinary men could not do.

This was in direct conflict with the religion the missionaries wanted to evangelize. The missionaries attempted to minimize their influence and convert the shamans to Christianity. This caused serious arguments between the shaman and the missionary. A real power struggle erupted between the two. The shamans were not giving God the credit for their power and this did not sit well with the missionary's Christian belief. The shamans were convinced that their power came from within the earth and the sky that gave them the existence they enjoyed. The missionaries won the battle of the power struggle. We knew there was a higher power, we just didn't have a name for it. It was the missionaries who gave us a name for this higher power. They told us about God and where he came from and resided. Over time they were successful in converting them to Christianity and by the time I was a little girl there were no shamans left in the village. There may have been one left. I think he was just old and senile which made him different from other men.

Pa did not pay much attention to the shamans. He did not believe that they were really possessed by supernatural powers. He did not seek them out for their advice. Their basic belief system did not make sense to Pa. Eventually the shamans died. They were not replaced as the missionaries made certain that their beliefs would not continue. Only the stories remain of what the shaman did during their lifetime. Their stories continue in the Eskimo dances that are still performed by the villagers of Emmonak. The shamans played an important role during sauna and potlatch by teaching the young people the importance of living their life right and listening to the elders when they spoke.

Naming the Eskimos
Pa talked about how the missionaries gave everyone a last name.

This occurred during my grandfather's lifetime. Prior to the missionary names, my father was known as James, son of Charlie. When we were given the last name of Hootch, my grandfather became known as Charlie Hootch. I am not sure if the missionaries gave us our first names at that time or not. I don't know if we had the option to choose our first name in the beginning of the naming process by the missionaries.

The missionaries obviously were trying to simplify for themselves what appeared to be a very disorganized naming system among the Eskimos. What they thought was simplifying for their purpose was very damaging to the people of the lower Yukon River area. Because last names were from that point forward used for family genealogy, it caused serious relationship problems for the Eskimo people. I was not able to trace our family tree to anyone beyond my great-grandparents time. This created a situation that caused families, which had a relationship in the past to become broken and unrecognizable in that relationship. We no longer knew who our ancestors were. Some families who were related suddenly became unrelated because their last name was not the same.

It is hard to understand in our modern day how this could have happened to us. Eskimos are a very trusting people and were not going to question the wisdom of the missionaries. The Eskimos were not going to be seen as a belligerent people, thus they simply went along with the naming of our people. Since we were seen, as a passive and loving people the missionaries were able to exert their power over us on this issue.

Some of the Emmonak Eskimo families had recent Russian origins and already had last names. The missionaries did not change those last names since they already existed and were in common usage.

Potlatches

In certain villages of the lower Yukon the missionaries tried to interfere with the potlatch celebrations. The missionaries even caused the potlatches to be stopped in some villages. The missionaries thought the potlatch was a pagan celebration because of the dancing that was performed. They thought the dancing was a worship to other gods. Over time the missionaries learned that the real purpose of the dancing was to perform and tell Eskimo stories. The potlatch was allowed to continue once the missionaries realized the great value they held toward the Yupik Eskimo society and their legacy.

Funeral Ceremony

Obviously death is a way of life. Someone told me that the hardest part of living is the dying of our loved ones. I never gave funerals a second thought until I witnessed how non-natives perform funerals. While I grew up along the lower Yukon delta there was just our way of funerals. I didn't know of any other way of conducting the funeral service.

When someone died in the village we tried to bury the body as soon as possible. This was especially true during the summer months. We did not embalm the body as they do in the large cities. There was no one that knew how to prepare the body through the process of embalming. It was not important to us that the body had to be prepared for burial. The elders of the church or the village would oversee the entire process of making certain that the Eskimo traditions were followed. There were certain traditions that were to be followed in order for the deceased to be properly cared for before burial.

If someone died outside the village, tradition dictated that the coffin and cross could not be made until the body was brought to the village and was allowed to rest in the village. Usually there was a person who did most of the casket making. The same person typically made the caskets for all the village families. That person bought treated plywood to make the sides, top and bottom of the casket. They lined the inside of the casket with very nice cloth suitable for the family. The pieces of plywood were screwed together to form a very strong box. Great care was taken to make certain that all the pieces fit together as tight as possible. The top of the casket was screwed down after the funeral service was complete. The final detail of the funeral ceremony was to have each male relative of the deceased take turns fastening a screw in the top of the casket lid to seal it. The village or church elders supervised every step of the construction of the casket. This made certain that the Eskimo traditions were followed exactly. The person who built the casket was usually the one to make the cross that was placed in the cemetery.

The Emmonak area is permafrost. The cemetery at Emmonak is located in an area of treeless tundra away from the river. Digging a grave in the tundra permafrost is very difficult work and requires a great deal of physical effort. At first the grave can be dug only about a foot deep. At that depth you hit permafrost and the digging stops. The casket was placed in the rectangular dug out area during the burial ceremony leaving most of it exposed above ground. At a period of time after the funeral a family member returned to the graveyard and dug the grave a little deeper after the permafrost had a chance to thaw. This process was repeated several times until the casket was completely buried under the ground. At any one time you found caskets of various stages of burial in the cemetery.

Missionaries not only changed the faith of the Eskimos but also their traditions. It was inevitable that missionaries would come to the lower Yukon River delta. Their influence in the region created conflict between their religion and the shamans. The power of influence shifted from the shamans to the missionaries. Long held Eskimo traditions promoted by the shamans came to an end. The missionaries challenged ancestral beliefs that formed the very essence of what made us Eskimo. I will not be the judge whether that was right or wrong as my own life is an example of the conversion of our people. Through the missionaries' efforts I have found my faith in God and live a very full and contented life because of their efforts.

Wise people think before they act;
fools don't and even brag about it!
Proverbs 13:16

Communal House

Qasgiq: Communal house

As a little girl the communal house was the center of the universe in our village. It was the gathering place for sauna, teaching, meeting and dancing for the entire community.

In Yupik Eskimo language this round, mud covered building was called the qasgiq. It was a gathering place for the village residents back when I was a little girl in Emmonak. It was one of the largest and most prominent structures in the village. People gathered there to take sauna, teach, meet and dance. It was a place that was filled with mystery to a young girl who did not quite understand these aspects of the Eskimo ways. There were a lot of memories that still remain regarding the communal house.

The communal house was built so that it had a round shape on the outside walls. It is shaped like the geodesic domes of today. This way there were no corners on the inside of the structure. It was built like an ordinary log house except that it did not have the four corners. The outside was covered with mud from the base where it meets the ground to the roof. The roof was also covered in mud. There was a hole in the top of the roof to let the smoke escape while being used as a sauna or fire house. There was also one main entrance to the building. The communal house in Emmonak had roofing tin or plywood placed around the sides of the building to contain the mud. Large poles were positioned around the building to keep the tin or plywood in place. The tin and plywood was a more recent addition to the building. I think by the middle 1970s electrical power was run to it. That was a huge advancement in allowing it to be used in many other ways. In Pa's day they had to maintain the mud on the side-

181

walls, as it naturally wanted to fall off with age. It was in continual repair and maintenance to keep it in good condition. It was the pride of the village. It was used often for many purposes. Everyone in the village, regardless of age, experienced the communal house.

Sauna

I remember one of the primary uses of the communal house was as a sauna. I think someone used it almost every night for that purpose. The men and boys were the first to use it. It was very segregated that way. Women and girls were not allowed to enter while the men and boys were using it. The elders of the village strictly enforced that rule. Actually, there was no question about this aspect of the communal house. You knew the rule and you followed it without question.

It was the primary, and for most villagers, only place, for bathing. Very few families had their own sauna. We did not have our own sauna while I was little. Pa did not have a personal one until the modern house was built. In order for us to bathe ourselves we went to the communal house. It was a competitive atmosphere at times I was told to see who could stand the heat the longest. The purpose of the sauna was to heat water placed in pans on the top of the fire. The boiling water raised the humidity in the communal house and made a person sweat. The hotter the fire and the more water that was boiling, the more a person would sweat. That was the cleansing effect of the sauna. It also made me very tired at the end of the session. All that sweating and heat really tired a person. I was so tired at the end that I wanted mom to carry me back to the cabin. The people said that the intense sweating was good for the body and spirit. It made the body release all the bad things that got trapped inside our bodies. I just remember that it could get so hot inside that I spent most of my time near the far edges of the building. If you really wanted to get a good sweat going then you sat closest to the fire and water. You were actually able to regulate your sweat by where and how far away you sat from the fire. If a person wanted to really get a hot sweat going then they brought in extra water and threw or poured it on the stove. The water instantly evaporated and raised the humidity almost immediately and lasted for a long time.

That is when the sauna really got you to sweating a lot and your body temperature rose dramatically.

When most of the people inside had had enough of the sweating, then we let the fire go down and removed the water from the fire. The sweat began to decrease and eventually stopped as the temperature inside the qasgiq dropped. We dried ourselves and put our clothes on and we were ready to leave and return to our cabin. The qasgiq was vacated for the evening.

Words of Wisdom

Sometimes the communal house was used for teaching or speaking words of wisdom which we called qanruyutet in the Yupik Eskimo language. They were planned whenever the elders thought one was needed. The elders or selected shaman used the opportunity to teach the young people. They explained to us the right and wrong way to live. It was a very good way to pass along to the young people the right principles for living. The boys received the most teaching while they were together with the other men of the village at sauna time. The elders were always using sauna as an opportunity to teach the young boys. It is too bad that that does not happen today with more regularity. I think every society would be much better off if that was more practiced. Qanruyutet was extremely important to the Eskimo people. It was a way of giving back the wisdom of the older people to the younger boys and girls. I am certain this is what made the Eskimo people the wonderful individuals we were. We had great respect for our elders and we listened to their every word. They knew from their own experiences as a young person what can go wrong if not taught the right way to live. Listening was important to the young person. Listening to our elders in the village taught us so much.

Shaman, or medicine men, used the communal house to demonstrate their supernatural abilities. They did their work during sessions held in the communal house. There were stories of the supernatural talents they possessed such as going to the moon and back. They could fly like a bird and see the earth from the air. They returned to the communal house and reported to the people about what they saw from above. After the missionaries were successful in stopping the powers of the shaman, the qasgiq was no longer the place of their supernatural work. My Pa did not believe in the supernatural powers of the shaman. It did not seem right that they could do the things they reported to be able to perform. That was one reason why he did not attend the sauna and teaching sessions when led by the shaman. He questioned their motives and ability to do what they reported to have been able to do.

Dancing

The communal house was also used for Eskimo dancing. Sometimes dancing was done after everyone had an opportunity to take a sauna. That was an important aspect of life. Eskimo dancing was our way of story telling. The movement of the dancers acted out a story of some aspect of Yupik life. The drummers, always men, started the dance with a drumbeat. The drummers told the story through their singing using the beat of the drum. The drum was made out of sealskin stretched around a wooden frame. A drumstick made of a piece of willow stick was used to beat the sealskin and a very unique sound filled the whole area. It was fun to watch the people dance to the drumbeat and listen to the drums. When the drummers and the dancers were in perfect synchrony it was a very heart-warming event to behold. The talented ones were very experienced. They have spent many years studying the movements and the drumbeat that were choreographed to tell the stories so important to Yupik Eskimo life on the lower Yukon River. As the dances continued into the night, the guests were invited to dance. As more and more people began dancing it seemed that something magical began to take over the atmosphere of the communal house. It was hard to explain the feeling that one felt. It made you feel very peaceful and content. Toward the end of the evening even the kids joined in on the dancing. This was encouraged because it was one way of teaching the young people the art and science of Eskimo dancing. One day the young people would take over the dancing and drumming.

Potlatch

Potlatches that Emmonak held with other villages were held in the communal house during my younger years. Those were important meetings between the villages. We shared each other's hospitality, stories, hunting and fishing exploits and family news during the potlatch. Food was shared between the invited villages. Dancing would follow the meeting. Each village brought their drummers and dancers and performed for the home village. The home village also demonstrated their expertise in drumming and dancing. Potlatch was a wonderful time of sharing between each other and between the villages. It was one of the primary methods used to communicate and associate the people of the villages of the lower Yukon delta.

Modern Water Plant

During the middle of the 1970s the village of Emmonak built a modern facility that had showers and a sauna. This building was also where we went to get fresh water. We carried our buckets there to fill them and carry the fresh water back to our cabin. We no longer relied on the river as our source of water. It was a wonderful advancement. Now we did not have to boil the water before we used it. What luxury fresh water was for us. It was really hard work carrying the full buckets of water back to the cabin. We started to go to the water plant instead of the qasgiq for a sauna.

The Passage of Time

As time passed the communal house became less important to our life in the village. As fewer people used the communal house, it became rundown. The communal house became less important as words of wisdom were spoken less frequently. It eventually started to collapse and fell into disrepair and was abandoned. There is no communal house in Emmonak today. People either use the modern sauna provided by the village or have built their own like Pa did at the modern home. The dancing is now performed in the community center building.

That part of Eskimo life, where everyone gathered at the qasgiq is gone. Only my generation has a memory of what that meant to me as an individual and to us as a village. It was a place that held the village together. It was the glue that kept people together. It gave each village and villager an identity. It made us who we are as Eskimos.

What I find most disappointing about the loss of the communal house is its effects on the teaching of the young people. The teaching by the elders helped each young person aspire to be a better Eskimo. The passing of the qasgiq along with the qanruyutet that was taught led to the end of a very important era in Eskimo life along the lower Yukon River. It was a most important building. It was the center of the universe of the village. It was a meeting place. It was a place to fellowship with your neighbor. It was a place to teach and learn. I now only have my memories of the times that I spent in the qasgiq or communal house.

 Above all else, guard your heart, for it affects everything you do.
Proverbs 4:23

Firsts

Ciuqlikacaarmek: For the first time

I feel fortunate to have lived in a time that saw so many advances that enhanced my life and the lives of everyone in the village. It was exciting to experience all the firsts to which I was so blessed.

Every generation has a claim that they are the first to experience the major advances of society. It was exciting to live at a time when our generation was given the opportunity to do so many things for the first time. It causes us to say that we had a part in the betterment of society. After a first was experienced, then succeeding societies can live a much better and productive life because of it. This chapter is about those firsts that occurred during the generation in which I lived. These firsts changed how life was lived on the Yukon delta from that day forward. I want to share them with you as I remembered them.

Northern Commercial Company Store

The store always existed as far as I know. It was built before I was born. The reason I mention it is because it changed everyone's life because of its existence. It bought the furs that Pa trapped from his trap line. It was a true general store in the sense that it sold everything that was required for living on the delta. It sold food, hardware, lumber, marine equipment, snowmobiles, clothing, just to name some of the variety. It eventually became my workplace when I turned sixteen years old and was able to begin work. Over time it was bought by Alaska Commercial Company to which it still is today.

It bought fish for as long as I remember. That was a big change to the people's livelihood along Kwiguk Pass. Pa did some commercial fishing for them prior to 1975. He did not qualify for a limited entry fisheries permit, thus he was not able to participate in commercial fishing. He spent his life fishing only for subsistence. Since Pa did not receive a limited entry fisheries permit he was not able to pass on the opportunity to commercial fish to any of his sons. This kept George, Teddy and Fred, my brothers living in Emmonak from being able to commercial fish when they reached adulthood. This had a drastic effect on each of their lives. They would not be able to commercial fish for salmon during the open commercial fishing season. This severely impacted my family. It shut the door to any commercial fishing income during my generation or any future generation of my Pa.

Power Plant

The village of Emmonak received their first electricity during my grade school years. A diesel-powered generator provided it. This made a great difference in the lives of anyone who chose and could afford to hook up to the power line. We were too poor to afford it until the modern home was built during my high school years. The first cabin I lived in did not have any electricity run to it. The second cabin did not have electricity either. Pa had bought a small gasoline powered generator to use sporadically at the second log cabin. We used it to run the lights and a few electric appliances on a limited basis. We did not have any electrical appliances that required electricity on a continual basis. There was no refrigerator or freezer at the second cabin. It wasn't until we moved into the modern house that we needed electricity on a constant basis to run the refrigerator and freezer. We eventually purchased other items that required electricity. Now I wonder how we lived back in my grade school days without any electricity. We just did not miss what we did not have. Getting electricity to the village was a huge event. It certainly transformed every aspect of our life. It changed everything. The old ways of doing things were changed forever with the availability of electricity.

Water Plant

We received the opportunity to have fresh water at our disposal during my grade school years. A water plant was built which gave us fresh water to use without having to boil it anymore. There was no need to carry the water buckets to the river or the lake to get water. We did not have to boil it either. In the wintertime it was no longer necessary to have to dig a hole in the ice to get water. No one needed to cut ice blocks out of the river and haul them to the cabin. Neither of our cabins had running water. It was not until we moved into the modern house that we had the luxury of running water. The water plant building also housed the sauna and shower facilities. This had a great impact on the use of the communal house. People began to take their sauna at the water plant rather than go to the communal house. This change caused a great alteration of peoples lifestyles. It eventually led to the abandonment of the communal house. Now we take fresh water for granted. Having access to fresh, clean water was almost like a gift from heaven. Fresh water from the faucet led to another major change in our subsistence lifestyle.

Freezer Ships

I remember the first freezer ship that arrived in Emmonak. It was called the *Polar Bear*. It started arriving in the village every spring during the late 1960s or early 1970s. I can't remember the exact year when it first arrived. The significance of the *Polar Bear* was how it changed the fishing in the lower Yukon River delta. It changed fishing from an entirely subsistence culture to an almost completely commercial one. This happened in just a very few short years. This changed the economy of the delta completely. Nothing was as it used to be after that. Money became the most important commodity to the Eskimo people. It used to be the food we gathered from the land and the river. Now it was the money that everyone sought after from the wealth of the commercial salmon industry. It caused countless changes to every family that was able to commercial fish for salmon. It simply caused everything to change from that time forward. The one lasting memory I have of the *Polar Bear* was that they sold ice cream cones for five cents. That was sure a wonderful treat when I was just a little girl. It wasn't long until more freezer ships came to anchor in front of Emmonak during the commercial fishing season. I remember the *Polar Bear* because it was the first.

Snowmobiles

Axel Johnson owned the first snowmobile I remember. That was during my grade school years. Prior to the first snowmobile it was the dogs and the dog teams that provided the only form of transportation for us. Every family had a dog team with a sled. It required a lot of work to maintain a dog team. They had to be provided food everyday. Dried fish was their primary diet. Dried grass was required to keep them warm and dry during the winter. They made a lot of noise when one of them decided to start barking. The snowmobile changed how far and how fast one could travel over the snow. The snowmobile was very expensive to buy. As families become wealthier from commercial fishing, more snowmobiles were seen in the village. By the time I was high school age the number of snowmobiles had increased greatly to the point where almost every family had one. Eventually the need for dog teams diminished until none are seen in the village anymore. Pa still had a purpose for building sleds. They were not pulled by dogs but by snowmobiles.

Automobiles

Only the businesses had pickup trucks during my grade school days. They were used to haul goods between the airstrip and the store. The trucks were ordered from the barge companies to be delivered on one of the barge's scheduled deliveries. Trucks and a few automobiles became very common after I left the village in 1978. More people began to own cars and trucks as time went on.

Oil Exploration

Around the year 1975 I remember Shell Oil Company came out to Emmonak to search for possible oil deposits. They used helicopters to shuttle their men and goods from Emmonak to wherever they were going on the Yukon delta. I don't think they found any major deposits during their search of the area. When they left they never returned. Nothing was spoken about whether they found anything at all. I think to this day no further work has been done to search for oil on the delta or the Bering Sea offshore area. I think our only claim to fame will still be our salmon resource.

Sewage Plant

A sewage plant was built after I left in 1978. The honey bucket was our only source of indoor plumbing. Today there is an entire network of above ground-insulated pipe that serves as the sewer line for connecting each home. Most homes now have indoor bathroom facilities because of that advancement. That has certainly helped the people clean up that part of village life. With the sewage plant in operation the need to dispose of the waste now belongs to the sewage treatment facility rather than the Yukon River. That was a big problem that had been solved by modern technology. It has also helped solve a major potential health problem for the village.

Telephone System

Communicating outside the village was not possible for a long time. Not until the development of the orbiting satellite was it possible to communicate with the outside world with any ease or regularity. The use of the telephone in Emmonak came after I left in 1978. Prior to the telephone the only real means of communicating was to use the KNOM radio station at Nome, Alaska. A person could write and mail a message to them and the station would pass it along to the recipient party. There was a telegraph available at the post office. I think Axel and Pearlie Johnson operated it. We used it a few times after Mom divorced Pa and was living in Anchorage with her second husband.

Television

Television came to Emmonak after I left in 1978. I never did experience any television during my grade school days. I did not see television until I visited Anchorage. It was captivating to watch. A person could sit and watch it for a very long time and accomplish very little. Today Emmonak has a complete cable system just like any city in America. It changed the lifestyle of the Yupik Eskimo. The people are more sedentary in their homes now. The kids do not play outside as much as they used to. They are basically glued to the television set. Video games can be attached to the television set and that has transformed an entire generation of young people. Instead of playing Eskimo games outdoors, they are inside playing video games.

How life has changed from the fish camp days when we played many games on the tundra. The young people are missing out on that very basic aspect of growing up among friends their own age. The television has also opened the door for a whole array of movie watching. You don't need to go to the local movie show anymore. You can watch any movie you desire from within your own home.

Health Services

I only mention the health services because it was the one memory I have that I remember most. I know the health service or health aid system was established before I was born. I did have to use it once while I was growing up in Emmonak.

I was a little girl in early grade school at the time. I was walking with two of my friends to see a movie at the old Catholic church building. A motorcycle hit me from the back. The impact hurled me in front of the motorcycle and then it ran over me again. I was hurt quite bad. I was taken to a nearby house, and then walked to the health aid building. They flew me over to Bethel the next day where there was a hospital. My arm was broken. They put a caste on my arm and sent me back to Emmonak. After a little while I was flown back to Bethel to have the caste removed. I was flown back to Emmonak for the final time. I still have a problem with that arm to this day. It doesn't get any better with age.

High School

During my junior year in high school we attended a one room building which acted as a high school. It did not work out very well, but represented good intentions. It was not until the Molly Hootch Case that high schools were built in the villages. The new, modern high school was completed for the 1976 and 77 school year. The construction of the high school was a great addition to the village as it kept high school age children in the village without them having to leave home to complete their education beyond the eighth grade.

Airstrip

It was always there as far as I know. It was created either before I was born or during my very early years. It was located along the east side of Emmonak slough. We could walk to it whenever we wanted to meet the airplane especially in the fall when we were curious about the arrival of the teachers. Who returned for another year and who was coming for the first time? The runway was bare dirt. Wien Airlines had a scheduled flight into Emmonak. They used a sky van or twin otter aircraft for the flights into the village. The ticket office was located in the home of Jake and Eunice Johnson right next to the airstrip across the slough. They maintained the airstrip and ticketing office. Boats used the slough separating the village from the airstrip. People were able to drive their boats right up to the bridge that crossed the slough and have easy access to the plane's cargo or passengers. Over time the slough dried up and was no longer able to handle boats. The Kwiguk Pass of the Yukon River was always changing the channel and the slough became another of the river's victims. By the time it dried up the airstrip was moved farther east of the village. The airstrip today is a very modern one with a real ticketing office with maintenance buildings for aircraft repairs.

I think the generation that saw the most firsts and came the farthest during those days had to be my grandpa and grandma. They witnessed a time before any modern conveniences were introduced. They lived at a time before the gasoline engine. They had to provide their own power, or rely on dog power. Yet they lived to see all the firsts that I witnessed. In my opinion they lived to see the widest range of civilization's progress from no motorized means to computers and video games. I wonder what they must have thought about all of those advances that they witnessed. It must have been impossible to conceive of so much change in their lifetime. How did they cope with all of it? We will never know, because it is all lost to history when they passed away.

Pa's Firsts

I remember Pa telling me stories about his first introduction to the things and events that occurred during his lifetime. Here are some of the stories that he told me regarding his firsts.

Pa's introduction to Sailor Boy® Crackers

Pa remembers when he was a young man out in the tundra out near the Bering Sea. He and his family and friends were first given Sailor Boy® Crackers. They didn't know what they were, much less being edible. They decided to use them as Frisbees and tossed them out into the ocean. He said they sailed over the water very well. Sailor Boy® Crackers eventually became the bread of the Eskimo diet.

Pa's Introduction to Flour

He also remembers the first time they were given flour. They had no idea what to do with it. His mother mixed the flour with water and made a paste out of it. They dipped their fingers into the paste and ate it that way. They weren't too crazy about the flour paste. It was some time before they realized they could bake it to make foods such as bread.

Pa's First Airplane Sighting

The first time my Pa saw an airplane was when he was a young man. He said that when he and his family were out in the tundra out near the Bering Sea they saw this thing flying in the air and flying right toward them. They all ducked down on the tundra frightened because they didn't know what it was. It was also very noisy and scared them even more.

Kosacks

Pa often told me stories about when the Russians began to show up on the Alaska countryside. He said his parents and grandparents would often talk about the time when the Kosacks came over from Russia. They treated the Eskimos badly. Pa also talked about Eskimos being beaten by Kosacks. Eskimos were forced to catch fur-bearing animals for the Kosacks and were not paid much for them. It was a happy day when the Eskimos became Americans. That stopped the Kosacks from coming around.

All the firsts had an impact on the community as each one moved us step by step from a subsistence existence to a commercial lifestyle. The advancement of new technology made us less dependent upon the land for our livelihood. This is why I feel it is so important that at least what happened during my lifetime as a young girl and the years following is written down to be passed on to the generations after me.

 A gentle answer turns away wrath, but harsh words stir up anger. **Proverbs 15:1**

Games

Aquigaq: To play

I loved to play games with other kids. As a little girl I didn't understand the real value the games meant to our development both mentally and physically.

As I look back upon my life as a young girl growing up on the lower Yukon River delta I remember the games I used to play. It was so much fun to play with my sister Joanne. We did a lot of girl play together. There were always others to play with in the village. It seemed I was always busy with the serious business of playing games.

Playing games actually served several purposes although as a young girl I didn't play with those objectives in mind. They just happened without me really knowing any different. Only now as I am older do they make sense to me. I now understand the importance of the games we played and how they shaped our young lives. The games we played assisted in our development toward becoming an adult.

Social Aspect

At an early age our parents, grandparents and village elders taught us the art of getting along with others. As we played group games this was of primary importance. We had to work together for the game to be completed as desired. The games required us to cooperate. We understood that each one had their individual strengths and weaknesses at playing the game. We encouraged the weakness and cultivated the strength of each player. This proved useful as we became adults in the village and required that every member of the village work together for the survival of all. This cooperation was most needed during whale and seal hunts. Each participant of the hunt had to work together with everyone else for it to be successful. Just as in a game there is the coach of the team as a team leader. That was also true during the hunt for whale and seal. Not everyone could be the leader. The hunt required that most of the participants play a secondary role as helper to assure success. When good well-trained helpers accompanied a good leader, a hunt generally ended up as a win for everyone. All the members of the hunting team came away with some of the bounty in food. Our games taught us those valuable assets that would serve us well during our adulthood.

Physical Aspect

Some of the games we played prepared us for the future when we became an adult. Playing games assisted in our physical development and conditioning which was crucial to living a subsistence lifestyle. We had to be physically fit to withstand the demands that were placed upon us. So much of the effort required of us came in the form of being physically fit. Since we had no modern conveniences we had to do everything through our own physical exertion.

Training Aspect

Some of the games we played provided valuable experiences that we may need to use as an adult. What we did as play while a child, would serve us in times of need as an adult. Some of the games we played taught us valuable survival skills. As a young person we built snow caves, snow forts and igloos just for fun. We built them for the simple joy of making them during our youth. These skills proved invaluable if we were called upon to use them during an emergency on the tundra. Being able to build an igloo when caught overnight on the tundra could mean the difference between life and death. As a young person, building an igloo was just a game. We never thought of ourselves as being in training.

Following are some of the games I remember playing as a little girl.

Boats

All Eskimo kids liked to play make believe boats. This was played at fish camp as well as in the village. Since the boat was one of the most valuable assets an Eskimo could have, it played a large part in the livelihood of our people. We were surrounded by water. We had the Yukon River at the front of the village. There were numerous streams that fed into the river. Lakes and ponds were located everywhere around us. We were never far from water and a chance to try out our latest skill at boat making. Our toy boats were no more than pieces of wood that we found and tied a length of string to it. All we needed was a source of water and we were ready to play. Playing boats became either very competitive or simply a social time to enjoy our creations.

Eskimo Yo Yo

This was a very traditional toy made from sealskin. Each Yo Yo was tied together with decorative string. The purpose of the Yo Yo was to have one end rotate in a circle going one direction while the other end rotates in the opposite direction. It takes a little skill to accomplish this at first. Eventually a person can figure out the proper hand coordination and it was amazing to watch a fluent performer. They were used just as toys to challenge the user to perfect the technique of making them rotate in opposite directions. They were never used to perform in front of a crowd.

Almost every family had at least one pair of Yo Yo's. The mother of the family usually made them. We had one pair that was shared by all of the family members. I don't remember Pa using the Yo Yo. Primarily the kids played with Yo Yo's. Adults usually did not play with them.

Playing Yo Yo's was never competitive. We played together just as we played with any toy. Those with a Yo Yo shared with the kids that did not have one.

Hide and Seek

We played this game at both fish camp and in the village. There were more kids available to play with in the village, which made it more fun than at fish camp, which had fewer kids available. There were more places to hide in the village than on the treeless tundra islands at fish camp. Playing at fish camp our hiding places were more limited to such places as our tent, smokehouse, behind fish racks, clothes hanging on the line, in a boat or in a lot of places where adults could not hide. Hide and seek was best played during the dark which was not readily available during the long days of summer at fish camp.

Hopscotch

We played this game a lot. It was an Eskimo child's favorite pastime. It was a lot of fun to play it as a group. We used a stick and etched the squares in a portion of the bare clay near the beach. We played it at fish camp as well as in the village. Wherever there were kids a game of hopscotch was likely to be played. It didn't matter where we were. We each had a rock we used for throwing at each square to play the game. I really liked the jumping and the concentration required to win. When I was young you could find throughout the village a hopscotch game etched in the dirt almost everywhere you went. The game of hopscotch is disappearing from the play of Eskimo children today. It is difficult to find a game being played by kids today because they seem more interested in playing video games or watching television inside their homes.

House

We played house whenever little girls were together. I especially enjoyed playing house with my younger sister. We could play it all day long it seemed. At fish camp we played it when our parents were not in the tent. At the cabin in the village we played house in our girls-only section of the bedroom.

Ice Hockey

This was played on the river in front of the village after the ice had frozen solid enough to be safe. We found a section of ice that did not have a lot of snow on it. It was faster and sliding was easier on the bare ice sections that were not covered with snow. Some of the kids had skates. Others that did not have skates just slid on the ice in their boots. I had a pair of skates that I shared with my sister. For sticks we used driftwood that we found. If we were lucky enough, we used broken broom handles. Essentially any long stick worked that was found lying around. The puck was anything that would slide on the ice. The game was more an opportunity to just pass the puck from person to person, rather than choosing sides and play competitively as teams. There was no need for goals. Actually we did not even know about hockey rules at the time. It was just something we did as kids playing on the ice together. It was usually a boy's game, but sometimes girls also joined in the play.

Jump Rope

What kid does not like to play jump rope? We played many different versions of it. Someone tried to see who could jump rope the most turns or be the most innovative in the jumps performed. We had songs that went along with the rhythm of the rope swings, which added to the fun of the game. Girls primarily played it. Younger boys were encouraged to join in and play.

Kick The Can

There were always cans left abandoned around the village and at fish camp. They tempted us to be kicked. We simply turned it into a game that every kid enjoyed to play.

Lap Game

I am not sure if that is the actual name for it. That is what I called it. It was a game that we played at the village because it required a lot of kids to play. There were not enough kids at fish camp to get a good game together. The game was played with a bat and a ball and two teams. The bat was no more than a piece of driftwood we found and we usually had a ball to play with. One team did the fielding and the other batting. We used a stick and make two parallel lines in the dirt about thirty or forty yards apart. Each team stood behind their respective line. A pitcher lobbed the ball to the batter. Once the ball was hit the runner went as fast as possible to the opposite line without being hit by the ball that was retrieved and thrown by a player on the opposite team. The runner had to run back to the batting line in order to score. Everybody got a chance to bat and field during the course of the game. I think some part of the game is similar to cricket with a combination of regular baseball mixed in.

Marbles

This was played on dirt. We played it in a circle as most people do or we played pockets. Pockets game of marbles was played in such a way as to require each player to get their marble in a hole in the ground.

Red Rover

This game was more fun played in the village since there were more kids that could play. We played it at fish camp occasionally. There were two sides of players. Each side all held hands and would shout to the other team "Red Rover, Red Rover send (a person's name) over." The person that was called out from the other team ran over to the other side and tried to break the connection between the two kids holding hands. If the person was successful then they got to pick one person and take him or her to their side. If the person didn't break the connection then he or she was forced to go onto the side of the team they couldn't break through.

Seal Hunting

For fun, the young boys went pretend hunting. They were not allowed to have and use real harpoons. They picked long grass, bundled it up and pulled it with a rope around on the ground. Other boys tried to spear it as a make believe game of seal or whale hunting. The harpoons used by the boys were nothing more than willow branches. This was good training for the boys to help them develop their hunting skills. This game was only played in the village because that was where the tall grass grew. The tundra islands near fish camp were not suitable for growing the long grass necessary for making the make believe seal. This was probably the most important game a young boy could play since it trained them in the art of seal hunting. Every boy would grow up to become a seal hunter.

Slingshot

A slingshot was a favorite item every Eskimo young person kept in his or her pocket. We looked for that perfect forked driftwood branch that we could wrap a strip of rubber to each fork to make the sling. With a slingshot, we were able to hunt just like the older ones. We were usually never very successful at hitting anything, but it was fun just to try and imagine ourselves as mighty hunters of the tundra. My parents forbid us to shoot at live animals or birds. I kept a slingshot with me at all times.

Snake

This was another game we played on the frozen Yukon River ice. We got a bunch of kids together and hold on to each other's hands and skate around in circles. The object was to see if we could twist and turn fast enough to make someone in the line loose their grip and break the chain of people

Snow Forts

We piled up snow in a mound if there were not enough already on the ground. We used our hands, or borrowed a shovel, to bore into the pile. This created a cave we could sit inside and pretend to play a lot of games. If there was a lot of snow on the ground, which there usually was by mid-winter, then we simply burrowed into the snow and made tunnels. This was a lot of fun to crawl through them and play games inside the tunnel. We also used the snow to make a snow wall and enclose ourselves on all four sides. This was also good practice for emergency igloo making. We could each make our very own snow fort and play that way.

Story Knife

This was one of the games I enjoyed playing as a little girl. It was played only among girls or older women of the village. I especially liked playing this game because it was usually played along with my sister Joanne. It was more entertaining to play the game with her around. I have many memories playing yaaruin or story knife during my grade school days. We played story knife at fish camp but the best games were played in the village where more girls could be gathered to play as a group. The more girls there were to play the more fun it was.

A story knife was made from either a stick or piece of metal. I made mine out of metal box banding straps that surrounded shipping crates. I cut them into about six inch pieces. This became my story knife. I kept it in my pocket at all times. You never knew when a story knife game opportunity presented itself when we met with other girls. If I was to lose my story knife, I made another one. It was important to have one at all times.

We used our story knife to draw illustrations in the dirt. This was the start of the story that we were about to tell to each other. It was a game played only by girls and older women. One person drew a picture with their story knife in the dirt while the rest of the group looked on and tried to interpret the story. Every girl had a story knife so that when her turn came to draw she was ready. It was usually spontaneous play. It just happened whenever a group of girls got together. It was usually never planned play or with a particular theme to guide the play. It was a popular game among the girls.

When we saw older women play story knife we played along with them in our own group. The women gathered at the riverside to play story knife. That is where we found them if we wanted to play next to them. The game was age segregated. Older women played with older women. The young girls played with young girls. The older women never played with the young girls.

It was a game that allowed us to use our imagination and creativity. We could be very creative while we were young girls. Our stories could be very serious or very funny. That was the beauty of the game. It was left to our own imagination. It was interesting to listen to the girl's interpretation of the drawing that was etched into the mud or snow. If the girls interpreted the story wrong then we laughed loud and long at each other. It was a very fun game that formed a real and lasting bond between the girls that played together. If the girls could not interpret the drawing then it was up to the girl etching the drawing to tell the others what it meant.

The game of story knife does not seem to be played as frequently in the village anymore. It is another casualty of the increasing amount of time that kids spend playing video games and watching television. They do not bother playing a game using a stick and drawing in the dirt. There are more entertaining things to do with ones time in today's society in the village. It is another lost art that has passed into the pages of history. I am pleased that I had the opportunity to play story knife. It is another game that remains as a memory to me.

Tag

We played tag with the same enthusiasm as any other kid would play. We played tag anywhere we found a bunch of kids playing together. It was most demanding when played on the ice. I was not the fastest kid on the ice. I did know how to ice skate but I wasn't very fast. My sister and I were fortunate to share a pair with each other. It was fun to chase each other around on the ice. There was always a lot of falling that occurred. I guess that added some to the excitement and challenge of the game.

As I grew older, play became less important to me. That happens to everyone. Our priorities changed, as we grew older. Playing games was for the younger kids. Certainly the modern conveniences of television, cell phones and video games have changed how young people grow up now. Young kids don't seem to play the traditional Eskimo games anymore. They spend their time with the modern electronic games inside their homes. There are fewer young people interacting with each other in today's society. There doesn't seem to be the desire to play games by the young people anymore. Playing games has become another casualty of the changing lifestyle of today's Yupik Eskimo children.

Kind words are like honey—sweet
to the soul and healthy for the body.
Proverbs 16:24

Epilogue

Certainly the village of Emmonak has changed since I was a little girl. The life I lived growing up during my grade school days during the 1960s was quite different from that of today. Society changes and civilization moves forward. It does not stop for anyone. I am not saying the era I lived as a young girl were the good old days. They were certainly different than they are now. There are so many modern conveniences today that makes the life that was lived back in the 1960s seem a long time ago.

Although society and the modern ways of living have changed the lifestyle of the village, one thing has not changed, and that is the warm hearts of the people. They are still as loving today as they were during my youth. That aspect of the people has not changed. Caring for each other as a community is alive and well in Emmonak. Nothing changes that aspect of a person.

The lifestyles my Pa showed me, and I experienced with him are now only memories of the past. That way of life will not return. Why should it return to be lived over again? It has been replaced with the conveniences of modern society. Surviving with a subsistence lifestyle is no longer a necessity. That may or may not be a good thing. I am not going to be the judge of that. It was certainly a different life than what is lived today. I am certainly an example of that. I remember when we had so little in material things, but we never complained. It was simply the way it was. We knew no different. We were so very content with what we had. We actually thought we had everything the whole world could offer. We were wealthy and did not even realize it! It simply did not make any difference to Pa, the family and especially me. I am a much better person because I lived with Pa and eagerly followed his ways. His skills of working with his hands are now a lost art. People today now buy the things Pa made with his hands. It is no longer required to possess the skills to build sleds and boats. They have been replaced with different wants, needs and skills.

I certainly live a much different life from the one I grew up. I now live in a very modern home. I live in a rural area and enjoy the outdoors with all the modern conveniences at my fingertips. How the cell phone, computer, automobiles and even a GPS have transformed me from that little girl with Pa to the working wife I am today. I have not forgotten my simple beginnings. We get out of life what we strive to put into it. All the experiences I learned from my Pa helps me each day of my life. They have not been forgotten. I still remember them although it has been approximately forty-five years ago.

I recognize the desire and need for change that has occurred in the village. I am no longer that little girl which grew up under Pa's care and influence. I can't go to fish camp with my family and play on Grandpa's Island. I am not able to pick berries in the shadow of Akulurak Hill. I don't need to harvest grass to keep my feet warm in the winter. I can't be next to Pa and watch him make boats, sleds, fish traps, harpoons, snowshoes and dog booties. The nights of going to Kwiguk to watch movies as a family with the dog team will not be experienced anymore. I can't watch a potlatch held in the mud covered communal house. I no longer play hopscotch, lap game, marbles, or story knife. I can't sit and listen to Pa or Grandpa talk about their firsts experiences. Those are all events of the past. Those moments are not going to return. Only the memories of them remain.

If Pa was still alive today I know there are some questions I would like to ask him. Did I learn all the things you wanted to teach me? Did I get them right? Did I live up to your hopes and dreams you had for me? Those questions will have to go unanswered. I think I know in my heart how he would respond.

These were the stories of my life while growing up a young Yupik

Eskimo girl on the Kwiguk Pass of the lower Yukon River. It was my pleasure to share them with you. If this book inspires you to write about the experiences you have lived, then my work has been successful. It is my desire that everyone can share with others those unique life experiences that God gives each of us. These stories came not only from my memory of how I remembered them, but also from my heart as I treasured them. You might say they are an opportunity to remember my Pa as a person who knew how to live and survive without any modern conveniences. He was able to live off the land and provide a comfortable existence for his family. It was that gift and talent I observed in my Pa. Writing about those gifts and talents are why I remembered these stories. They were too important not to be recorded so future generations of my people may be reminded of our past.

I hope you found them informative, enlightening and entertaining. They were the memories I had of those times that I can say, "I remember when."

Molly Agnes Hootch Hymes

The Molly Hootch Case

Introduction

The final section of my memoirs is about that portion of my life that included the Molly Hootch Case. I never thought myself as an activist or someone looking for a moment of fame. I didn't have a battle to fight or some terrible wrong that needed to be set right. When the opportunity came to do something about the lack of high schools in the villages, I simply signed my name to a petition.

I am sure that every person who signed the petition possessed a hope that someday the dream of a high school in Emmonak might become a reality. I was not someone special or stood out from all the rest of the signers. I just remember my name was the first one on the petition.

I admit I was surprised to be the one whose name was chosen to represent the court case. I really didn't expect it to become so well known throughout the state. I was surprised to hear my name mentioned and written about in all the major newspapers of the state.

The court case took on its own life. Where ever I went I was always associated with the case. People that were complete strangers to me would stop me and ask if I was Molly Hootch. It was nice to be associated with such a good deed. I was surprised by how thankful the people were toward the construction of high schools in their villages.

This portion of my story follows my life to the beginning of the court case and concludes with the life that I now live. As I moved on with my life and lived away from Alaska, the Molly Hootch Case always followed me. The news media had a way of finding me as a follow up to the case. It was doing the *right thing* which brought me to the rest of the story of my life. The following pages tell the story of what became of that little girl who grew up on the Kwiguk Pass of the lower Yukon River.

The Molly Hootch Case

The school in Emmonak only allowed for grades one to eight. If a student wanted to continue on to High School they had to leave the village and go to a boarding school somewhere. That meant going to Anchorage or possibly out of state to continue education at the high school level.

The fall of my first year of high school found me leaving the village. I looked forward to going to school in Anchorage as a new experience in my life. I was ready and willing to leave home for school. I was going to leave my whole family back at Emmonak while I went to high school. I was a bit sad having to say good-bye to the family while I boarded the plane at the airstrip. It was just one of those things that were required if you wanted to go on to high school.

When I arrived at the Anchorage airport a representative of the high school met me. I was taken to the home of my host family. I would spend the next nine months of the school year with them. I don't remember exactly where they were located in Anchorage. I attended Wendler School. My host family was made up of a husband and wife and three very young kids.

The host family treated me nicely. It just wasn't the same as being with my real family. Actually, I thought I functioned more as a free baby sitter for the three little kids than as a real member of the family. I was usually left out of their family activities. It was a very odd feeling. I had always been used to being a part of a real and complete family. This was so strange for me and I really did not feel good about the situation.

I don't remember being able to go back home at all during the entire school year. I know my family could not afford the ticket to have me come home for even a short break with them. All the holidays were spent with my host family. It made Christmas especially hard to be away from my family. Sometimes I felt like a stranger in a strange land. My only contact with my family back home was to write. There was no way to communicate with them, not even by telephone.

I would say my experience at the high school was okay Going to school was not my favorite interest, but it needed to be done so I managed to get through it. Most of the time I would say my school experience was fun. If I met the right kids it was a really good experience. As anywhere, there were bad kids. I just tried to avoid them. Being an Eskimo and from a small village had its down side. It was difficult to adjust to the big city way of life. That made us appear as odd to most of the kids who grew up their entire lives in Anchorage. There were difficulties assimilating into the big city life. Some kids made fun of us as being from a small village.

The experience was made more tolerable as I had never been exposed to a big city atmosphere. The big city has a lot of activities that were completely new to me. It was fun to experience those things I never encountered in Emmonak. It was a learning experience. That part of the time I spent in Anchorage was fun. Doing new things helped overcome the other problems I had to cope with.

It was still difficult being away from home. Not having my family and friends that I knew back home with me all the time was hard to deal with. I especially missed not being with Pa. I missed all the great experiences we had together. It was hard not having him with me. I had many memories of the times he and I spent together. That was simply not going to happen with me in Anchorage.

My mom had divorced Pa a few years earlier. She lived in Anchorage. I was able to visit her sometimes. That helped a little in missing my family.

When my first year of high school was over and I was able to return to Emmonak for the summer made me feel great. I was so happy to come home and be with my family for the summer. It was so nice to come back to Emmonak for the summer between my freshman and sophomore year. You never realize what you miss until you experience that void in your life.

I felt so free to be home for the summer. It was wonderful to be a part of the family again. Going to fish camp was just what I needed to get myself recharged. Just being with Pa and my brothers and sister made the summer so refreshing.

That summer of 1971, two lawyers representing the Alaska Legal Services came to Emmonak to explain a proposition that would provide villages the opportunity to have a high school. I went to listen to them. Their names were Chris Cooke and Steve Cotton. The idea sounded great to me. The thought of not having to leave the village to attend high school was wonderful. The experience I just had with my high school year made me desire a high school in Emmonak. It would be a dream come true if that could happen. The two sounded as if the possibility could become a reality. They gave all of us a real optimistic outlook that it might happen. At the end of their discussion they passed around a petition for each of us to sign if we wanted to be a part of the court case. My name was the first one on the list.

The rest of the summer went as usual for me. I did what I was supposed to do for the family. Since mom had left I was the oldest female member of the family. The job of being the mom of the family rested on my shoulders. I was too young to work outside, so I simply worked around the cabin and did the work that mom would have done.

Late summer came too soon and it was time to leave and go back to Anchorage for my next year in high school. I was going to have a different host family this time. That made me feel better about the next year ahead of me. I was also going to be transferred to a different high school. I would be attending Dimond High School. I was not sure how that was going to work out for me. Was it a good idea or not? I was about to find out as I left Emmonak for another year in Anchorage.

I settled in to another year with a new host family. That required getting used to. I liked this family better. They treated me nicer.

Going to Dimond High School was again another challenge. New friends had to be made. As expected, there were bad students that gave me a hard time. There were also nice kids that made for good friendships.

One day while at school one of my teachers asked me if I was going to quit school. That question really surprised me. Why would they ask me that question? The news had gone out that a court case was going to start that would require each village that desired a high school could have one built. The court case was named after me. It became known as the Molly Hootch Case.

After my sophomore year was over, I returned to Emmonak. I was sixteen years old then. I got a job with the Northern Commercial Company store. The money I made helped the family a lot. After working there for the summer I realized that my family needed the money more than my returning to Anchorage for school. I made the decision to stay in the village and not return to high school in Anchorage for my junior year.

Instead I attended a one-room high school during my junior year in Emmonak. A man named Alex Tatum taught the high school classes. He was very nice. His pleasant personality and zeal to teach us high school subjects was a wonderful experience. The old Catholic Church building was the site for the one-room high school. I don't know how the idea of having high school subjects taught in Emmonak came to be? The building was not really capable of providing us a quality educational experience. It was better than no attempt at all. It was the first time we could attend some high school without leaving the village. It was a generous beginning. Mr. Tatum tried his best to give us as much education as the circumstances allowed. We all applauded him for the great job that he did considering all the obstacles he faced. Eventually I had to quit going to high school because Pa needed me at home and I needed to work and earn money to help meet the household expenses. It was not possible for me to go to school and work full-time at the same time. It was a painful decision to make, but one I had to make in order to keep the family financially together. Without a mother in the family, I had to fill that position as best I could. The decision was not easy to make. I really wanted to complete my high school requirements and perhaps get a high school diploma. That meant a lot to me. But it was just not going to happen, at least not for now. I had to be at home.

I knew that decision would keep me from getting a high school diploma. I also knew I could earn a General Education Development (G.E.D). diploma if I worked hard enough for it. So I began the process of working toward that goal. I enrolled in a G.E.D. program with the Kuskokwim Community College at Bethel. I took it as a sequence of correspondence courses while I was living and working in Emmonak. I was determined to do it all on my own. I studied at the village jailhouse. It was very quiet there. I could study without any noise or interference. Robert Moore was the village policeman at the time. He was a friend of my family, so he was willing to let me use it for my personal study toward my G.E.D. He gave me the key to the jail whenever I wanted to go there to study. That was really nice of him to do that for me. I made every effort to study hard and do well on all my exams so I could pass each of them and eventually graduate with my G.E.D. While I was working toward my G.E.D. the Molly Hootch Case was in full swing working its way through the Alaska judicial system.

Eventually the Molly Hootch Case came to a final conclusion in October of 1976. It was decided that each village that desired a high school and had enough high school age children could receive appropriations to build one. Emmonak received authorization for its High School, and construction began during 1975. I was still working toward my G.E.D. while it was being built. I decided not to attend the new high school because of the same circumstances as before. I was needed at home. I continued to study in the village jailhouse almost in the shadows of the new Molly Hooch high school. What a strange set of circumstances that presented me. In May 1977, I completed my G.E.D. coursework. I successfully passed the examinations and received my G.E.D. diploma.

After The Molly Hootch Case

In October 1976 the court approved the Molly Hootch Case and it was then settled. Villages that wanted a high school and had the necessary number of high school age children would now be able to have one. No longer would high school age kids have to leave their village and most importantly their parents and family members to go to high school. Some had to go far away to boarding school. Some even went out of the state of Alaska to go to high school.

The first complete year of attendance at the new Emmonak high school was during the 1976 and 1977 school year. The high school body decided to dedicate their first annual yearbook to me. It was a great honor to be selected as the recipient of this award. I wish I could have been a member of that graduating class, but it was just not to be. I would take my G.E.D. and apply that toward the future God had in store for me. I had no idea what awaited me next while I walked toward my future.

I never dreamed that the petition I signed that summer of 1971 would make my name a household word throughout the entire state of Alaska. I simply wanted to do what I thought was right. It was not right for a young person to have to leave their home and family behind just to go to high school. It was one of the most traumatic events in my life and for every Eskimo young person to have to experience.

The successful conclusion of the court case, overnight made my name known throughout the entire state. I could not envision how it was going to affect my life from that point forward. It seemed that every reporter in the state wanted to talk with me and get my opinion regarding the case. I never wanted such celebrity status. I was just doing what I thought was the right thing for my fellow Eskimo children. As the schools were built in each village, they became known as Molly Hootch schools. When I met people from those villages and they blessed me and told me how proud they were to have their very own high school, I knew the right thing had been done. It kept families and entire villages together rather than breaking them apart. This had to be a good thing for every village that received a high school.

While the initial excitement of the new high school construction was going on throughout the entire Yukon-Kuskokwim Delta I was working at the Northern Commercial Company store in Emmonak. I was also the mother of the house. I enjoyed the work at the store. It provided a very important source of income for the upkeep of the family. During those years there was a significant shift from subsistence existence to commercial enterprises. That changed the economic basis of the entire lower Yukon River delta. More people had more money to spend. Commercial fishing was attracting more freezer ship activity and more people were moving to the area for the improved fishing opportunities. We were experiencing our very own boomtown days. I was eventually promoted over the years to dry goods department manager. I really enjoyed working in that department. I got the opportunity to travel to trade shows as far away as Anchorage where we bought merchandise for the next selling season. I had found my niche in life working for the company. I was very pleased when I was promoted to the position of assistant manager of the Emmonak store. It was a very successful store. It was a very needed store in the village of Emmonak. I was happy to be a part of that growth and prosperity. I tried to never lose sight of the humble beginnings where I had come from as a little girl. Progress and economic development was quickly changing the lifestyle I knew as that same little girl of years past. Emmonak was moving to a future that no one really fully understood its ramifications. I was being moved or shoved right along with it.

The Molly Hootch Case became a political football by the end of the 1970s and early 1980s. Each political party had their version of a Molly Hootch plank of their political platform. Some politicians were strongly in favor of the bush school system while some were very opposed to it. During election time I heard my name mentioned quite often. I was highly regarded by some and very disliked by others. I came to accept that as the price I paid to do what I thought was right.

I did not realize it at the time, but the summer of 1975 would be the beginning of the rest of my life. The court case had not been completely decided by then. The end of the court case was in sight for most of us. Emmonak was in the process of building its new high school. My life was going on like normal for me. Every summer the Alaska Department of Fish and Game brought their personnel to Emmonak for commercial salmon monitoring. That summer I met a fisheries technician named Alvin Hymes. He was just another fisheries guy. At least that is what I thought. When we met in front of the Northern Commercial Company fisheries cutting house, I thought nothing of it at the time. How wrong I was. This fisheries technician would change my life forever.

He did not come back the following summer of 1976 to Emmonak to work. He was stationed out of the Bethel fish and game office that summer. I remember he showed up at my house one summer afternoon while he was assisting on a fish ticket run to Emmonak. I was washing clothes at the time. I was so excited that he had come to see me. At that point, I think our lives started to become more involved. We wrote letters to each other. Every summer he requested the KNOM radio station play our favorite song on my birthday. I listened all day for it. Even though we were hundreds of miles apart it seemed we were really never separate.

This continued for the next two summer fisheries seasons until the fall of 1978. Alvin asked me if I wanted to come to his home on his Illinois farm with him. I accepted the invitation and the two of us left Alaska that fall of 1978. This little girl from Emmonak was going to experience the life as an Illinois plowgirl. I was simply following the love of my life. As the jet left the runway of the Anchorage airport I was reminded of the words of an Old Testament girl with similar feelings, as I was experiencing.

> ... I will go wherever you go and live wherever you live. Your people will by my people, and your God will be my God. Ruth 1:16

In Between

The portion of my life that existed after Alaska and before Minnesota I call In Between. It was a quiet time of my life. I was able to simply hang out at Alvin's farm house in Illinois and just enjoy the simple life on his farm. It was so peaceful living there among the other Illinois farmers. I enjoyed that a lot. Alvin's parents were so nice to me. His father, Russell Hymes, had lived and worked on a farm his entire life. His mother, Frances Hymes, had likewise known no other life aside from that of being a farm wife. And best of all, I had my very own room at his farmhouse. I did not have to share a room with anybody. It was all mine. How different it was from the two-room log cabin from which I grew up, as a little girl, in Emmonak.

Life on the farm was nothing like I expected. I had no idea what I was expecting anyway. The farm animals were nothing like the wildlife I grew up around on the Yukon delta. The Black Angus cattle on the farm were so big. I didn't want to get too close to them for fear they would attack me. I was really scared of them because of their size. Alvin and his father would just walk right up and touch them without any fear. I just couldn't bring myself to be that bold. I remember one time we had to haul two calves to the slaughterhouse. They were constantly moving around in the back end of the pickup truck. The truck would go back and forth the whole trip. I really thought they were going to tip the truck over or at least make it go off the road before we got to our destination. They also had pigs on the farm. They were very nosey and wanted to follow me wherever I went. They spent a lot of their time with their nose in the dirt. I remember we had to check the fence all the time because they dug under the fence constantly and tried to get out of the pen.

Their family had a firewood business they operated during the fall and winter months. I remember we went to other farms and cut and split their dead trees and hauled them back to their farm where they would stack it in neat rows to be loaded onto their pickup truck for delivery. I remember one time we cut the wood and split it in a barnyard where there were lots of pigs. The pigs were always getting in the way of our work. They would also cut and split a lot of the wood from their own woods located on their farm. They used a tractor and cart when they drove to the back end of the farm. I tried to learn how to drive a tractor but I just never could get the hang of clutching and shifting gears. I always thought I was just too short to reach the clutch and brake pedals in order to shift the gears.

During winter on the farm it could get a little slow. When the local stock ponds froze over Alvin and his father went ice fishing on them. They caught bluegill sunfish or largemouth bass in the farm stock ponds. These fish were so tiny in comparison to the salmon we caught in our nets on the Yukon River. They had a hand operated ice auger to cut a circular hole in the ice. Using the ice auger was much easier than using the ice pick my Pa had to use in order to cut his holes in the Yukon River ice. I never caught any fish even though Alvin and his father was catching fish constantly from their holes. I switched holes with them and I still did not catch anything, yet they caught fish from the hole I just left. Alvin's father told me that I was not holding my mouth right to catch fish. I remember one time while we were fishing for largemouth bass on the ice that a bass actually jumped right out of the hole onto the ice. That startled me so much I did not know what to do. These were strange fish that lived in the stocked ponds in Illinois.

I usually helped Alvin's mother make supper for all of us. One time she had to go somewhere and could not make supper. She asked me to make it for her. This was the first time I had to make supper by myself for the two of them. Everything went all right until I tried to make the gravy. The gravy was so awful that none of us could eat it. Alvin's father did his best to appear to like it. Even the dog would not eat any of it. During Sunday nights Alvin's father made supper. His usual menu for that night was a sandwich that they called the all-time favorite. It was made of bologna by frying it in a skillet. Two pieces of bread were toasted. The fried bologna along with a slice of cheese was put between the two pieces of toast. Usually mayonnaise was added as seasoning and that was the sandwich that was called the family favorite. Another favorite food made on Sunday evening was chocolate covered popcorn. That also became one of my favorite foods.

Christmas day of 1978 was one of the most joyous days of my life back on the farm in Illinois. That morning Alvin came up to my room and recited to me the story that he had written called The Cabin. It was about a young man that was trying to find his way to a cabin that was the home of his sweetheart. There was a terrible blizzard outside and he almost did not make it to her cabin before he suffered the effects of the cold and snow. The young man eventually made it to the cabin. He untied the little package wrapped in Christmas paper and gave the gift to his sweetheart. It was a ring with which he proposed to her for marriage. Our engagement began on that Christmas morning on Alvin's farm.

I learned to drive a car the following spring. Alvin let me drive his little blue AMC Gremlin car. We took the back roads that were never traveled by anyone. I thought I was never going to learn how to drive, let alone get my very own driver's license. Alvin was very patient with me. He was a good teacher. When I went to the driver's license office to take my driver test I passed every part of it. I was so thrilled that I passed the very first time.

We set the date for the wedding to be held on June 30, 1979. That would be the last Saturday in June and Alvin thought he could always remember that date. We planned for the wedding the rest of the year. I couldn't be happier. It was such a wonderful time of my life. My aunt Rose Rice of Anchorage made my wedding dress. I wore her veil during the wedding ceremony. All of Alvin's family had some part to participate in the planning. None of my family could make it for the wedding. I had Susan Meyer as my bridesmaid. She was one of Alvin's best friend's wife. She had become my very special friend during my stay in Illinois. The wedding was held at Alvin's church. It was held at Concord Christian Church in Concord, Illinois. Since none of my family could come it was an exclusive Hymes' only wedding. I didn't care; it was the most wonderful day of my life.

Life in Minnesota—Part One

Almost immediately after our wedding we packed our most personal belongings and headed to Minnesota in Alvin's parents' pickup truck. Our destination was the northern Minnesota town of Bemidji. We simply chose it from several towns that we had an interest in living at, and off we went. We found an apartment in Bemidji and settled in to life and work in this wonderful small town nestled among the tall pines of northern Minnesota.

Alvin went to work at a lumberyard owned by United Building Centers. I found work at the local J.C. Penney store. I worked in the shoe department. I felt like I was back doing somewhat the same work as I did in Emmonak. It was a wonderful time in my life as we began our lives together.

We attended the Bemidji Church of Christ in downtown Bemidji. It was a small congregation just like the one back in Concord, Illinois. I liked the small size. It offered a wonderful sense of togetherness among the church families.

Most Influential Person In 1970s Decade

The Molly Hootch Case found me eventually. I am not certain how I was tracked down in Bemidji, but they have their ways of finding people. In the late fall of 1979 I received phone calls from reporters and journalists from Alaska who wanted to interview me in regards to being selected as one of the most influential people of the decade of the 1970s. It was hard to believe at first that what I did warranted such an honor. I knew the case was big and had a great impact on the education of children of western Alaska. I just didn't think it would make me that famous. I was the most influential person of the decade in Alaska? What an honor. I couldn't believe it was true.

I still did not think it was for real until I received a copy of the article that was written in the December 5, 1979 issue of the *Anchorage Daily News*. How shocked I was to see the headline Molly Hootch alive and well in Bemidji. It was never covered in the Bemidji hometown newspaper, so it went unnoticed by the local people. Only a few of our close friends ever knew of the honor that had been given me. I did not have a current picture of myself to give them so I sent our engagement picture featuring Alvin and I as the photograph of choice to use with the article.

I was pregnant with our first son, Alvin Eugene, at the time. I was also working at the local J.C. Penney store in the shoe department. I was at least still working in something related to dry goods. I know that by 1979 not all the schools had been built that were eligible under the case. The rulings of the case would affect over one hundred villages along the Bering Sea coast. It changed the entire way of providing education at the high school level in those villages that opted to have a school built for them. High school age kids no longer had to leave their village just to go on to receive a high school education. In that sense it was a big event. It would impact every child of high school age. Families no longer had to be separated from their children. They could stay home with their families and attend high school. That was a priceless opportunity considering the alternative of being away from home for nine months at a time.

After the excitement generated by the selection of me as the most influential person of the decade newspaper article; my life in Minnesota became very routine. We eventually bought a small house in the city of Bemidji in 1982. For the first time in my life I was able to live in a house that was my very own. I felt so blessed by having our own little house. I loved its small size and simple design.

We were blessed with another son in our family with the birth of Daniel Alvin on October 22, 1983.

We had a garden in the back yard. Alvin had dug by hand a thirty by thirty feet garden area. I knew nothing about growing anything. That was Alvin's skill-set he learned from the farm. It was fun growing our own vegetables. I remember the first frost that occurred in the fall. We did not cover the tomato plants because we did not know it was going to get that cold. Alvin called me from work the next day and asked me to look at the plants to see if they had frosted. I told him they looked great. When he came home from work and looked at them he said to me, "They are all dead from the frost!" How was I to know since I had no experience with tomato plants? That Thanksgiving we decided to have fresh carrots from the garden. When we went to harvest them for the dinner we discovered they were frozen in the ground. We had to use a spade and an axe to dig them out for our Thanksgiving dinner. It was really hard work harvesting those carrots. It also took a lot of cleaning to make them ready for cooking. But they were are very own homegrown vegetables.

During the summer of 1984, my sons, Alvin Eugene and Daniel, and myself went to Emmonak to visit. We spent the entire summer living at Emmonak. I worked at the local Alaska Commercial Company store in the bookkeeping department. My brother George was the store manager at the time. Working at the store allowed me to earn enough to pay for our airline ticket back to Bemidji. We left Alvin back at the house in Bemidji as he was undertaking a remodel project of the front room while we were gone. I think the remodel work went smoother without us there to interfere and get in the way of the work. The boys and I arrived back in Bemidji by early fall.

During October of that year Alaska Commercial Company offered Alvin a job managing a lumberyard in Kotzebue, Alaska. We thought that would be a good opportunity for all of us so he accepted the offer. We had many preparations to complete before we could leave Bemidji. We had a house, car and lots of personal items too big to bring along with us that needed to be sold. We managed to sell, barter or give away to friends and family everything else that we owned. Before Thanksgiving we found ourselves back in Alaska.

The Kotzebue Experience

We arrived in Kotzebue, Alaska during November of 1984. I remember the cold wind nearly blowing me over with Daniel in my arms as I descended the steps from the Alaska Airlines jet. My first thought was "What have we done?" It was so cold I was ready to get back on the jet and go back to Anchorage from where we had come.

Eventually we settled into life in Kotzebue. Alvin managed the lumberyard owned by Alaska Commercial Company while I performed the bookkeeping duties for the store. It wasn't long before the long winter night settled into the arctic region.

I thought it was cold when we arrived in November, but much colder weather was to greet us in the months to come. It took a lot of work to oversee the store in the depth of winter. We spent a lot of our life at the store. The heaters had to be checked at least every night to make certain they were operating especially on the very cold nights.

I thought northern Minnesota had tough winters, but they were nothing in comparison to the Kotzebue blizzards that blew in from the Chukchi Sea. We kept ourselves constantly informed of any approaching winter storms. Since all of our lumber and plywood was stored outside, we were required to nail and weight everything down to keep it from blowing away during the blizzards. Anytime we sold lumber or plywood we had to get our shovel and dig it out of the snow. I remember a customer calling one winter morning and wanted to know if we had a certain amount of lumber. Alvin spent

226

all morning digging it out so he could count it. When I called the customer to tell him that we had enough, his response was that he just wanted to know if we had enough in stock. That required a lot of work to simply answer the customer's inquiry.

Summer brought the first barge of the year that arrived around the fourth of July. It brought all the lumber and building products we hoped would last for the summer building season. The last barge came in early fall to deliver our inventory for another winter. Summer, with its constant daylight, kept us busy almost around the clock. Many times we had to return to the lumberyard and make a delivery around midnight. Carpenters did not want to stop work just because the clock said they should be home in bed. Those were sure long and tiresome days. It was difficult sleeping at night since the sun never set. It just spent the entire day circling the horizon. The boys wanted to play all day long.

Even in Kotzebue the Molly Hootch Case caught up with me. The University of Alaska at Fairbanks wanted to interview me on my thoughts regarding the court case. They sent a film crew to our home in Kotzebue to conduct the interview. The university was responding to several local radio stations broadcasting that they had heard rumors that I was living in Kotzebue. I proved their rumors correct by calling the radio stations to confirm that indeed I was back in Alaska. Our quiet life in Alaska just came to an end. People would come to the lumberyard just to see me so they could say that they actually met Molly Hootch.

We purchased a three-wheeler ATV that became our family vehicle. I used it to make the daily post office and bank trips for the store. It was the vehicle of choice to getting around the village. Once, the Kotzebue police stopped me because I was speeding on the three-wheeler. I didn't think I was going that fast. The policeman just gave me a warning. I drove slower after that incident.

When the economy took a turn for the worse our work at the lumberyard came to an end. It was time to leave Kotzebue and move on with our lives. The United Building Centers lumberyard in Bemidji, Minnesota indicated they would rehire Alvin if he returned to Bemidji. In the spring of 1986 we packed up our belongings and headed back to Bemidji in the little Geo Metro automobile we purchased in Fairbanks.

Life in Minnesota—Part Two

The spring of 1986 found us back in Bemidji, Minnesota. We found an apartment to rent while we settled in to a routine. We enrolled Alvin Eugene in the kindergarten program at the local Lincoln Elementary School that was just down the street. In a few weeks Alvin went back to work at the lumberyard that he had left just a couple years ago. After a few short months we bought our old house back from the people we had sold it to. It was as if we had never changed anything. We were almost back to the same life we had left before the move to Kotzebue.

Twenty Years Later Hootch Still a Name

In recognition of the twentieth year since the conclusion of the Molly Hootch Case I began to receive phone calls from reporters of the *Fairbanks Daily News-Miner* newspaper. The paper was preparing a six-part series on education in rural Alaska. It was focused on the success and failure of the rural school system. Its focus was primarily centered on the Molly Hootch schools. They were asking me the same questions again regarding what happened during the court case. They were interested in my opinion and what I was doing after twenty years. I thought that after twenty years the dust would have settled on the case and no one would be interested in it anymore.

The Molly Hootch schools were still there and educating young people during their high school years. The village life had changed since the kids did not have to leave home just to attend high school.

I do know that not all the schools have faired well. Some suffered from low attendance because of the lack of high school aged children. There was much political pressure to do something different for those villages. The cost of educating those high school age kids was very expensive. Politicians were questioning the wisdom of spending so much money and getting poor results from the schools. It was difficult listening to the failed effort talk that seemed to swirl around the capital in Juneau regarding the Molly Hooch schools. The villages were caught in the middle of a debate that was more about money than helping the valuable resource of our high school age children. I will forever rest on my conviction that I did the right thing for the children of western Alaska.

Ranking the History Makers Since Alaska Statehood

As the year 1998 began to close the reporters and journalists began to compile a list of the most important people since Alaska's statehood. It was in celebration of the state's fortieth birthday. In the forty years since statehood a lot had changed and shaped the state of Alaska. I am happy to have been one of those people. Not that I set out in 1971 to become one of those famous people. It just happened to be me that I was the first to sign the petition that was circulated in the village of Emmonak to build high schools. It was not right that we kids had to leave our homes, families and villages just to get a high school education. I wanted better for the next generation of high school age kids than I had been given.

When I first learned of the list containing forty names, I assumed I would be lucky to make the bottom half of the list. Of course I was anxious to know who came before me. How famous were they? How important were they to the history of Alaska? When I learned I was ranked number fifteen, I was quite startled that I finished that high on the list. I was especially honored to realize that the fourteen people above me were very famous politicians and history makers in the state. I was certainly not more important than them. They certainly deserved the honor of being ranked above me.

I particularly enjoyed the quote about me that said "She made history before she was even old enough to vote." Twenty-four years since the Molly Hootch Case was settled and it was still an important issu in the state of Alaska. Education is always an important issue for everyone. It just goes without saying that any victory for education will not go unnoticed. I was pleased and honored that I was able to do my part and that people still remembered it almost twenty-five years later.

Alaska was not a state yet when I was born in 1956. I was too young to remember the events that surrounded our statehood in January of 1959. I only remember what Pa and Mom would talk about it. I am sure it was a big deal in the big cities of Fairbanks, Anchorage and Juneau. For us along the lower Yukon River it was just another day during the winter of 1959.

Thirty Years Later

As the year 2003 closed I was receiving phone calls again concerning the Molly Hootch Case. This time it was to recognize the thirtieth anniversary of the court case. Again I had to ask myself the same question. They still remember me after thirty years? The Alaska Native Heritage Center wanted to celebrate the anniversary of my court case with a two-day seminar at the center in Anchorage. What an opportunity to come back to Alaska for a visit in the middle of winter. The event was going to require two days of my presence. One day at the Alaska Native Heritage Center and another day at the Hotel Captain Cook as part of the Alaska Teaching Justice Network program.

The two events covered February 27 to March 1, 2004. It was a wonderful opportunity to meet the people connected with my court case and others that had played such an important part in my educational experience. I had not called ahead to alert any of my relatives that I was coming to Anchorage for the event. Once the television and newspaper coverage was broadcast around the Anchorage area, it was obvious that my arrival in Anchorage had been released. I had a lot of explaining to do when I arrived back in Bemidji to answer the many phone calls from people asking why I did not tell them that I was coming.

The opportunity allowed me to see people I have not met in such a long time. They were:

Chris Cooke and Steve Cotton

It had been a long time since I saw Chris Cooke and Steve Cotton.

These were the two lawyers who in 1971 came to Emmonak and presented the idea of building high schools in the villages. They both had many wonderful things to say about me. I really didn't expect to be so highly acclaimed by them. They were the ones who did the hard work. It was them who made the case a success for Alaskan children. I signed their petition and the rest is history. We stayed in Chris Cooke's home during the seminar and he was a wonderful host to Alvin and I.

Georgianna Lincoln

She has been an Alaska State Representative and Senator. She lived in Rampart on the middle Yukon River. She was our hostess while we stayed in Anchorage during the seminar. She made our stay an excellent experience with her bountiful kindness. She is a very good cook. She makes very good sour dough pancakes and waffles. Her moose stew tasted great. It was a real pleasure talking to her and having her tell me about her many stories of her life along the middle Yukon River.

Marshall Lind

He and his wife were teachers during my grade school days in Emmonak. I had his wife, Lois, as a teacher. She was very nice and memories of her have lasted a lifetime. Marshall would go on to become the Commissioner of Education for the state of Alaska and would then position himself as a defendant in the court case. He was also a chancellor of the University of Alaska, Fairbanks campus.

Alex Tatum

He was my high school teacher when Emmonak tried to bring high school curricula to the village. I have lots of memories of him while he lived in Emmonak. He was one of my favorite persons to know as a teacher from the village. I have a great admiration of the work he did while he taught in Emmonak. He was a strong inspiration to my life.

What surprised me most about the seminars was the joy I sensed from the native people because their villages have a high school as a result of my court case. They gave me such a warm feeling that what was accomplished through the case was beneficial to all village residents. They brought me so many items of their choice for me to autograph. Some just wanted to see me because they could not believe I really existed. Some desired to simply shake my hand and tell me how proud they were of all that had been accomplished because of the Molly Hootch Case. Many simply wanted to have their picture taken with me to prove to their people back home in the village that they actually met Molly Hootch. Some simply came up to me and said, "I can't believe I am standing next to Molly Hootch."

Into the Future

I don't know if there will be future recognitions of the Molly Hootch Case. Will anyone really care about celebrating it into the future? Honestly, it does not really matter to me. As I have said numerous times before, "I know I did the right thing by signing the petition." I am ready to live my life into the sunset of my years, pleased with what was accomplished.

I currently live with my husband, Alvin Hymes, and our beagle we call Tippy, in the northern woods of Minnesota east of Bemdji. It is a quiet existence for me. I love the serenity of the peaceful existence I now experience. The northwoods provides us with numerous birds, squirrels, chipmunks and rabbits of both cottontail and snowshoe hare varieties. Whitetail deer ramble through our yard as if it was all their territory. We get an occasional black bear that checks out our bird feeders every fall. Gray wolves and red foxes use our yard as a passageway to the game refuge across the road in front of our home. When the trees leaf out in the spring we are completely surrounded by green. I love the tranquility it gives both to my husband and me.

Our oldest son, Alvin Eugene, is married to a beautiful young lady from Malaysia. Her name is Shien and they now live in Singapore. Our youngest son, Daniel, is now out of the Army after a seven-year tour of duty. He lives in what we call our town house in Bemidji preparing for his life after the armed forces.

Now that we no longer have anyone in school, it is strange that t

Molly Hootch Case is the only connection I now have with education. It seems appropriate that I only have the memories of those days that have now passed me by. I will always remember when the idea of a high school in Emmonak could only be envisioned as a dream. And then it happened. Compared to my lifetime it occurred so suddenly. It is like the blinking of an eye in the passage of time. I am so happy it happened. If it weren't me who gained the fame it would have been someone else. It was only a matter of time before it would be inevitable that high schools would be built in each village. It just wasn't fair that we had to leave our village just to go to high school. I am glad I signed that petition.

Where does the future of bush education go from here? There are discussions of changing how education is delivered to the village children. Will some of the Molly Hootch Schools be abandoned? Some say the system is not working and that it costs too much. There are real concerns that have no simple answers. As always the solution is difficult to achieve without harmful effects being administered. I hope that whatever resolution is decided the children will not have to make the difficult choice that I had to make in order to attend high school. Those are the memories I would rather put behind me and not have anyone forced to repeat them.

As far as my future is concerned, I do not know. Although I currently do not live in the state in which I was born, my heart is always there. That part of me never left. Wherever the love of my life is found, my husband, there I will be also. That happens to be northern Minnesota for now. I love going back to Emmonak to visit my family and relatives. I love and miss each of them very much. I make certain to visit the Emmonak High School during each visit.

Each time I return to Emmonak I am met by the changes that keep occurring within the village. Progress within the village is that one constant which I can always be assured of each time I visit. There is one constant that never changes. That is the love of the people, their compassion for each other, and their hearts that never stops giving. I hope my life has also been an example of those very qualities that I earned while growing up a little girl on the Kwiguk Pass of the lower Yukon River.

Where or how I go into the future is anyone's guess. I am happy that it is not I to predict. I do not know what God has in store for me. The legacy each of us leaves behind for the future generation ahead of us is what counts. Not many of us can lay claim to fame. Few have schools named after them or dedicated in their honor. Few have their names stamped into history as a reminder of what they have done or accomplished with their life. It is rare that anyone leaves behind a legacy that will last long into the future. I have been so blessed.

As I consider my future after the Molly Hootch Case, I am reminded of a dialog that I heard from the *Back to the Future III* movie. In the movie, the professor was discussing the future with a young couple and made the most profound statement that has stuck with me ever since. He said to the young couple, "Your future has not been written yet. So make it a good one!" That thought inspired me and I have decided to spend the rest of my life making my future a good one.

My wish to all the young girls growing up on the Kwiguk Pass of the lower Yukon River:

PLEASE MAKE YOUR FUTURE A GOOD ONE ALSO!

Quyana

To contact Molly for book signings or to arrange for her
to be a guest speaker for your group, email:
ahymes@paulbunyan.net

Use this Coupon to Order Additional Copies

Please ship to:

First Name _____ *Last Name* _____

Address _____

City _____ *State* _____ *Zip* _____

Phone Number _____ *email* _____

Orders shipped via Air Mail the day they are received.		Quantity	Total
Molly Hootch	$17.95 each	_____	$ _____
Shipping and Handling	3.00 each		$ _____
No S and H with purchase of two books or more.	**Grand Total**		$ _____

Credit Card Number _____ ❏ VISA

Expiration Date _____ Signature _____ ❏ MC

Publication Consultants

8370 Eleusis Drive, Anchorage, Alaska 99502
phone: (907) 349-2424 • fax: (907) 349-2426
www.publicationconsultants.com — email: books@publicationconsultants.com

Made in the USA
San Bernardino, CA
13 November 2015